The Architects

The Architects
by Apollo Harrison

FANTASTIC
BOOKS

Fantastic Books
1380 East 17 Street, Suite 2233
Brooklyn, New York 11230
www.FantasticBooks.biz

Simultaneous hardcover and trade paperback publication
trade paperback ISBN 978-1-5154-5813-5
hardcover ISBN 978-1-5154-5814-2

First Edition

Chapter 1

Life consisted of the same shirt, jacket, slacks, and tie for Albert. Perhaps that explained why he wanted to spend more time in New Orleans, to experience all that the city had to offer. His visits here were always brief and secretive, never permitting him an opportunity to absorb the spectacle and revelry. After returning home to Munich, he often dreamed of foods flavored with spicy ingredients and brass instruments creating jaunty music that was both foreign and alluring. These mysteries teased him during every visit.

During the night, seen only by the moon, Albert slipped into the city to meet with his American partner, Howard. By sea was the easiest; the New Orleans port asked the fewest questions. Alas, Albert would have only enough time to complete his mission and return home, no prospect of enjoying the city.

As a professor at the University of Munich, he knew little about mooring a ship. Standing on the boat's deck, he watched the crew and dockhands scurry about to make the docking procedure as smooth as possible. His disguise of a thick, off-white cotton shirt and jeans gave him anonymity, not ability. There was little he could do to aid the crew except to stay out of their way.

Waiting on the wharf, Howard met Albert as he disembarked. Twenty years of age, Howard had a long face with rounded chin. A slight under-bite and perpetually furrowed brow gave him an air of determination, resolute that his ways and ideals were the only ones that mattered.

"Your trip?" Howard asked, his tone clipped as if courteous small talk pained him.

"Uneventful," Albert answered.

"Good. Follow me."

"Carriage, train, or another boat?"

"Foot. The site is only a mile this way." Howard slung a satchel over his left shoulder and started down the road, the contents of the bag clanking in muffled rhythm with his gait. As they walked, Howard offered the details of their mission in hushed tones to mimic the silence of the night. Albert had hoped to glimpse the city, even for a moment, to see how the denizens celebrated the arrival of comet Halley. Instead, he listened to his partner as they walked among the warehouses, the streets desolate this time of night. Alas, sightseeing was simply not meant to be, as Howard led them to a deserted warehouse tucked away in the armpit of the district.

The building stood as a monument to yesteryear—two stories tall with plank wooden walls, the only windows located immediately below the roof. Howard sifted through the contents of the satchel. He pulled two weapons from the bag and handed one to Albert. "Here."

Albert took the gun, as he had done so many times before, but he never felt comfortable with it. Shaped like any pistol, it had a silver handle and barrel. However, the cylinder was bulbous, pregnant with a battery that displayed its contents—green and black liquids swirling about, but never mixing. The battery contained what he and Howard had dubbed "dark energies." Howard had discovered the energy and pulled it from a different plane of reality, and Albert had created the battery to contain it: the metaphysicist and the physicist working together to develop guns that harnessed the energy. When dark energy was discharged in controlled bursts, it was a formidable weapon. Albert detested wielding the gun, but he knew it was a necessity, for his foes would possess great power as well.

Slinging the bag over his shoulder, Howard skulked to the nearest door, a rotted chunk of wood hanging from rusted hinges like a scab upon the building. Albert followed, crouched and ready. The door made nary a creak as they opened it, and what noise it did make was drowned out by the humming of voices emanating from the center of the warehouse.

The stale smell of mildew hung in the air. Mold conquered the stacks of wooden crates resting in pools of dank water, their origin and purpose long forgotten. The men took care not to make a noise, moving from behind one stack to the next, inching their way closer to the center of the warehouse. Howard moved with caution, fastidiously trying not to sully himself with any of the omnipresent filth.

The duo found the best vantage point behind a pile of boxes that formed a sloppy pyramid tall enough for them to stand behind without being seen. Thirty feet away, in the center of the warehouse, was their target.

Oil lamps placed upon crates and boxes threw illumination about the open area, but it was quickly consumed by the rippling darkness. Around the perimeter, a dozen hooded figures swayed to and fro, their cloaks and cowls as black as decay and trimmed with red piping, the flickering light giving the illusion of blood flowing through veins. They all chanted in unison, "Eeeeeya. Eeeeeya. Eeeeeya. Eeeeeya."

More lamps were arranged in a smaller circle, close enough for the glow of the light to converge. Standing in the center was the man Albert and Howard sought: Szilveszter Matuska. He wore robes as well, void black with green piping that writhed like tentacles as he moved.

"He's barely an adult," Albert whispered to himself.

"Evil knows no age," Howard replied. "Need I remind you that I am a scant year or so older than he."

"I fear your words are too true. Too true indeed," Albert muttered, unable to look away from the spectacle.

"Brothers!" Szilveszter addressed the hooded figures, his thick accent similar to Albert's. The chanting stopped, the followers allowing their leader to continue. "Tonight, Halley's comet passes by Earth, weakening the cosmic fabric between our reality and that of the one imprisoning our ancient god. Tonight, we shall call him forth. He will hear our unified plea to reshape the world to his vision. Tonight, we shall free our master. Tonight, we will be rewarded with unfathomable power!"

Howard sneered and whispered to Albert, "His accent is as deplorable as yours."

"Need I remind you that he is Hungarian, while I am a son of Germany?" Albert whispered his reply.

"I hardly recognize the difference. At some point in time your ancestors were cast from the same set of Bavarian loins."

"Now is not the time, Howard," Albert mumbled. "What are they doing?"

Five hooded figures oozed from the shadows. One of them held a tetrahedron filled with the same green and black swirling liquid found in Albert's and Howard's guns. Once close enough, the hooded figure bowed and placed the pyramid at Szilveszter's feet. He then rejoined the ranks of those at the edge of the shadows. The other four men dragged a naked woman before their leader. Her black hair, a nest of tangles, flopped around as she shook her head from side to side, back to front as she cried for help. She twitched and trembled with every head jerk, changing the language in which she shrieked. Snapping her head to her right shoulder, she screamed for help in French. Mere seconds later, her head peeled backward and she moaned her pleas in German. Snap to the left. Spanish.

"She seems to know more languages than the average person. Have they bewitched her?" Howard whispered to Albert.

Tightening his grip on the gun, Albert shifted his stance, readying himself to rush from behind the boxes and stop this ceremony. "I don't believe so. It appears that she is mad, touched by different personalities. I have read cases about people with different personalities being able to speak different languages, sometimes never knowing them beforehand. This poor woman seems to be one such case. That hardly matters now, we need to stop this."

Howard grabbed Albert's shirt sleeve. "Not yet. We need to see what Matuska is doing, which Forbidden Knowledge he's attempting to access."

The hooded figures tied the woman to the floor in front of Szilveszter, strapping her wrists and ankles to metal stakes, and then moved away to join the others in the shadows. Flopping on the floor in jerking spasms, she continued to scream in ever changing languages. The low chant of "Eeeeeya" started again, but quieter than before.

"Madness! Madness begets madness! Madness and pain!" Szilveszter shouted.

The hooded men all stepped forward, each holding a large glass jar. They weren't close enough to the lantern light for Albert to see what the jars held; he only saw movement within them. A jar shattered by the woman. Shards of glass cut small slices into her skin, blood slowly oozing from the fresh wounds. The contents of the jar scattered over her. Insects.

Another jar crashed to pieces beside her. Then another. The hooded figures all threw their jars to the ground, each exploding like a glass grenade and throwing insects over the woman. Flying, crawling, squirming, stinging insects swarmed on her, making their way into her mouth, ears, bloodied cuts. The insects buzzed as the woman howled and thrashed.

The liquids in the pyramid swirled, churning faster as if controlled by the volume of the woman's screams, rising to a crescendo.

With the gleeful look of a satisfied child, Szilveszter took the pyramid from the floor and raised it over his head. Thunder rolled around outside, each rumble growing louder than the last, shaking the building. In a crackling explosion of noise, a hole formed in the roof, wood and shingle raining down. A column of blazing white light shined though the hole to the pyramid.

"Ia!" Szilveszter shouted. Upon his word, the light refracted from the pyramid into dozens of tiny beams shooting outward, each piercing the chest of a worshiper. The intensity of the insects' humming ratcheted up another notch.

"Ia!" Szilveszter shouted again. Another beam shot from the pyramid, green light swirling with black arcs of electricity, and shined upon the woman staked to the ground. The buzzing intensified, rising in pitch, as the insects began to dissolve, desiccating mid-flight. The screaming woman fared no better. Chunks of flesh covered sinew popped from her legs and arms, then exploded midair into a red mist. She was being deconstructed piece by piece until she was no more than slimy pink strings swirling with the insect particulate.

"Ia!" Szilveszter bellowed one final time. The whirlwind remains of the woman and insects twirled and formed thin strands. The strands spun together, cording into a single rope of carnage. Both ends of the rope anchored to the floor, forming an arch tall enough to accommodate the height of any man in the room. The air under the arch rippled, then split, discarded like tissue paper and giving way to an inky darkness, a whirlpool of green swirling within it. Two gray tentacles covered in sizzling goo wriggled from the archway, striking out with purpose toward the closest of the hooded celebrants. With a bone-crunching grip, the tentacles wrapped around the man and squeezed. A river of blood poured out from under his robes. The tentacles retracted and pulled the corpse into the darkness, leaving slick red streaks along the floor.

"How much madness and death must we witness?" Albert asked Howard as he moved to intervene.

"I believe we have discovered all that we need," Howard replied.

Leaping from behind the pile of boxes, Albert and Howard both shot at Szilveszter. Their aim was off, shaken by a burst of thunder rattling the building. The beams of dark energy crackled through the intervening space, striking a crate and a celebrant. The crate exploded into splinters; the robed figure's chest exploded into gore.

"No! Not again. You shall not stop me. The Ancient Lord of Madness will walk the Earth!" Szilveszter yelled. He wielded the pyramid before him, light beams still connected to each of his minions like shining marionette strings. The hooded figures all snapped to attention and turned to Albert and Howard. They rushed as one to attack.

Albert and Howard ran, weaving around boxes and crates, knocking them over to slow their pursuers. Looping around the perimeter of the warehouse, they continued to shoot at Szilveszter's minions, missing more than they hit.

Szilveszter continued to use the pyramid like a puppeteer yanking on the strings of his followers. He pulled left and right, snapped up and down. The tendrils of light cracked like whips as he commanded his charges to protect him and thwart the interlopers. Albert and Howard used their weaponized dark energies to destroy his drones. With each fallen worshiper, the duo advanced. The number of puppets dwindled.

A stray beam struck a crate, and the oil lamp upon it fell. Flames engulfed the surrounding wood and corrugated paper-board. The blaze found purchase immediately, consuming more and more of the warehouse. Fire climbed the wooden support posts and blanketed two of the four walls.

Heat rippled the air. Wood popped. Ash and glowing ember rained down. The fire danced behind Szilveszter, growing larger by the second and eating into his chances for escape. Hope bloomed within Albert's chest as he and Howard drew closer.

Szilveszter rushed to the portal and cried out, "Master! Great Lord of Madness, hear my plea! I wish to free you, to be your harbinger, but my enemies... *our* enemies ruined it. Save me!"

In response to his begging, the archway portal throbbed, and the buzzing grew louder than the raging flames and cracking wood. The green and black within the portal swirled, blending together into one sickly color of milky fester. The whirlpool of decay spun faster, subtle shapes formed in the murkiness. The color darkened, shifting back to black as the spiraling slowed. Finally the maelstrom stopped, and within the portal was the view of a desert wasteland. No sun to illuminate the barren ground. Without hesitation, Szilveszter lunged through, the image rippling like waves in a pool.

The portal began to fade. The organic archway slowly sloughed apart, the flesh flaking away and mixing with the floating ash. Albert and

Howard arrived too late to snatch their prey. Albert pushed aside the frustrations of defeat while he scanned the warehouse for an unencumbered way to exit. Finding a tenuous path through the flames, he grabbed his friend's arm and yelled, "This way, Howard! If we hurry, we can—"

"No!" Howard yanked his arm away and pointed at the collapsing archway. "We must pursue."

"You're as insane as he. This is a portal to the unknown crafted from mystics and madness. We must run before the fire robs us of all chance of escape."

"Szilveszter escaped through the portal and we must follow. We must put an end to his plans. Nothing else matters."

"I have two children and one on the way, that's what matters! My wife is pregnant and I must go back home to be with her."

Howard regarded Albert, his expression pleading more than his words. "Albert, you saw. You saw with your own eyes what Szilveszter intends to do. If we do not follow, there will be no *world* for your wife, your children."

Tears welled in Albert's eyes. He looked at the dissipating portal. What horrors lie beyond? To what world, dimension, or universe must he travel? "My family."

"Yes! Your family will only survive if we do this. I cannot track and defeat him alone, Albert. We must traverse through the portal together. And we must hasten our pace!"

Gritting his teeth, Albert grabbed Howard's arm again, his strength born from fear, frustration, anger. Without another word, Albert Einstein and Howard Phillips Lovecraft leapt through the portal just as it vanished and the fiery ceiling collapsed.

Chapter 2

William McCarty, Jr. had a face that seemed a half-decade younger than his twenty years; oval in shape, with eyebrows arched in a way that implied youthful curiosity. His sandy hair was shaggy and unkempt, just long enough to tickle the bottom of his neck and peek out from under the front of his slouch hat with dented crown. His front teeth were a bit more prominent than he cared for, but they did nothing to diminish the charm of a smile disarming enough to get him out of, and sometimes into, trouble. But his smile alone was not enough to put food in his belly. For that, he needed to call upon other skills.

William played poker with four other men at a round wooden table, the top rippled with warps and dents from years of sweat and spilled drinks that worked into cuts and cracks, testaments to the many years of bored or nervous patrons picking away at it with a knife. The evening crowd at the saloon took little notice of the men at the table, partaking in various forms of merriment from drunken tall-tale telling to small groups singing to ogling the girls dancing to the upbeat tunes of the piano. Nary a hand in the bar could be found bereft of a sloshing mug of beer.

Across the table from William sat a burly mountain of a man with hands so large the playing cards he held looked like postage stamps. Eyes the color of coal squinted at his cards while the left side of his black handlebar mustache jiggled each time he mumbled his intent from the corner of his mouth. "Raise ten," he said sliding two five-dollar notes into the pot at the center of the table.

The next two men folded, but the third, the cheater wearing the bowler hat, matched the bet and raised it another five. William smiled and said, "Well, don't we have some very impressive hands amongst the three of us? I reckon I'll bump it up another five to get myself an idea of how impressive they are."

As he suspected, the other two men raised as well, further dwindling their funds. The man with the mustache had four sevens while the other man had a full house of aces over kings. William knew this, since he was the one who gave those hands to them.

William had controlled the game ever since he sat down, rigging the deck when it was his turn to deal or distracting the other players with pleasant conversation while plying them with jiggers of whiskey. The man with the bowler hat cheated as well, but nowhere near as well as William. During one hand, the man dealt himself a flush, yet William had convinced him to fold. But now William grew weary of cards, and wanted to tickle his fancy with the other dalliances the bar had to offer, so he decided on one last hand, and dealt the sevens right to the handlebar mustachioed monster. The man drew one card anyway, trying to convince the table he was trying for a straight or a flush. Seeing that the fellow with the bowler had a few aces up his sleeve, William dealt him two kings and an ace. Knowing the bowler man couldn't resist the temptation, he drew two. William watched from the corner of his eye while the man quickly switched the cards. After a few more rounds of raising, William had enough. "Well, I'm gonna go ahead and call so I can have me a gander at your cards."

The brute smiled, the curls of his mustache shifting toward his nose. "Four sevens."

"Horse shit!" the man in the bowler yelled, slapping his cards down on the table to reveal his impotent full house.

Knowing that the simmering joy of his large opponent could boil into bubbling ire at any moment, William decided not to tease; instead he quietly placed his four jacks on the table. Forcing back a smile, he collected the pot, and grabbed his satchel from under his chair. Standing, he tipped his hat and said, "Pleasure doin' business with you gentlemen. I now find myself in need of other forms of entertainment. Good day."

William wove his way through the jostles of partially inebriated patrons and sidled up to the bar, taking a spot right next to one of the dancing girls sitting on the corner. Her hair was long and black, loose ringlets framed her tan face and flowed over her shoulders. Her full lips were soft pink and her makeup emphasized the sparkle in her green eyes. Ruffles and frills abounded, her dress was red and the off-the-shoulder short sleeves emphasized her cleavage. The outfit finished with black boots that went up to her knees. William unleashed his smile. It was time for some trouble. "*Hola.*"

"*Hola*," she replied with a purr that suggested she liked what William had to offer.

Always feeling the need to press his luck, William continued, "*¿Si compro una bebida para usted, usted hará el desayuno para mi?*"

She laughed. "I will always accept a drink. But I will need more than a 'hello' to make breakfast for you tomorrow."

"Well, that is certainly promisin'."

"Is it?"

"You didn't say no, so that means there is a chance for a yes."

"Well, that is certainly true."

Extending his hand, he said, "My name is William. William H. Bonney."

Placing her hand in his, she uncrossed and then recrossed her legs. "Rosalina."

Looking directly into her eyes, William kissed the back of her hand. "Rosalina? Just Rosalina?"

"What more do you need?"

"What if I want to find you after tomorrow mornin'?"

"You ask for Rosalina, I will be found."

"So—" William started, but the large hand clamping down on his shoulder interrupted him. Squirming his way out of the grasp, William spun away from the bar. The swindled poker player, looking none too happy. Only coming up to the angry man's chin, it was time for William to test the charm power of his smile. "Now, what seems to be the problem?"

The music stopped. The dancing stopped. The singing, bawdy jokes, and uproarious conversations all stopped. All eyes turned to the large man with the handlebar mustache and the young man in the center of the room. The man pointed to William with a meaty finger and grumbled, "You cheated."

William ran his hands over his vest and shirtsleeves to smooth away wrinkles that didn't exist. "Whatever do you mean, sir?"

"I counted the deck. I counted fifty-four cards."

"Well, did we all hear that? This fine gentlemen demonstrated that he, indeed, did receive enough schoolin' to be able to count to fifty-four."

The crowd laughed. The scorned man did not. Fists clenched, spittle sprayed past his lips as he fumed. "Not funny!"

"All right, all right," William said, gesturing to the crowd to cease with the laughter. "So, I must ask, which cards were duplicated?"

"The aces. Two extra."

"And what hand did I win with?"

"Four jacks."

"Well, friend, there you go. Why would I put extra aces in the deck when I had no need for them? Now, I reckon the fellow in the round hat may have had somethin' to do with the extra aces, since he had an ace high full house."

Both men and many of the patrons looked to the table at which the game had been played. All the seats were empty. Scowling, the big man yelled, "You're trying to trick me!"

Sighing, William put his hands on his hips, pulling back the bottom of his vest to expose two Colt six-shooters. "It has become quite obvious to me that you might not know who I am, so let me introduce myself. I am sometimes referred to as William H. Bonney, but most people know me as Billy the Kid."

Between his erubescent face and his devilish mustache, the man's countenance began to resemble that of Satan. Hellfire burning behind his eyes, he shouted, "I do not care who you are! I will kill you and your whore for stealing from me! I will——" The empty whiskey bottle smacking the back of his head cut him short.

Rosalina hopped down from the bar and hit him again on the top of his head. He crumbled to the ground and curled into the fetal position to protect himself as the crowd collectively winced and said, "Ooooooooooo!"

After gently placing the bottle on the bar, Rosalina kicked his exposed rump and said, "Do *not* call me a whore!"

William barely had time to grab his satchel and sling it over his shoulder before Rosalina took his arm and led him toward the exit. The crowd parted to give them unimpeded egress; William smiled, occasionally tipping his hat and nodding to the patrons as he passed.

The night air was crisp and cool. Hanging oil lanterns lit the main street, but did little to penetrate the darkness of any side alley. Laughing about their harrowing escape, William and Rosalina remained arm in arm as they scooted down one of the alleys to a secondary road. Catching his breath, William slowed his pace and placed his hand on hers. "So where to?"

"Whichever inn you would like. I know them all."

"Inn? So, you're not a local either?"

"Oh, I am. I do not care to bring business into my home."

"Business? You mean…? I thought you hit that brutish man because he called you a name you found a mite unsavory?"

Rosalina giggled. "Despite speaking it in Spanish, did you honestly think your line would work?"

William stopped walking. His smile disappeared. "Oh. Then… then why'd you hit him with a bottle?"

"I just do not like the word. Nor the tone in which he used it. So, do you have a preference of an inn, or shall I pick?"

Dismayed that his charm did not work quite as well as he thought, he mulled over her offer anyway. There were many other fellows to bed at the bar tonight, yet she chose him. Plus, he was the big winner at the poker table, so a few dollars to slide down her bodice for a night's worth of company seemed very acceptable. Just before he could articulate his desires, a patch of air toward the edge of town rippled, then split open.

An oval shaped hole with glowing amber edges hung in the air, flames reaching out from the center. A young man wearing black and green robes fell through the hole onto the dirt road. Rosalina shrieked and ran away screaming, "*¡El Diablo! El Diablo!*"

"It's not the devil!" William yelled to her. "It's just some fool dressed like a carnival geek! Probably a circus magic trick gone wrong!"

Rosalina disappeared behind the next building, and William cursed his luck. This fool who ruined a fun night was going to pay. The fall had knocked the wind out of the stranger as he lolled on the ground gasping for air. William drew one of his guns and walked toward the man, but stopped when something on the ground caught his eye—a pyramid-shaped object. He picked it up. It was half as big as a head, and light enough to be held by one hand. The swirling liquids mesmerized him, black and green and refusing to mix together.

"Mine!" the man barked as he jumped to his feet and lunged at William.

William sidestepped the stranger with ease, and then trained the sights of his gun on him. "Stay where you stand, sir. I would hate to have the blood of a stranger on my hands tonight, even though you did ruin my chance to peek at Heaven with a mighty fine Mexican dancer."

"Heaven?" the man spat the word from his mouth as if it burned his lips. "My name is Szilveszter Matuska, and I tell you that Heaven is a mere fairy tale, told by uneducated cretins slogging about the muck beneath my feet!"

"Oh my, what an accent you have there. You certainly have a less than delicate way about you, don't ya? Well, I—" Szilveszter lunged again, but this time William pulled the trigger. The bullet struck the earth by Szilveszter's feet, the spray of hardened dirt flicking his robes. Szilveszter stopped and glowered. Fixated on the pyramid, his eyes glowed with madness.

"Hey now. Didn't I just tell ya not to do that?" Just as William thought he had the situation under control, two more figures flopped from the hole in the air right as it winked into nothingness. Szilveszter took advantage of the distraction and ran down a darkened alleyway before William could react.

"It's as if every hair on my ass turned into a briar tonight," William mumbled as he put the pyramid into his satchel. Gun still drawn, he walked over to the two men helping each other to their feet. They looked harmless enough, but their guns concerned him, like none he had ever seen before. "Now, who the hell might you two be?"

Panting, the men frantically looked around. The one with the mustache spoke first. "I don't see him. I don't see Szilveszter."

"You mean the fella wearin' odd lookin' clothing and seemed a bit touched in the noggin?" William asked.

The other man, the one with the long face, looked at William's gun and took a step backward. He slowly opened the satchel slung over his shoulder and placed his own gun inside. "I do believe your description of the person we are searching for is an accurate one. You've seen him?"

"Yup. Came fallin' through that hole a bit before you two did. Said somethin' about Heaven being a fairy tale and then ran away. Had an accent a little like your friend's. Now, who might you two be?"

The man with the mustache put his gun in the satchel as well and stepped forward, "I am Albert Einstein. My young friend is Howard Philips Lovecraft. And your name is…?"

"Pleasure to meet you, Albert, Howard. I, myself, am William H. Bonney, but you can call me Billy, which is short for Billy the Kid." With a tip of his hat, William holstered his gun.

Despite his brow furrowing deeper, Howard's eyes grew wide. Albert wore a look of confusion. "Billy the—? I understand the question I am about to ask will come across as quite peculiar, but I beg that you answer it honestly—where are we and what is today's date?"

William winced as if Howard had splashed him with water. "You're right. I do find that question rather queer. We're standin' in the town of Santa Fe in the New Mexican territory of the United States of America. And today is the fourteenth of March, 1879."

Albert wobbled as if he had forgotten how to use his legs. Howard grabbed his friend by the arm for support.

"What the hell is wrong with you?" William asked.

"Today," Albert said, voice but a whisper, "Today… I am born."

Chapter 3

Martha Jane Cannary fiddled with the empty shot glass in her left hand while she absently played with the corner of the poster in her right, as she had been doing for the past two hours. She barely felt the textures of the beige parchment as she rolled the corner inward a couple inches with her calloused thumb, then unrolled it over her index finger. Ignoring the printed words, she stared at the image and tapped her shot glass on the much maligned bar top.

The barkeep ambled over and filled her glass with an amber colored whiskey. "You see her show yet?"

Moving only her eyes, Martha glared at the barkeep. "Not yet. Headed there soon."

The tips of his walrus mustache fluttered with every "f" and "s" that passed over his lips. "It's a good show, for sure. Easy on the eyes and hard on the targets with them irons of hers."

Martha responded by slugging her shot and tapping her glass again, her sticky stare conveying her lack of appreciation for his comments.

Smirking, he poured another shot. As he walked away, he said, "She puts on a helluva good show."

Stewing, Martha looked at the girl on the poster. She found the pose ridiculous, the girl training her shotgun on something off the right side of the paper while wearing a frilly dress, bodiced in the middle to accentuate her hips and bosom.

Martha thought about being that young once, that attractive too. Sure, some might think she wasted her youth bouncing from bedroll to bedroll, but she eventually found Bill Hickok. She loved Bill; loved him enough to step out of the way when he wanted to marry another woman. Their time together was brief, but intense. It had been three years since Bill was shot in the back, but Martha still felt alone, her only friends being whiskey and beer. She felt old, too old to garner the same level of attention she could so long ago.

Hell, at twenty-seven, she could hardly be considered an old maid! So her waist jiggled a bit more while riding her horse. Somewhere along the way, her breasts went from "full" to "floppy," but she could scarcely remember when. Her thighs spread and her ass added extra padding anytime she sat down. "More cushion for the pushin'," Bill would have said. She snorted to herself and tossed her shot back, the whiskey burning from tonsils to tailbone. She missed Bill something fierce.

Martha removed her hat and used her sleeve to wipe the sweat from her brow. She ran her fingers through her short hair while looking at the flowing curls of the strumpet on the poster. The starlet's hair was hardly the reason why Martha traveled from South Dakota to New Mexico, nor was it because of the girl's pretty face, perky tits, or shapely gams. No, Martha was here because of the girl's gun.

This girl was from Ohio! What did they know about shooting east of the Mississippi? Big stupid creatures like deer? Black bears slow from hibernation? Large and easy targets, in Martha's mind. Nothing like what she plugged in her days like snakes ready to inject their venom or wolves desperate for their next meal.

Ire whirling around in her guts and mixing with the whiskey, Martha stood from the barstool and needed to shift her feet to keep from falling. She put her hat back on, used both hands to center it, and shoved the paper in the pocket of her tanned leather jacket. The dozen strings of turquoise beads clacked against each other as she walked out of the bar. She needed to wear a cotton undershirt to keep her nipples from being rubbed raw by the thick hide, but the matching leather trousers were far more comfortable.

The sun wobbled in the sky, as it often did around noon and after too many shots of hootch. Martha shielded her eyes from the brightness and with short jerky steps wobbled from the bar at the edge of town, across the stretch of plains grass, to the temporary setup of the carnival.

With the edges of her vision rippling, she squinted to focus on the center of her world. Her first priority was getting to the carnival; she'd find the girl once she got there. Streamers of every color flowed from the rows of canvas tents, going from limp to lively any time the slightest breeze kicked up. Past the first layer of tents was the main path, grass flattened or worn away, dirt packed hard from usage. People of all shapes and sizes and ages and skin tones and careers bustled along. Sticky faced children with handfuls of candy zipped about the ever moving maze of adult legs, rushing from one rigged game to the next or trying to get a free gander at what lurked within the arcane tents advertising various freaks of nature. Men in overalls walked equal with men in ties, nary a hand bereft of treats like stick-speared pickles or grease-soaked bags of peanuts, all with salted lips in dire need of the quenching powers of overpriced beers and fruit juices. Women clung to the arms of their respective men, guiding them from vending tent to vending tent, listening to the pitches of snake oil salesmen with their tales of adventures in far off lands to procure the exotic perfumes or spices that could be theirs for a price that was but a pittance of the treasure's value. Martha found zero interest in any of that, never yielding from her quest to find the girl on the poster.

Noises and voices blurred into one dull rhythmic thrum. Once in every twenty or so paces, a caller's booming voice made itself known, but was quickly drowned out by the surrounding cacophony. Martha even ignored the harsh words thrown her way by passersby whom she jostled or stepped on, mere collateral to her mission until she finally found what she was looking for.

With a glassy-eyed snarl, Martha paid her two bits to the fast-talking man in front of the tent, and followed the throng inside. The patrons filled the benches in an orderly fashion, starting with the rows in the front and working their way back. There was no back wall to the tent, just an opening with a five-foot gap to the stage, thirty feet long, as wide as the tent itself.

Almost a quarter hour early, Martha found herself sitting in the middle of all the benches. The time passed quickly as she tried to formulate a plan. Or maybe she took an alcohol-induced nap, she wasn't too sure. She jerked with a start, pretty sure she was awoken by a snort, and also pretty sure it was her own. The glares of disgust from those seated closest to her as well as the line of drool down her chin lent credence to her theory.

The tent wanted to spin on her, but she anchored herself by gripping the bench with both hands and focusing her attention on the center of the stage. Her stomach throbbed to the beat of her heart, making it difficult to think. However, she ran out of time for thinking or planning when the same man she had paid sauntered his way to the center of the stage. "Ladies and gentlemen, I know you have traveled far and wide, from every corner of this great nation of ours to witness the magnificence of the performer you are all here to see. Since she needs no further ado, I give to you the greatest shot from ocean to ocean, all the way from Cincinnati, Ohio, the one, the only, Miss Annie Oakley!"

The crowd erupted with applause and cheers and whistles and one lone boo as the curtain raised. Frozen in pose was the girl on the paper, the girl Martha had been hunting and hating, Annie Oakley. She stood facing the crowd wearing a flouncy dress much like the one in her picture, left foot propped up on a wooden crate no taller than her knee, both hands holding a rifle. She smiled so broadly it was as if the gun were made of gold. Loose curls of black hair fell about her face, and a tiny top hat, five inches in height, adorned her head.

A phonograph played scratchy trumpet music, upbeat and meant to keep the crowd's emotions high, but the crowd itself soon drowned it out. Applause and cheers filled the tent, some patrons even standing to demonstrate their ovation. Martha jeered, but she, too, was drowned out.

Annie remained in the same pose as when the curtain lifted, a statue carved from pure glee. The cheers died down, but the booing did not. Annie started the show.

Still smiling, Annie rested the barrel of the rifle on her shoulder and held the butt of it in her right hand. With a perky spring in her step, she marched around the crate in time to the music. As she did, the backdrop—a cartoonish depiction of the desert painted on a six-foot tall canvas strapped to two rolls—scrolled along as she marched. The audience clapped in time to the music, loud enough to cover up Martha's continuous booing, as Annie mimed her journey.

The music changed to encourage feelings of suspense and trepidation. The crowd stopped clapping. From the right side of the stage, a wooden pole pushed a taxidermied coyote onto the scene. The canvas backdrop stopped scrolling. Annie stopped marching and reeled back, pantomiming fear. Gasps, and one jeer, came from the audience.

Muzzle molded into a permanent snarl, the coyote held a menacing pose, ready to pounce. The pole prodded the back legs, moving the stuffed animal from side to side while inching it closer to its prey. Annie cocked her rifle and pressed the butt against her shoulder, lining up the sights to defend against the vicious predator. The pole disappeared. She squeezed the trigger. Many in the audience jerked in their seats, startled by the thunder of the rifle. A burst of fur exploded as the bullet struck the already dead animal, sending it careening off stage. The crowd erupted with excitement, except for Martha shouting, "What a bunch of horse shit! She's standing twenty feet from her target!"

The lively trumpet from the phonograph returned, as did Annie's cheerful march around the crate, the scrolling backdrop, the clapping, and the booing from Martha. After a minute a new threat appeared. A rogue with a handlebar mustache glued to his face, tips spiraling inward, and a top hat, two feet tall. Brandishing a handgun, he demanded money from Annie. The audience booed and jeered the outlaw while Martha continued to boo and jeer Annie.

Wearing a face of bravery, Annie trained her rifle again. The base villain froze. Annie squeezed the trigger. With another booming crack of her rifle, the scoundrel's hat flew from his head. Arms wind-milling for comedic effect, he retreated.

Appreciating the storyline, the audience again cheered and laughed. The change in music cued Annie to return to her journey, however it would be stopped again. Not by the story-line, but by one cantankerous audience member.

Not able to tolerate this farce any longer, Martha stood and jumped onto the bench seat, yelling, "Liar! This is all horse shit and lies!"

The audience gasped as if the desert bandit had returned to exact his revenge. A scratch came from the phonograph and the music stopped. Searching for answers, Annie looked to her crewmembers off either side of the stage. She received shoulder shrugs in response.

Martha yelled again, "You ain't the best in the country! You ain't some sharpshooter. You ain't no good at all. I might not be the best in the land, but I sure as shit am better than you."

All eyes were on Martha now, including Annie's. Squinting, she regarded the loud woman. "There's something mighty familiar about you, ma'am," Annie called out from the stage. "The way you look and dress. You seem a bit too far along into a bottle of spirits. Maybe too much for my show? But why are you yelling about your gunmanship? Wait… wait a gosh darn second. You…? You wouldn't happen to be Calamity Jane, ma'am?"

"I am!" Martha said, straightening her body as best as her inebriation would allow. "But I ain't no ma'am."

Martha took a bit of pride in making the crowd gasp again.

Annie offered a sugary smile and said, "Well, it is certainly a pleasure to have a fellow sharpshooter among us."

"Girlie, you and I ain't equals."

Annie jerked her head back and blinked, still playing to the crowd. "Surely you must have been here long enough to have seen my skills so far."

"Skills?" Martha barked as if insulted. "You're shootin' things that ain't more than twenty feet from your face. They ain't movin', neither! You got no gun skills. I got gun skills." With that, she drew her revolver.

The crowd cringed, those closest to Martha scrambling to get away from her. The men in the crowd tried to shield or shuttle away fussing women and crying children. Martha used her shaky left hand to steady her rubbery right arm. She closed her left eye to reduce the number of Annies she saw from five to three. Aiming for the tiny top hat of the middle Annie, she lined up her sights as best her quaking arms allowed. Screams ripped through the crowd.

Martha squeezed the trigger.

Chapter 4

Feet shoulder width apart and with a slight bend at the knees, Howard stared at the brass pot on the floor, half filled with liquid. This was a form of Hell for him, Albert knew. Attempting to perform such a private act in the corner of a rented room with two other people in it was too great a mountain to climb. Howard drew in a deep breath and exhaled slowly. Much to Albert's surprise, the sound of splashing water filled the room.

No sooner did the stream start, William offered a smirk and a wink to Albert and said, "Don't splash."

Howard winced and the stream stopped. "Damnation! The savagery of this place is reprehensible!"

Leaning back in his rickety chair, William added a few more scuffmarks to the already scuffed table with his boots and laughed. "Ah, come on. I'm just joshin' ya."

Fighting the urge to join in the razzing, Albert stifled a smile and offered, "There is an outhouse behind this inn, Howard. I can't imagine it being any more comfortable, but it should at least offer privacy."

Buttoning his trousers, Howard stormed out of the room's lone door, all the while mumbling about the barbarism of this period of time in America.

Wiping away a tear, William said, "Your friend sure ain't cut out for this kind of living, is he?"

"No, I'm afraid not."

The next few minutes around the room's lone table were spent in silence. Fingers folded together over his chest, William squinted at Albert, regarding the mustachioed man. Albert knew that William didn't trust him. How could he? Two men burst from the sky, chasing a third and claimed to be from the future? Preposterous. From the legends of Billy the Kid, Albert considered it a minor miracle that William didn't shoot everybody and walk away. Instead, William had asked very few questions when they met last night, and reacted to the information given to him as if he had accepted it. He even rented this room for the three of them.

Even though Howard was the same age as William and more physically suited for sleeping on the floor than Albert, he was ensnared by the trappings of the modern era whence he came and expressed that he could tolerate nothing less than the bed, barely large enough for one person. Allowing Howard the comfort of the bed, Albert took the floor, but slumber was elusive as his mind churned with the notion of traveling thirty-one years into the past. William slept in a chair, placed between the bed and the door, with his feet propped on the bed. He kept his satchel under the chair and looped its strap around the chair's legs.

When they had been awoken by dawn's first pale rays, William was well rested while bags resided under Howard's and Albert's eyes. They ate breakfast in the dining room of the inn. Albert enjoyed his bacon and eggs that had been cooked in the same unwashed iron skillet while Howard enjoyed nothing and unceasingly expressed that sentiment. William sat and watched, a beer and two shots of whiskey accompanying his breakfast. After they finished, they returned to the room to plan what to do next, William bringing the whiskey bottle with him.

Now William stared at Albert, stopping only to sit forward and pour himself a shot. He slugged it back, poured a second one, and slid it to Albert. Offering a polite smile, Albert slid it back. "I am from Germany. I'm afraid I have more of a taste for dark ales rather than American whiskey."

"Germany," William repeated. "Explains your funny accent. So, other than chase spooky men who want to raise demons from other dimensions with your friend, what do you do in Germany?"

"I am a physics professor for one of our colleges."

"Physics?"

"Physical sciences."

"Ahhhh, yes." William lifted the bottle stopper and dropped it on the table. "Gravity is all I truly need to know about the world of physical sciences, because that's one of the few laws I can't break. Now, studyin' biology with a cute cantina chica... well, that's a different story."

Albert chuckled, acknowledging the truth in William's statement, in an effort to put him more at ease. "Unfortunately, we are slaves to many of the laws of science, including the laws of biology regarding man's desire for women, especially how they can reduce our minds to mush with a single word or the slightest of touch."

It was William's turn to chuckle. "I'll certainly drink to that!" He tossed back the shot meant for Albert, and went back to observing his new companion. "Germany, huh? So, how did a professor from Germany and a scary-story writer meet?"

"Well, I have had a few papers published—"

"Papers?"

"Theories, and proof to substantiate those theories. All regarding physics. Howard took note of my papers and contacted me to discuss them at great length. Then our conversations turned more philosophical, moving into metaphysics."

"Do I even need to ask?"

"Sorry. It is a form of conjecture, discussion, to explain the world around us that can't be explained."

"So, you mean like God? Or don't you got that in the future?"

Albert smirked. "We still have God. However, metaphysics is more like a stop gap between creating a formula for an answer and accepting an answer purely on faith."

William leaned back in his chair again, crossing his arms and pursing his lips. After heaving a sigh, he said, "Sounds like you future folk got too much time on your hands."

Albert nodded. "Sometimes, my friend, I feel that you are right."

"So, you and Howard started talkin' about... how to calculate God?"

"Not something quite that lofty, but you are not far off on your assessment. One of the topics we went back and forth on was the notions of good and evil. Are these ideas tangible? Calculable? Controllable? So, Howard and I decided to begin with the pineal gland."

"The what now?" William asked, face contorted as if he were in the midst of a headache. Forgoing the glass, he took a swig straight from the bottle.

Albert slowed down, making sure to keep his voice tempered and even so he wouldn't come across as condescending. "The pineal is a gland at the base of the brain about the size of a piece of rice. For centuries, it has been hypothesized that this is, for lack of a better term, 'the third eye.' Howard and I produced formulas and created machines, experimented and explored. We stimulated the pineal gland in rabbits, mice, cats, dogs and—much against my better judgment—monkeys."

Albert paused, working his jaw muscles as he turned his gaze to the morning sky outside the window, the sun shining on his dark memories. He whispered, "I'll take that whiskey now."

William filled the shot glass. Still watching the world beyond the window, Albert downed the alcohol and continued his story. "There is nothing natural about an animal experiencing madness. But why? What happened to them, we wondered. We felt that we had to continue to understand. While doing this research, we discovered that there were other individuals besides us performing similar experiments. However, they were experimenting on humans."

Not needing to be asked, William refilled the shot glass and then took a pull from the bottle himself. Albert's fingers slowly spun the glass as he continued, voice heavy from guilt, "Human beings should hardly suffer madness either, but it was learned that with their pineal gland enlarged and excited, they were able to peer into a whole different reality. Howard and I were determined to find answers, so we created a way to see what they saw, to peel back the fabric of this reality and peer into the other one. This other reality… it is one filled with darkness and vile creatures. A reality that possesses powerful monsters that our ancient societies worshiped as mad gods."

Albert drank the whiskey. "We opened a small hole into this other reality, just big enough to gather data. We even collected what could only be described as dark energy, a fuel of swirling green bile mixing in a pool of black ink."

Sitting back in his chair and slouching, William's hand fell to his side, fingers gliding over his satchel. "You experimented with that stuff? Even though you knew it was evil?"

"We did recognize that this knowledge was forbidden, and wished to cease our quest. However, the other explorers, whom I mentioned earlier, wish to rend the membrane of the realities and release the mad gods. Howard and I have been conducting covert operations ever since, stopping men such as Aleister Crowley, Grigori Rasputin, and Szilveszter Matuska."

William sat up again and brought the bottle to his lips for a long pull. Wiping his mouth with his shirt sleeve, he said, "Now, this fella that you were chasing last night, he is one of these men?"

"Indeed it was. Szilveszter Matuska. He's the worst of the lot, so far."

"Yeah? Judgin' from the funny robes he was wearin', he seems too touched in the head to be taken seriously."

"Touched he may be," Albert started, pausing to accept the bottle from William. A minor thought crossed his mind about how much easier the alcohol was going down, but it was washed away by the whiskey. "But his faculties are far from handicapped. He is mad. He is evil. And he is frightfully intelligent, having a penchant for demolitions."

"You mean explosives? Well, that is certainly a tricky trade to ply."

"Oh, to the best of my knowledge, he made no money from this passion of his." Albert leaned forward, the whiskey warmth flowing through his body, and looked directly into William's eyes. "He destroys things and kills people, simply because he enjoys doing so."

William swallowed hard. "He… enjoys it?"

"All too much," Albert said, satisfied that his words were having the desired effect. "Even though he is young, about your age, he has been linked to more than one event of mass deaths, including train wrecks. Witnesses even reported that he… that he…."

"Was less than gentlemanly with his privates as he took pleasure in watching the fruits of his labor," Howard said as he entered the room, the top of his shirt pulled over his nose from his trip to the outhouse. In his right hand were rolls of rough paper. "Albert, I feel the need to warn you—you and I have walked through a veritable field of rotting carcasses during a mission once before. The stench in that outhouse is far, far less pleasant."

William's face twisted with disgust. "You mean he was chokin' his chicken while watchin' trains wreck? Ugh! That is one sick sonuvabitch."

"Well put, William," Albert said. "Therein lies our dilemma. We don't know why his god of madness chose to transport him to this time period. We don't know what he knows or if he has a plan. We don't know where he would go. All we know is that he is sick and demented. We need to find him and stop him."

Stroking his chin, William eyed the ceiling in contemplation. "Yeesh. I have no idea where a fella like that would go."

Howard dropped the rolls of paper onto the table and tugged at the bottom of his shirt. "Well, I believe this may be a good place to start."

William and Albert unfurled the papers. Black ink on tan paper, one advertised the sharp-shooting abilities of Annie Oakley. Another, the horrors and wonders of an elephant man, a lizard woman, and a rotund bearded lady. One showed an image of a man with bulging pectoral muscles bending a metal bar, his flexed arms larger than his legs. The final paper advertised Zarkahn, a magician touting his skills in the black arts.

"The carnival," Howard said. "A menagerie of freaks and deviants. I don't think there is a more compelling place for Szilveszter."

William clapped his hands together and jumped from his chair. "Well, gentlemen, it looks like we're goin' to the carnival!"

Chapter 5

Children squealed as they ran about the meandering crowds, faces slicked and fingers gooey with remnants of sugary treats. Happy couples laughed, taking in the sights and sounds, savoring these tender memories to revisit in the future. Groups of friends whooped and hollered at every game of skill and chance, whether they were winners or, more often, losers. Camaraderie and good tidings flowed through the air as freely and vigorously as the flags that adorned every carnival tent. Howard hated this.

Walking beside Billy and Albert, winding their way through the ever-shifting throng of humanity, Howard groused to himself about people's base desires to revel in such frivolity. Every once and again, an example of the finer elements of what humanity had to offer could be found among the muck. One astute couple caught his eye. Fine looking coat over a well-tailored shirt, ascot tucked in neatly below the neck, smart trousers, and topped by an exquisite piece crafted by a talented haberdasher for the man; the lady on his arm would carry about a bundle of her dress in her free hand to keep from dragging it through the muck. Even though she wore boots designed to endure such terrain, the cobbler still made an effort at style. The lacing of her dress's bodice crisscrossed in an aesthetic pattern while ivory hued frills peeked from the sleeves. She, too, wore a flattering hat. A moment's reprieve, then around the bend came a crushing reminder of the demise in civility.

Another couple trotted by, equally content in their ungainliness as they were in their unseemly way of living. Both as portly as livestock, with sloppy and dull faces to match, they wore breeches thick and stained. Howard assumed them to work as butchers or behind the closed doors of a slaughterhouse; faded crimson handprints speckled their once-white shirts. Shades of yellow swirled from under each of their respective armpits and faded browns from the grease of past lunches and dinners splattered their chests.

Or maybe, the dead being eternally envious of the living, the butcher shop carcasses arose, unable to tolerate life's ambulatory hubris one iota longer, and marched themselves into the daylight. Meat simulacrums parading about, having discarded their shackles of being on display. He, nothing more than an upright swine bloated and distended by death gasses. She, an amalgam of other discarded pork products, breasts slabbed upon her pig belly like greasy chunks of ham, lolling from side to side as she walked.

"Ya know, they're just hard workin' folk," Billy said to Howard.

"Excuse me?" Howard snapped back.

"The… bigger… couple you been glarin' at. They're just regular folk, probably with thankless, backbreakin' jobs. They're just here to blow some steam off, like everyone else."

"If they spare the dollars between 'no longer hungry' and 'belt busting full,' then maybe they would have to break their backs less. And afford better attire."

"So, you have no workin' folk from your time? Or those on the constant edge of poverty?"

"We do. However, they don't celebrate their own offal by parading around in it."

"That is not true, Howard," Albert interjected. "In my country as well as yours and all other countries, past, present and future, there will always be those whom you would deem less savory due to their choice of lifestyle."

Howard scowled, his under bite jutting out even further. Billy walked beside him, satchel slung over his shoulder, while he ate peanuts from a funnel of thick brown paper. Howard had a satchel over his shoulder as well; the weight of the bag irritated him, but not as much as Billy's laissez-faire attitude. "Maybe if you spent more time focusing on the mission at hand and less time shoveling detestable snacks into your gullet like the rest of these dirt-wallowers, we could find Szilveszter and stop his undoubtedly nefarious plan."

Billy took a handful of the pre-shelled nuts and dropped them into his mouth one at a time as if loading ammunition into a weapon of disgust. Once full, he chewed in exaggerated chomps and proceeded to speak, shooting nuggets of nut with sprays of spittle. "Well, if you'd be kind enough to share with me exactly what we're lookin' for, I'd be more than happy to oblige."

Howard reeled back, upper lip curled in disgust from Billy's eating habits. Albert laughed and said, "Unfortunately, we have little to go on, so just keep looking for anything unusual."

Five clowns loped by on stilts tall enough to step over most people. Voracious maws of lunacy painted upon white powdered faces made Howard's skin crawl. The clowns shrieked and cackled as if speaking to each other through some arcane language of witches. A few of the clowns carried thin tins of soapy mixture and large hoops. Drawing the hoops through the air, they created bubbles with rainbow sheens that bobbled freely into the sky. Howard said, "Well, it seems that the definition of 'unusual' is subjective and in a constant state of flux."

Billy waved to the clowns and laughed along with them as they passed by on uneven spider legs. "Oh, lighten up, will ya?"

Howard stopped and snarled at Billy. "Lighten up, did you say? My partner and I have chased a lunatic *through time* into a part of America that exemplifies why we should have never left the comforts of British rule, where the aforementioned lunatic is determined to summon from another dimension a great and terrible creature capable of incomprehensible evil. Now I find myself stuck with you, who is more focused on frivolous foods than assisting us in searching for anything out of sorts!"

"Yeah?" Billy asked, still displaying his easy going smile. "You haven't found anythin' out of sorts?"

"No, I loathe to confess that I have not."

"So, it's completely natural and normal that durin' the busiest time of day, there are at least half a dozen attractions that are closed."

Billy was right.

The carnival layout was that of a horseshoe, the walkway wide enough to accommodate eight people shoulder to shoulder. The outside tents were reserved for special attractions, while the inside tents held games of chance and skill, more rigged than not. Between the two ends of the horseshoe shape were two larger tents as well as a pavilion with a stage and bench seating.

Finding it vile that human nature would compel an individual to willingly lay down a portion of their hard-earned wages to ogle at the repulsiveness of those burdened by a physical malady, Howard had given the tents along the outer rim, reserved for the sideshow freaks, nothing more than a cursory glance when he first arrived. A hand painted canvas affixed to the one tent next to the entrance depicted a human brain with two eye stalks, a menacing gaze cast to all who observed. The phrases "Living Brain in a Jar" and "See the Eyes Move" were scrawled across the top and bottom of the advertisement. Howard felt confident that the attraction was mere costume and mechanics, but he did find it odd to see the tent flap shut, guarded by a sign reading "Closed" on a pedestal.

The adjacent tent housed the strongman from one of the parchment posters Howard had collected. A "Closed" sign stood in front of that tent as well. Two tents away was the lizard-woman, a human-reptile hybrid with scales instead of skin, if the emphatic advertisements were to be believed. Howard guessed it to be a poor soul blighted by full body psoriasis. Like the others, that attraction was closed. Closed signs also blocked the entrances to Madame Sulola, the mystic fortuneteller, her clairvoyance coming from beyond the realms of the dead, and Zarkahn, the master of magics who professed to manipulate the cosmic membrane between dimensions as if it were made of mere tissue paper. These two concerned Howard. If they did possess even a modicum of the power purported via the advertisements, then they would make quite enticing allies for Szilveszter.

"Well done, William," Albert said, his gaze moving from tent to tent. "Now if we could only surmise were they might be congregating."

After tossing another handful of peanuts into his mouth, Billy used his head to gesture to another tent. "What if we just follow that fella over there?"

A thin man wearing an oversized shirt and belted trousers, making him look even thinner, popped out of the Bearded Woman tent with a "closed" sign on a post in hand. After placing the sign in front of the tent entrance, he closed the flap and walked around the side.

Albert and Howard exchanged glances; Albert smirking, Howard grimacing. Albert said, "Again, William, excellent observation. Now, let's see if he can lead us to Szilveszter."

The trio weaved their way through the crowd. As inconspicuously as possible, they slipped between tents to the outside of the horseshoe. A few other stray attendees wandered around and handfuls of hired help milled about in tight groups. Careful not to trip over the web-work of ropes anchoring the tents to the ground, the trio followed the curve of the tents to where the carnival's transportation cars were stowed. Fortune smiled upon them as they found the skinny man and followed him to a section corded off for employees and performers.

Voices. One particularly familiar voice stood out. Stopping beside one of the carnival's wooden transportation cars, the trio listened and poked their heads around for a better view. In an alcove formed by the carnival vardo wagons and cages containing animals were the missing sideshow freaks, congregating around Szilveszter.

Albert whispered, "Our suspicions were correct. We're too far away to engage, but we have the element of surprise. I suggest we press forward, and hopefully we can set an ambush."

"Agreed," Howard whispered back. He rummaged through his satchel and procured two guns, one for himself and one for Albert. "I believe you should go left. I will sneak around to the right."

Rolling his sleeves up, Billy whispered, "I'll go right up the middle."

Howard frowned. "Your idea is ludicrous. Do you plan to sprint to them with guns blazing?"

"I can be more subtle than that." He crouched down and, with a wink, disappeared under the transportation car. Albert and Howard crouched down as well to see that the cars were set up on wheels high enough for Billy to crawl under them with ease. As they readied their weapons, Albert smirked. "The history books do say he was cunning."

"Even a broken clock is right twice a day," Howard mumbled. A quick stride to the back of the car and he was in position. Stepping with purpose and resolve, he focused on making nary a noise as he crept along the length of the car. Once at the end, he judged the gap between this car and the next. Three paces, he took with hastened step when no one was looking his direction. Success! Again, he slunk along the length of the car, getting closer to Szilveszter and his newfound cabal, taking great care to avoid the animal droppings that grew in number as he got closer to the cages. Curious about Billy's whereabouts, he crouched down and looked under the wooden cars. The ruffian was as close as he could get to the target, his guns drawn and ready to use at a moment's notice.

The offensive animal smells gagged Howard, but he forced down the ripple in the back of his throat and clung to his determination. Deftly, he navigated the five paces of open space to the next wooden car for a much better view of his target.

Despite routinely seeing the impossible and the unnatural since partnering with Albert, it still held him confounded when he witnessed it. He wondered if exposure to the madness in others condemned him to descend into it. The sideshow attraction of the brain in a jar could no longer be considered a charlatan's trick; it was indeed alive and moving. As were the eyes attached to the stringy, pink stalks floating with purpose in the jar's liquid. As was the body that the jar rested upon.

Ants skittered down Howard's spine, each extoling the virtues of fleeing. The abomination moved. The bare-chested body was that of the carnival's strong man, fists the size of the head that once belonged on top of it, now on the ground like a discarded organ at an abattoir. Now, the jar containing the brain and eyes on stalks was fastened between carnival's strong man's muscular shoulders.

Dead center in the sternum set a circular mesh of copper, a crisscross pattern running the diameters, the skin around the newly inserted ring mangled and inflamed. The device was a speaker, the metallic voice for the abomination. The eyeballs moved independently at first, but then focused on the carnival magician. A hollow voice reverberated from the speaker, "I am impressed. I always assumed your magics to be smoke and mirrors, Zarkahn, but with Matuska's guidance, you have yielded magnificent results." The newly created monstrosity held up his hands and wiggled his fingers before the jar. "My name is Dr. Sivkas. A laboratory accident took my body from me. I had left instructions for my assistants to preserve my brain and eyes, should such a circumstance arise. Unfortunately for me, I didn't finish the instructions, so after doing the bare minimum, my assistants sold me to this circus. Now, I believe I will indeed join Matuska in greeting the great god of madness he wishes to usher into our realm."

Still wearing the black robes with green piping, although no longer as clean as before, Szilveszter walked a circle around the unnatural creature, his eyes gliding from top to toe again and again, admiring the beauty of the ugliness. "That is wonderful to hear, Dr. Sivkas. Your talents will aid me in bringing about a new age for man. To you, Zarkahn, I say well done. Even more incredible than I imagined. The god of madness will have great use for you."

Zarkahn wore a garish jacket, crushed velvet dyed a bright scarlet with gold filigree woven through it, the tails past his knees. With an equal affront to style, a chartreuse top hat adorned his head. As he smiled from Szilveszter's encouraging words, his fingers traced the waxed curl of his mustache. "Excellent! I am glad this was successful."

Szilveszter finally peeled his gaze away from Dr. Sivkas and addressed the small crowd around him, consisting of the bearded woman, the lizard woman, Madame Sulola, and a dozen carnival employees. Surrounding them were ten cages of animals: two alligators, a rhinoceros, two zebras, a leopard, two gorillas, an anaconda, and a tiger. All the animals paced or slithered about their cages, baring fangs and offering rumbling growls of agitation. "All of you have accepted my invitation to become the harbingers of a new era. Our master has set before us a cryptic quest, one I believe must lead us to Europe, but first we must depart immediately for the east coast."

The small crowd cheered. Except for Madame Sulola. Howard found her curious. At first glance, she was very unassuming; the most fascinating thing about her being her attire, dozens of veils and scarves, all sheer and varying in size and length overlapped each other from her head to her feet. Despite each one being a different color it was impossible to tell where one ended and another began. But the most puzzling detail about her was her face; covered by only one thin veil the color of fire at twilight, it hid little more than her skin complexion and eye color. However, when she turned to the right, she had the countenance of the most beautiful Mediterranean maiden Howard had ever seen, yet when she turned to the left her visage was that of a ragged and weathered crone. Then he noticed that she now looked directly at him.

Voice holding the toll of a funeral bell, she said, "We are not alone."

Howard threw himself around the corner of the car, but it was too late. With the wave of Zarkahn's hand, all the doors of the animal cages unlocked and opened.

Chapter 6

A tiger. Howard never fathomed that his demise would come from the crushing jaws and shredding claws of a rogue jungle cat. Yet, stalking closer to him was a tiger in all its primal splendor, flexuous muscles rippling beneath its striped pelt.

Behind the tiger, nine other animals sprung from their cages, feral and angry. Howard remained focused on the approaching tiger as it ranged closer, snarling with every step. He fired his gun, the green beam blasting the ground in front of the tiger. The animal lifted its front paw and growled, pelted by the resulting spray of dirt. The distraction worked, and Howard ran.

Clutching his satchel with his left hand, gun in his right, he weaved among the transportation cars. The cracks and pops of Billy's six-shooters filled the air, followed by a jubilant, "Yeeeee-haw!"

Billy's cavalier attitude angered Howard. How could a person charge forth so blindly into the maw of death? Then a stray thought gnawed at Howard's mind—he knew a minimal amount of history about Billy the Kid, but he knew well enough that he did not die at a carnival. Did that mean Billy could act with impunity, a free pass given by Fate over the next few years? Or were they now in a divergent time line with an alternate set of historical circumstances? Or did—?

The roar of the pursuing tiger reminded Howard that now was hardly the time or place for such cogitations. He slipped between two transportation cars, and the great cat crashed into the side of a car. Death closer to him that he realized, Howard spun and fired his gun again. He missed, the beam striking the ground and throwing more dirt at the cat. Ahead of him was the unmistakable sound of a rifle, and he assumed some form of authority was taking control of the situation. Howard sprinted from the conglomeration of carnival cars to salvation. He had assumed incorrectly.

Knowing the tiger was but a few bounding strides behind him, Howard found no other option than to continue to sprint toward the open pavilion and stage. A young brunette, gussied up in a dress with frills, stood upon the stage with rifle in hand. The crowd watching the show suddenly stood and screamed and fussed. Not because Howard led a rampaging tiger in their direction, but because a woman among the audience members pointed a gun at the young brunette upon the stage. When people finally noticed the tiger chasing Howard, it only made matters worse.

Pandemonium ensued. Women grabbed children. Men shielded women. Everyone ran in different directions, often colliding with each other. Howard had no choice but to run right for the screaming chaos. He tried to stay close to the stage, running between it and the seating area. Halfway along, a chair bounced from the audience area into Howard's path. Even if he possessed the skills of the most seasoned athlete, avoiding the obstruction would have been impossible. Howard tripped and toppled to the ground, his gun tumbling from his grip. Tail twitching, the tiger stopped and readied itself to pounce, coiling its body like a deadly spring. Hopelessness petrified Howard, unable to do anything other than face his inevitable end.

The tiger lunged, but as soon as its feet left the ground, two bullets struck the beast, one tearing through the right side of its head, the other punching a gaping hole through the left side of its chest. Falling limp as if it had never known life, the now dead carcass flopped to the ground before Howard, splashes of blood streaking the bottom of his pants.

"Ha! Look at that shot!" the woman from the audience yelled as she ran to the dead animal. "Right in the head!"

"I must confess, Calamity Jane, that was indeed a well-placed shot," Annie Oakley said, crouching down while still on the stage. "However, it's clear to even the casual observer that I was the one to kill the beast."

"What?" Jane yelled, the force of her exclamation knocking her off balance. Eyes glossy and unfocused, she scowled at Annie. "You shot it in the chest. I done enough huntin' to know that a chest shot ain't a kill shot. That's why I shot it in the head."

"Jane, you know as well as I that I got it right through the heart."

"You were all but standing right next to it! I shot this thing from way over there!" Jane pointed, the momentum of her action causing her to struggle with her balance again.

"Exactly. Waaaaaaaay over there. With that little peashooter of yours, your bullet probably bounced right off its thick ol' skull."

"Peashooter?" Jane snorted, looking at the gun as if somehow it could have been substituted for another. "This here is a Colt. Top of the line!"

Conflicting emotions wrestled within Howard as he watched the argument. His first inclination was to question the sanity of both women, clearly more concerned about some sharp-shooting competition than safety amidst the lunacy that befell the carnival around them. He was a bit ashamed that he, too, forgot about the maelstrom when he got a better look at the dazzling brunette upon the stage. Soft midnight cascaded about her porcelain face in long, loose curls, and her eyes possessed the sparkle of stars. The direness of the situation waned every time she spoke, her voice that of an angel. Smooth, with a refined accent found in the northern states, her thin lips moved over glistening pearls. Then she disappeared.

Howard blinked, his spell broken. One of the escaped gorillas found its way to the stage and had approached Annie from behind. Latching on to a fistful of her hair, he yanked. Screaming and thrashing, she dropped her gun and grabbed the animal's arm to keep it from separating her scalp from her head as it dragged her across the stage.

Heroism welled within Howard's chest, a rare opportunity to rescue the damsel. He commanded the use of every aching muscle to fling himself to his gun. As soon as he grabbed it, he twisted and pulled the trigger. Direct hit, the emerald beam charred the left half of the gorilla's face.

Standing as if dazed, the animal relinquished its grasp of Annie. Hurriedly, she freed herself and scrabbled away from the beast. The gorilla wobbled, its right eye lolling up into its head while spurts of blood flowed from a hole in its chest. With a gurgling moan, the creature fell, its legs giving one last death twitch.

Confused by the excess of blood, Howard wondered how his energy beam could have produced such a result. It didn't. Billy was also on the stage, wisps of smoke dissipating from the barrel of his handgun. With his crooked-tooth smile, Billy looked at Annie and used his gun to tip his hat. "Howdy. You okay?"

Annie stood and ran her hands through her hair. "A bit sore, but I do believe that the miscreant monster took from me no more than a stray lock or two."

"Well, that's wonderful news. I am happy that I arrived in time to kill that gorilla before it did any permanent damage."

"You?" Howard shouted as he stormed to the stage. "You think that it was you who killed that beast?"

"Sure do. Who else would it have been?"

"Well, obviously me."

"You? With that little ray gun of yours, shootin' little green lights?"

"I assure you, the power that this weapon wields is far superior to what can be found in this time period."

With the exaggerated movements of an actor, Billy sauntered to the fallen gorilla and leaned over to peer at its head. "You gave the ol' monkey here a nasty burn. I guess that means your special future gun can do the same thing as a big box of matches. Good to know."

"Box of...? Despite your limited intellect precluding you from making a suitable comparison, you can surely observe that I shot the beast in the head, thusly delivering the kill shot."

"All I see is a burnt monkey face. Now, if you 'observe' farther down here, you will 'thusly' notice a mighty big hole in this here chest, where a beatin' heart used to be, where I shot it."

"Of course you were able to shoot it in the heart! You were standing not but ten feet from the target!"

The argument was terminated by the crack of a gunshot. The Gorilla's foot twitched as a bullet passed through its leg, blood oozing sap-like from the newest hole. All eyes snapped to the source: Jane's gun. With one eye still shut from aiming, she swayed and shouted, "There. I shot the gorilla, too. Annie! Shoot the gorilla, then we'll all have shot the gorilla."

Howard could only gawp at the spectacle.

"Ah-hem," Annie cleared her throat just loud enough to garner attention. "I must thank both of you gentlemen for coming to my rescue. Although it is unclear who actually felled either of these beasts that lay before us, I believe I must ask—do we know how these animals came to be here?"

"Actually, we do," Albert weaved his way through overturned benches and chairs of the now empty audience area. Close enough to the others, he sat on the edge of a bench and looked at Howard with the unspoken question of, "Should we tell them?"

Howard knew as much about Calamity Jane and Annie Oakley as he did Billy the Kid. Just stories he believed to be embellished to elevate fact to fiction. Yet he stood before all three of them, and there had to be a reason more than coincidence. A force greater than he guiding him? He couldn't say, but if they were to be a part of his life, then they deserved to know why. He agreed to Albert's question with a nod.

Albert stretched his legs and told his story. As he spoke, Howard watched the listeners. Jane seemed drunk and refused to sit, but her wobbling lessened while her focus intensified. Annie approached the front of the stage and sat, feet dangling over the ledge. She absorbed Albert's story, the intelligence behind her eyes obvious as she weighed and measured Albert's every word.

Once Albert finished offering what he knew, Annie was the first to speak. "Your story is a might farfetched. However, you two do have yourselves quite a set of rather unique guns. The moment I came to visit this carnival, I found both Zarkahn and Madame Sulola positively unnerving, so the thought of them dabbling in the darker forces of nature comes quite easily for me. And if you convinced the infamous Billy the Kid to join your posse, then that must mean he's buying what you're selling."

Billy offered a cheeky grin and sat down next to Annie. "Why, I'm much obliged."

Jane and Howard shared a groan and an eye roll.

Annie continued, "But that is hardly a solid selling point for me. Let us say for a moment that I might believe what you're telling me. What is your next course of action?"

"Well," Albert said. "We overheard Szilveszter say that they needed to get to Europe but with a stop somewhere on the east coast. During the commotion of releasing the animals, they fled in one of the carnival's transport cars. It had six horses pulling it, so I'm sure they're long gone by now. I'm assuming they're heading east to find transport to Europe?"

"Then our next move is obvious," Howard said. "We head east as well."

Albert sighed. "Therein lies the dilemma. We have no transportation and no money to purchase any."

Annie smiled, her eyes fox sly. "East, you say? Well, I may just be able to help...."

Chapter 7

Albert told the story again and Annie listened, her eyes never looking away from his, never offering the slightest glimpse into her thoughts and feelings. Thin lips drew across her porcelain doll face, matching the emotional elusiveness of her eyes. Howard had no idea what parts of the tale she believed, if any. Jane, on the other hand, kept her mind on her next drink, judging from her nonstop imbibing. Both of her eyes held the sheen of freshly cleaned plate glass, as well as a pink glow that could only be the harbinger of a blood-shot hangover. Howard could hardly guess how much of the story she even heard, let alone processed.

"I know our story sounds impossible, fantastical at best, but I cannot express enough gratitude for offering us transportation," Albert said.

Howard chuckled to himself, amused by Albert's sugary compliments, as if the horse drawn coach were something more opulent. Cushioned seats and tasseled curtains, the only luxuries found by Howard's descrying eye. As with any coach, whether owned by celebrity or pauper, the terrain determined how it pitched and the horses determined how it jerked, the combination making the passengers bob like marionettes commanded by a drunken puppeteer. On his lap was his notebook, more than a few words rendered unreadable due to stray marks created by a sudden jolt.

"Well, Albert, after the unfortunate... *calamity*... at the carnival, I find no other recourse but to head home. I would be remiss if I failed to offer aid where I could," Annie replied, the edges of her lips curling into a subtle smirk.

"Where might you be callin' home?" Billy asked.

"Cincinnati. Where my betrothed, Frank Butler, and I work together on our show."

Billy sat to the right of Annie; Howard to the left and across from them were Albert and Jane. The carriage was large enough to fit the three youngest in the party on one bench without any one person's thigh touching another. Even at a scant five feet tall and possessing the slight build of an adolescent girl, Annie still wore a corseted dress, frills abundant. Howard and Billy each had a leg engulfed in the material, but that didn't stop Billy from shifting in his seat, angling himself inward, so his knee touched Annie's. "Betrothed, huh? So, you ain't married?"

Unable to stop himself, Howard leaned forward to direct his comment across Annie to Billy. "Betrothed means that she is indeed spoken for."

Billy leaned forward to address Howard with a glimmer in his azure blue eyes. "I thank you much, good sir, for the clarification. However, I already knew what the word meant, and even if I didn't, I know that it don't mean 'married.'"

Leaning back, Billy continued, "So… your betrothed… he sure don't seem to be here with you now, does he?"

As if trying to stifle a laugh, she leaned a bit closer to say, "No he does not, since he cannot be in two places at once."

Howard fumed, although he certainly could not pinpoint the reason for his ire. It either stemmed from Billy and his lack of couth for continuing to flirt with an unavailable woman, or Annie for encouraging such attentions from the lout. Who was to blame—the hungry cur ready to pounce, or the morsel so willingly traipsing into an obvious trap?

"So, where might he be?" Billy asked.

"He 'might' be anywhere the imagination wills him to be. However, where he 'is' is back home working on advertising our act and attempting to find other shows willing to display my talents."

Billy's smiled widened as if he had no control over it. "Oh, you do indeed have an overabundance of talent."

Howard was disgusted by Billy's ability to take so much of her attention with so little to offer; his bright, boyish face marred by buckled front teeth and sweated mats of unkempt locks plastered to his forehead. Comparatively, Howard had the visual lumber of a permanent sneer. To his defense, though, he had never tried not to sneer, for fear of overcompensating and creating a maniacal look, or one of insincerity at best. But Billy was dazzling her with words, an area that Howard considered to be his forte. So, he used his words.

"Your talents are mellifluous poetry indeed."

Annie turned to him and chuckled. Albert's face went wan as he discretely shook his head. Billy leaned forward again to peer across the carriage, this time with the soured expression of biting a lemon, clearly confused by either what Howard had said or why he had said it. Howard assumed it was the latter. Luckily, the carriage lurched and caused Jane to belch, pulling everyone's attention to her. Noticing all eyes upon her, she turned to Annie and said, "Well, I guess after word of the carnival disaster gets out, you'll have to come up with new talents."

"Oh, Jane," Annie said. "You may know quite a deal about hunting and trapping and living off the land, but what I'm referring to is the business of putting on a show. The theatrics I perform on the stage pale in comparison to the theatrics happening behind the stage."

Jane crunched her face. "Now, what in the hell does that have to do with the price of tea in China?"

"That means that the carnival will come up with whatever excuse is convenient. If eyewitnesses say that the animals escaped, then the animal trainer will take the blame. It matters none that it happened during my show, or that you tried to put a bullet in my head. It only matters what the newspapers print. The Annie Oakley act was long gone before the newspapermen could even catch wind of it. It's as if I was never there. Control the newspapers, control the world." Upon finishing her statement, she addressed Albert. "Unless that was a misstatement?"

Caught off guard, Albert shifted in his seat. "How do you mean?"

"Was it ever noted that I was in New Mexico this day and the three prior?"

It was now clear that Annie Oakley was indeed no morsel traipsing into a trap.

Albert squinted, regarding the diminutive young woman before him. "Why would you assume history even cares?"

"Well, the three of us each have had articles printed about us and tales told of our actions. I must confess that I am quite curious about the staying power of that fame."

"Miss Oakley, we come from a time of progress, where the entire world changes every day. Maybe we can't remember with any clarity the details about history or newspaper articles or tale telling."

"You have a thick German accent, yet use English words to weave quite an impressive tapestry. And Howard here," she turned to Howard, then shifted her gaze to his book of notes on his lap and continued, "has quite a mastery of words as well, proclaiming that not only is my smile 'the panacea that will save him from the anathema of this wretched time period'—for that compliment I must thank him—but that I also have the type of beauty that should grace something called celluloid. You two are very intelligent men, quite capable of recollecting if any of us tagalongs are worthy footnotes in history's tome."

"So, this is why you decided to help? To get a glimpse into the future?"

"Well, if you gentlemen are truly from the future, then you possess knowledge that is not only unique, but could prove invaluable," Annie said. Howard gently closed his notebook. Annie was not prey, but indeed a predator.

"We do, Miss Oakley," Albert replied. "But I do not believe it would behoove us to share such knowledge with anyone."

The coach pitched hard to the right, then lurched to the left as it righted itself from a rut wreaking havoc with the wheels. During the jolt, Billy's hand found its way to Annie's knee. When she regarded his action with raised eyebrows, he removed it while smirking and said, "For support."

Annie smiled.

Howard frowned.

So did Jane.

"So, William," Annie purred. "What is your motivation for coming along?"

Billy shifted again, tucking his left foot under his backside so he could face Annie, only Annie. "Well, that there is a mighty fine question. I must confess, the part of Albert's story where he first mentioned my good name is true, God as my witness."

"Is that so?"

"It indeed is."

"A wild man in black and green robes fell from the sky, followed by our mysterious new friends here?"

"That is an accurate account, yes. We tracked him to your carnival and we were attacked by the animals. It seems like this Szilveszter fella made some new friends as well. A crazy lot, them sideshow freaks. Had a hundred and one evil ways about 'em."

"So, your propensity for doing God's work is what is driving you to join up with Albert and Howard, I'm guessing?"

Billy chuckled. "Yep. That's me. I'm all about doin' God's work."

"You have no interest in trying to learn what destiny has in store for you?"

Placing his hand on Annie's knee, he leaned forward as he said, "Miss Annie Oakley, unmarried from Cincinnati, I try to live my life like destiny's gonna put a bullet in my back. We ain't promised no tomorrows."

"At least one of us is."

Jerking up straight as if Annie had splashed ice water in his face, Billy squinted and asked, "Now, what do you happen to mean by that?"

"Well, it was you who gave us their last names. Once they realized where—I'm sorry, *when*—they were, they only gave out their first names. Logic would dictate that is because at least one of the three of us is still alive during their time period, else there would be no harm in freely giving out that information. They claim to have traveled back thirty-one years. You and I would be watching the sunrise of our fifties, while Jane could be in her... what? Eighties...? as unconceivable as that may be."

Scowling, lips pulled tight against her teeth, Jane hissed, "I'm twenty-seven."

Annie scanned the woman across the way, the action adding insult to her words. "My apologies."

Not considering himself to be an expert in the ways of the "fairer sex," and now reconsidering the validity of that epithet after witnessing such sprays of venom, Howard knew enough to recognize the escalation of the situation. He felt the need to make an attempt to defray it, no matter how paltry or obvious. "So, Jane, why have you decided to join us?"

"Thought I could use a little adventure. See where the road takes us," she replied, placing her hand on Albert's knee.

Trying to be deliberate, but not rude, Albert took her arm by the wrist and moved it to her own lap. "I apologize, but this road is inaccessible. I am a married man."

Jane moved her hand back to his knee. "Ain't stopped men I known before."

With the same care as before, Albert moved her hand back. "I am afraid that it will stop this man."

"Fine," she snarled, crossing her arms over her chest. She nodded toward Annie and said, "Then I guess I'm along to prove that she ain't a better shot than me."

Annie simply turned to Albert as if Jane's words offered nothing worthy of a response and said, "I just want to remind you that this carriage driver is taking us to the train station, where I will be more than happy to purchase each of us a ticket to Cincinnati. If you believe this Szilveszter fellow is heading someplace other than there, please let me know before we get to the station."

Albert frowned. "Unfortunately, we're working on speculation. Before our skirmish at the carnival, Szilveszter mentioned nothing more than heading to the east coast."

"The east coast has quite a few big cities with quite a few offerings. What do you believe he wants?"

"Power."

"What about Washington, D.C.? The President?"

Albert pondered the question. "I don't believe the President would be Szilveszter's target. Getting to the President would be loud and messy, and I don't think he would garner anything from that. At best, he would have a high profile and important hostage, but that wouldn't be a logical step to meeting his needs. Szilveszter would be more interested in technology."

"Technology," Howard spat with soured tone, staring at the barren plains outside of his window. Every rock grouping that passed by made him feel as if he rode upon stone slabs, every bump in the road an explosion within his nerves. Technology meant alleviating himself from this perpetual state of discomfort. "They don't have airplanes, useful electricity, or automobiles." His words gave glimpses to the future as he had written them for everyone to see, doing the very thing he and Albert agreed not to do. Shifting his eyes to his companions, he beheld three confused looks and one of concern. However, Albert's frown shifted from disappointment to contemplation.

"Howard. Something you said. Didn't Thom—?"

"Yes!" Howard cut off Albert in a burst of excitement. "He did. But it was at the end of this year when he unveiled it to the public."

"To the public, yes. But surely he has to have working experiments and prototypes. Plus, he has the greatest laboratory in the world."

"Agreed." Howard's smile was broad and genuine as he turned to Annie. "Miss Oakley, if you were sincere in your offer to finance our little expedition, then we have the destination."

"Indeed I was, Howard. And where might we be going?"

"New Jersey."

Chapter 8

Albert chuckled, slightly ashamed with himself for finding humor in Howard's perceived suffering, but it took little effort to recall any one of the derogatory comments Howard had made in the past regarding Albert's ancestry. In fact, Howard quite often made less than flattering statements about everyone's ancestry if it did not originate in England. The jibing at Howard's expense was well deserved.

Similar to their carriage ride to the train station, the seating arrangement on the train developed from different motivations. The men let the ladies enter first, allowing them to choose their seats. Annie chose a bench seat halfway closer to the front of the train car; Jane sat in the corresponding seat across the aisle way, and eyed the younger woman with contempt. Jane had found a fresh bottle of whiskey, and Albert wondered if she could even see the woman she glared at.

After Annie made herself comfortable by tucking under the frills of her dress, Howard hurried to sit across from her, smiling as he claimed his seat. As it so often was, this rare facial expression was short lived, flipping upside down into a forehead-wrinkling frown as William slid onto the same bench. William hipped Howard hard enough to shove him against the train car's wall, his right shoulder smacking the thick window. Albert resigned himself to sit across from Jane. At least he would be able to know the whereabouts of her hands. Although, he was just grateful to sit and rest.

Determining that they needed to go to New Jersey made the rest of their travel plans fall into place. Annie commanded her team of coaches to the closest station so they could catch the first train heading east. Since neither Albert nor Howard had any current era currency to pay for tickets, Annie paid, but not before they worked off their debt in fair trade. They helped her load her show paraphernalia into the cargo cars of the train and her horses into the livestock cars.

Never shying away from physical labor, and still dressed as a harbor man, Albert felt quite comfortable, even thankful for the exercise. His companion, on the other hand, was not. Every time Howard complained of sweat, William offered a handkerchief, but not before blowing his nose into it. Any time Howard paused to examine a newly formed blister on his hand, William poked it. And when the emotionally penurious Howard displayed a smile while enjoying conversation with Annie, William interjected, commandeering her attention.

Howard pontificated about ancient philosophies to which William would reply, "Milquetoast."

Howard put on display his knowledge of world history to which William would reply, "Dandy."

Howard recited poetry with pronunciation perfection to which William would reply, "Fop."

The insults ended with a red-faced tirade. "You let your hyperactive libido guide your troglodytic demeanor like a compass, one in a perpetual state of disrepair, as you would rather choose to micturate on the face of homogeny!"

Albert always felt he had a rather strong grasp of English, but there were more than a few words he couldn't translate. He also doubted that William had a formal enough education to know the definition of Howard's angry words either. Whether Annie understood the meaning of every word or not, she offered the softest of smiles, giving the appearance of both sympathy and satisfaction. Regardless of specific definitions, all felt the weight of Howard's words, and that was enough to keep the rest of the loading process shrouded in silence.

Despite Albert's sympathy, there was a certain amount of justice in Howard being dished the same meal he so often doled out. Compassion reached deeper into Albert as he contemplated how conflicted Howard must be feeling—a driven young woman blessed with both beauty and charm appeared in his life, yet he felt bound to keep his emotions in check since she was betrothed, while simultaneously trying to compete for her attention against a dashing young rogue who made it clear that he didn't give a damn about her betrothal. Although, Albert also had to deal with an individual who didn't respect the sanctity of commitment.

All during the loading of Annie's equipment, Jane offered a lewd proposition to Albert twice an hour or more. Upon the completion of loading the equipment, she gave a meaty smack to his rump, stating that it was to signify a job well done. No other worker celebrated in such a way, so Albert was dubious of that explanation. Now, as he took the seat across from her, he felt the need to be perpetually vigilant.

After a few hours into the train ride, Jane slurred, "Look at Annie. Look at her, just eatin' up all the attention that the fellas are feedin' her. Like it's food keepin' her alive."

"You disapprove of her celebrity?" Albert asked, genuinely curious.

"I 'disapprove' of her showiness. It's almost like she's tellin' the world that what she's doin' is important, more important than what the regular people do who come to see her prance around on stage. I'm a better shot than she is."

"That makes you a better person?"

"No. I'm a better person because I don't charge people money for me to tell them that I'm a good shot. I'm a better person because I helped travelers keep from gettin' killed by Indians. I'm a better person because when someone shows me affection, I appreciate it and… and I don't take it… take it for granted."

A lone tear slid over her cheek as she struggled with her last words. Albert felt the loss in her words. "You miss him."

Jane took a long swig then wiped her mouth with the back of her hand, brushing away the tear as well. "Yeah. Yeah I do."

"Good man?"

Eyes glassy and unfocused, Jane turned to Albert. With a bit of head wobble and a twitching smile, she said, "The best. Kinda reminds me of you. Except he didn't need to make himself feel better by usin' big words no one understands. And he had a much better mustache. What the fuck is goin' on with that thing on your lip?"

Taken aback by the sudden turn in the conversation, Albert said, "You disapprove of… my mustache?"

"Hell yes I do. Be a man and grow a real one." Jane gulped from the bottle again and turned her attention back to the younger trio across the aisle, mumbling to herself, "Sorry excuse for a mustache if I've ever seen one. Like a caterpillar died on his lip."

Albert could find no rejoinder, his fingers brushing over his upper lip, and wondered how his partner was handling his own frustrations.

Howard remained silent, shifting his attention between writing in his notebook and glaring at William. William, on the other hand, leered at Annie while she was fixated by the world outside the train windows. He then looked at Howard's notebook and his perpetual smirk twisted into a smile. "This is why I called you a fop."

Tone even and calm, Howard did not look up from his writings. "I hardly believe you have the acuity to even know the definitions of half the words I've written."

William shrugged a shoulder. "I got the general gist of it."

"That's how you move through life, isn't it. Getting by on the 'general gist' of things. Never investing your time or energy into trying to better yourself. Taking the path of least resistance. That certainly explains why you were with a whore the night we met you."

William's demeanor changed, his posture becoming rigid, his nonchalant smile fading. "I told you that I didn't know she was a whore."

"Would it have mattered if you did know?" Howard's words started to flow faster. "Your motives for her company were purely carnal, whether you had to pay for it or not was inconsequential."

Almost growling, William replied, "You know nothin' of my motivations."

"I know what I observe, and I've observed a scoundrel who manipulates and uses people to meet his basest desires. I've observed an egocentric xenophobe who would rather tear down new ideals than learn about them."

Face awash with concern, Annie turned away from the window. "Howard?"

"If Billy disagrees with my assessment, I would be more than happy to examine evidence to the contrary."

Eyebrows knitting, William clenched his jaw and flared his nostrils. A storm brewed behind his eyes, lightning ready to strike. Just as quickly, the clouds dissipated as William turned his attention to the window. "Does it feel like the train is slowing down?"

"Please do not change the subject," Howard snapped.

Annie looked out the window as well and said, "I believe Billy is right. We're stopping."

Albert and Jane looked out the window closest to them. Dry brush sprouting from dry ground across the flat plain. An idea of a town seemed to form in the distance, but Albert assumed it merely a mirage. "Maybe something blocking the track?" he hypothesized.

"Only thing in these parts is tumbleweeds and trouble, and tumbleweeds ain't never stopped a train before," William said, fidgeting in his seat.

"Trouble?" Annie asked. "What kind of trouble?"

"The bad kind." William skittered across the aisle and leaned over Jane and Albert to look out their window. He moved on to a set of unoccupied seats, again looking out the window. The two dozen other passengers in the car mumbled among themselves, either pointing to William or looking out their own windows.

"No need to get your hackles up. The porter will be along soon enough to keep us abreast of the situation," Howard said to William. "Now sit down. You're upsetting the other passengers."

The train slowed to a stop. William rushed back to his seat and grabbed his satchel, frantically looking for a place to hide it, jostling Howard with every move.

"Will you please settle down? I find no need for this behavior. Look. Here comes a porter now," Howard said, pointing to a figure approaching from the other side of the smoked glass door separating the train cars.

For the first time since their initial meeting, a no-nonsense look washed over William's face. As the figure rapidly approached, William removed his gun belt. He threw it under the seat and kicked it close to the wall. "That ain't no porter."

The door flung open, kicked by the man on the other side. He wore a dirt-stained white shirt and brown pants. His Stetson did nothing to hide the glee dancing behind his eyes or the smile as wide as his face. The revolver in his right hand danced around as if it were the one speaking. "Greetings everybody. My name is Jesse James, and I'll be robbing you today. My associate is coming down the aisle from the other end of the car with a bag in his hand. Gentlemen, if you'd be so kind as to drop your watches, rings, and cufflinks into it. Ladies, the same for any and all your jewelry. And, as always, any kind of cash you might have."

Albert glanced to the back of the train car. Sure enough, a man with a sack and a revolver of his own stopped by each occupied seat, taking collections for the church of larceny. Albert slid his left hand out of view to hide his wedding band.

Jesse James stayed toward the front of the car, supervising. He looked at Albert and his companions the way a coyote looked at a lame rabbit, then sucked his teeth with disappointment. Using his gun to point to William's satchel, he said, "Well, son, it looks like you and your friends ain't wearing anything shiny, so how 'bout you give me your bag?"

Still clutching his satchel on his lap, William didn't move.

"I don't think you heard me, boy. Let me have the bag," Jesse repeated.

William scowled, but his youthful appearance made him look more like a petulant child than a man making a stand. "Nothin' in this bag of value to you, mister."

Jesse cocked the gun, the click of the hammer being pulled back, a metallic warning. Slowly, Jesse grabbed a fistful of the bag's material and pulled. Billy refused to relinquish.

"William," Albert said. "I think it would be best if you just let him have the satchel."

Eyes wide, his back against the window, Howard said, "I concur with Albert."

Even though she sat tall and proud, fear painted a portrait upon Annie's face. "Billy. Please. Let's all just get out of this in one piece."

Jesse tugged again, but William remained firm. Until another click of a retracting hammer sounded next to him, the gun of Jesse's partner pointed at Annie.

Howard's jaw muscles rippled. Albert tried to calculate what he should do if the gun discharged. Where to dive? Attack? Protect? But William acquiesced.

Jesse took the bag and backed out of the doorway, keeping a watchful eye on William. His partner followed. Less than a minute later, six men on horses rode en masse away from the train.

The passengers in the car breathed a collective sigh of relief, everyone unharmed. Despite the stupidity of William's actions, Albert recognized the unintended benefit—had Jesse not been so involved with William, he might have noticed Howard's satchel. The travesty of the dark energy weapons falling into the hands of Jesse James would have been unparalleled. Relief blossomed behind Albert's chest in warm blooms.

"Dare I ask what was so important in that bag of yours you were willing to risk the lives of everyone on this train car?" Howard snipped at William.

Still looking out the window, in the direction that Jesse and his gang rode, William said, "Remember when we met?"

"Of course, I do. It was only—"

"Remember how you and Albert were talkin' about some power source, or somethin', that Szilveszter used to bring himself and you two into this time period?"

"Yes. It—"

"Well, he did have it. It was a pyramid shaped thing with black and green swirlin' liquids, like what you two got in your guns."

Albert stood and took a step toward William. "How do you know this?"

"Because I took it. It's in my satchel and right now, Jesse James has it."

Chapter 9

Harold grumbled a curse, a superfluous pleonasm like all the others he uttered during this tortuous trip. As if offended by being the source of Howard's contempt, the horse he rode retaliated by swishing its tail to the side and releasing a slushy blast of flatulence. With the shortest insult hurled within the past two hours, Howard crinkled his nose and muttered, "Damnable beast."

Billy laughed and complimented the horse's good taste. Howard did his best to ignore the indirect chide. Every time he responded to Billy's antagonizing, he felt like he distanced himself from the group. Even though he cared not a whit for Billy, nor much more for Jane, he knew their value in what needed to be done. Despite him being German, Howard respected, even liked, Albert, for he was truly a good partner and very close to being the best that humanity had to offer. And there was Annie, an exquisite flower blooming alone in a field of feces. Finding in her a woman he would deem nearly his equal, she made his heart swell, filling it with anticipation every time she spoke, anxious for her next words, thoughts, ideas. Just as quickly, his heart deflated any time he thought about how a future with her was destined never to be. Not only did he respect her betrothal to another man, but he could not recall the history books ever mentioning "Howard Philips Lovecraft" as her beloved. But he refused to pass up any opportunity to enjoy her company, and felt a sense of obligation in attempting to fend off Billy's advances. He slowly concluded that he needed to stop underestimating that miscreant, for he was far more astute than his lackadaisical persona let on. It was especially frustrating when Billy used Howard's own words against him.

Another shift in the saddle and groan by Howard prompted Billy to say, "Seems to me horse ridin' is a new experience for you. Also seems to me that you're tearin' it down and not tryin' to learn from it."

"Now, Billy," Annie said. "It's rather clear that he is certainly trying his best at equestrianism."

Howard's feelings ripped into two—happy that Annie regarded him suitable enough to defend, yet more than a bit humbled that he presented a need for her defense. He straightened his posture to defy Billy. But even at the horse's slow pace, the necessary coordination to flow with the animal eluded Howard. The constant slamming of his tailbone against the hard leather saddle forced him to lean forward, choosing to look awkward for even the slightest bit of respite from the pain.

Wearing the smirk of a skilled pickpocket entering a crowded parlor, Billy rode alongside Howard. With Billy's youthful visage, Howard couldn't help but feel transported back to the schoolyard, face to face with a ruffian. However, Billy offered a bit of benevolence by saying, "Well, I guess he's in luck. We're here."

Never had a ramshackle town looked like such an oasis. The sun had moved from late noon to early evening, but it had yet to take the heat with it. Howard was happy that he would be getting off the horse soon enough. Finding resolve in the fact that the end was nigh, he sat straighter in his saddle and tried to ignore the conflagration burning within his thighs.

The buildings were all two stories tall and built of wood with gaudy advertisements of what they had to offer. From dry goods to cobbler to tailor to tavern, the town seemed to lack nothing the inhabitants could desire. Howard saw a doctor's sign and thought about seeing him for the pain, until he remembered the medicinal teachings of the time period went no further than leeches.

The group stopped at the nearest hitching post and tethered their horses. Dismounting proved a challenge for Howard, calling upon Albert's help, but the cessation of pain and the ability to stretch tightened muscles bordered on heavenly. "So," Howard said, hands on his hips, twisting the knots out of his lower back, "Where do you suggest we begin our search, Billy?"

With omnipresent smirk, Billy said, "I ain't the smartest of the bunch of us and I'm certain no one here would consider me the leader. So, why you askin' me?"

"Simple reasoning mandates that it takes a criminal to catch a criminal."

"I may have swindled a card player or two who deserved it, and I'm a little too quick to draw my irons, but I'm no liar, cheat, schemer, or robber."

"You blatantly lied to us about stealing Szilveszter's source of power."

Billy's smirk grew as he gave a lazy shrug and looked around the town. "I didn't lie to you. I simply didn't share those specific details. He dropped it. I found it fair and square."

Howard snorted in derision. "Now you sound like a lawyer."

Billy stopped, turned on his heel and pointed at Howard. With his index finger an inch from Howard's face, Billy growled, "Don't you ever compare me to a lawyer!"

Neither man moved, even blinked; Billy simmered with anger, Howard in shock. Annie sauntered over to Billy and placed a hand on his shoulder. "Now, Billy. Don't you think you busted his chops enough today?"

Billy's bright smile returned as he gave Howard a good-natured pat on the cheek. "Yeah, I guess you're right. Just tryin' to lighten the mood, is all."

Howard replied as he so usually did to Billy—with a scowl.

Jane laughed as she took a swig from her bottle of whiskey. Howard assumed it was a container of infinite portions because he had never seen her without it, and she constantly drank from it.

"I do have an idea, though," Billy said. "There were quite a few in that gang, so when they came into town, they musta been noticed. I have a feelin' the first thing they're gonna want is a drink, followed by a room for the night."

Howard hated to admit it, but Billy's logic was sound, and he appreciated the contribution until the rapscallion continued, "There's a saloon down the road, so why don't Albert, Howard, and Jane go take a peek in there. Right over here is an inn that's sure to have a bar in it, so Annie and I will go have a look see in there."

Jane shrugged her shoulders and took another swig. "Come on, Albie. Let's go find us a train robber." She punctuated her statement by smacking Albert's posterior as she started to the saloon.

Billy offered the crook of his elbow to Annie. She reacted with an eye roll and a smirk, but accepted his arm anyway and they headed toward the inn. Howard went with them, walking on the other side of Annie.

Billy looked around at the cloudless sky, but addressed Howard, "You sure don't listen well, do ya?"

"Well, as you so eloquently put, you are neither the smartest one in the group nor are you our leader," Howard replied. For the first time during this unholy trip, Billy responded with silence.

They made their way up the creaky steps and across the creakier porch. As soon as they entered through the swinging wooden doors, the stench of sour sweat hit Howard first, followed by the stale yeasty odor of spilled beer. If he concentrated, he could detect hints of vomit. It hardly surprised him that Billy found solace in a place like this, and wondered about Annie's level of distaste. She seemed unoffended, simply observing her surroundings.

The floors were made of squeaking planks, scuffed and stained, an occasional nail twisted free, ready to catch an unsuspecting boot. On the left side of the room was the bar, the shelves behind it stocked to the brim with bottles. To the right, a wide staircase led to a second floor landing with three doors. Underneath the landing were at least two more doors in the dusty shadows past the bar. Round tables with wobbly chairs speckled the floor. Only two were occupied: one by a vagrant, passed out and drooling; the other by two gruff looking men minding their own conversation.

The trio went to a table away from everyone else. Howard pulled one of the chairs out for Annie to sit upon. "What is our next step?"

"I'm gonna ask the barkeep if he's seen Jesse James and his gang," Billy said.

"That's it? That's your plan?"

"You got a better one?"

Howard hadn't given it any thought. "No. But I'm joining you."

Billy shook his head and strode to the bar. Howard followed. Feeling as though his knees would never meet again from the horse ride, he hoped his gait appeared more as a limp than a waddle.

"Well, hopefully you know well enough to keep your mouth shut," Billy said as he sidled up to the bar. The barkeep strolled over, absently running a rag over a mason jar. The sunlight spilling in through the windows cast a sheen across the man's bald head. A thin line of perspiration glistened on his upper lip as he said, "Afternoon, gentlemen."

"Afternoon. My friend and I were wonderin' if Jesse James and his gang happened through these parts recently."

The bartender offered a chuckle as his eyes shifted downward. Still wiping the glass jar, he said, "I'm sure I woulda noticed if he had. Now, can I get you fellas anything?"

Howard didn't like how the conversation was going, but this wasn't his forte. He had to trust that Billy was getting something meaningful from just staring at the bartender. Billy's face lightened and he offered a bright smile. "Sure can, sir. How about three whiskies and just as many strips of jerky?"

"Sure thing."

The bartender poured whiskey into four squat shot glasses, then grabbed five strips of dehydrated beef from a long glass container. Billy paid and grabbed all the merchandise, then exchanged a courteous nod with the barkeep. Without another word, Howard followed Billy back to their table.

"Well?" Annie asked.

"I think they're here," Billy said dispersing the glasses and jerky, giving the extra strips to Annie while keeping the extra shot for himself.

"What?" Howard asked. "Why do you think that?"

Leaning forward, Billy took a sip from one of the glasses. Minus his usual smirk, he looked to Annie and said, "Miss Oakley, would you kindly ask Howard to keep his voice down, lest he brings upon us unwanted attention. I have a feelin' if I were to make that request, it would somehow make him even louder."

Howard sneered and leaned in as well, but looked over both shoulders before speaking in a softer tone, "Point taken. But that hardly explains why you believe Jesse James is here."

Taking a large chunk of jerky and chewing it like a cow with cud, Billy answered, "First of all, even though it's a nice sunny day, it's hardly warm enough to break a sweat, yet the barkeep is glistening like a frog in a pond. Second of all, he gave us way more than I ordered. I don't care where you are or if you're in the back pocket of Christ, no bartender ever gives you extra, unless he's scared of you or for you."

Howard glanced at the jerky and drinks. "So, this is some kind of secret bartender code? What is he trying to tell us?"

Exasperated, Billy said, "It's a cryptic gesture, not a handwritten note. My only thought is that since there are nine total items, he may be tellin' us that there are nine men we need to be aware of."

Howard looked around again. The bartender had his back turned to them, busying himself with something Howard couldn't see. Was he trying to help them? Or was he involved, setting them up? "So, if you think the bartender is trying to warn us, why are we still sitting here?"

Billy leaned back and finished his shot. He lifted the second one with one hand and took a bite of jerky with his other. "'Cause we just got here, and I need to take the load off my feet. Plus, I'm hungry and thirsty."

Annie sipped from her glass and ate a bite of jerky. After glancing around the room a few times, she leaned forward and whispered, "Billy? I agree with Howard. Let's go find Albert and Jane and formulate a plan of action with them."

Another bite of jerky, a few bits falling from the corners of his mouth, Billy leaned forward again. "If they are here and we leave, what do you think will happen? The bartender warns them and they either leave or ambush us when we come back."

"How do we know that we're not currently in the middle of an ambush now?"

Billy smirked, but then his eyes shifted to the happenings behind Annie. His smile faded into a frown and he gulped back his second shot. "Damn it."

A voice came from behind Howard and Annie. "The l'il lady's right. You're smack in the middle of an ambush."

The other three patrons, including the letch previously thought to be passed out, stood with their guns drawn.

Chapter 10

Jane knew how squirrelly she made Albert, and that tickled her. Sure, at times it disappointed her that her feminine wiles had no effect on him, but the idea of a man turning down a free and easy bed partner because he loved his wife was quite the new concept for her. Like a child with a new toy and no adult supervision, she played with Albert. As they walked side by side on the packed dirt road to the tavern, she'd occasionally close the gap between them, and then Albert would re-open the gap, keeping a distance just outside of her reach, obviously trying to avoid being mauled by her grabby hands.

Albert differed greatly from most of the men she associated with. He was neither a blurry-eyed stranger at the end of a bar, nor a horny miner at a mining camp, nor a lonely religious zealot doing Mission work with the Indians. Albert was a virtuous man, driven by his heart, not his crotch. She staggered three steps closer to him; he slid away by three steps. She giggled and took a sip of whiskey.

"Is that truly wise?" Albert asked.

Jane belched. "What? Me drinkin'? Gotta quench my thirst, ya know."

"At the cost of your skills, though, lest you forget that we are openly trying to ferret out the whereabouts of a gang of train robbers."

"Pheh!" Jane snorted. She then swiped her sleeve over her spittle glistened lips and chin. "I'm a better shot than Jesse James or any in his gang."

"I find it hard to fathom that you could outshoot anyone if you're face down in a pool of your own drool."

Incensed, Jane scowled at Albert. She drew one of her pistols and said, "Shooting ain't about eye or feet or hands or even what's in here," she tapped the tip of her gun against her head, then continued, "It's about what's in here," she then pressed the barrel to her heart. To prove her point, she finished off the whiskey and tossed the bottle high into the air. Without so much as a glance skyward, she fired and the bottle shattered, raining broken glass into the middle of the street.

Townsfolk out and about froze when they heard the gunfire, but then hurried back to their business once they figured out what had happened. Women shooed along children whose curious eyes were still looking at the gun-toting woman. Men gave huffy glares toward Jane, but hastened their step as well, quick to remove themselves from the situation. Albert stood frozen, eyes as wide as the overhead sun.

Jane couldn't get her eyelids to blink at the same time, but she looked at Albert and said, "Well?"

"I stand corrected," Albert muttered and continued to the tavern, one building away. Jane holstered her gun and caught up with him on the porch stairs. They pushed aside the swinging doors together.

The room was bustling with life. Not a single chair in the place was empty as men and women milled about, chatting and laughing with one another. The only thing Jane noticed, though, was a small opening at the bar, large enough for her and Albert to squeeze into. As soon as they did, a smiling middle-aged barkeep asked, "Howdy, folks. What was all the commotion about outside? Sounded like a gun shot."

"Don't know. Didn't hear nothin'," Jane said.

"Hmm. Okay. What can I getchya?"

"Jesse James been 'round?" Jane asked, slurring her 's's.

The bartender laughed. "Can't say that I've seen him."

"You sure? None of these people is him?"

"No, ma'am. I think I would have noticed if he and his gang came in. You sure he's in town?"

"Just robbed the train I was on, and we saw him head this way. Figured he'd be here at the tavern or at the bar over at the inn."

"Well, I gotta be honest. This is the most crowded my place has been for a while, and everyone does seem a tad agitated. Nothin' special happening in town, so if I gotta guess why, then maybe everyone is avoiding the inn?"

Albert said to Jane, "We should head over to the inn."

All business all the time. So serious. If he and Howard were truly ambassadors from the future, then their perpetual seriousness acted as a wet blanket for what tomorrow held. She might as well have some fun now since there didn't seem to be much of it in the future. Turning back to the barkeep, she slapped some cash on the counter. "This is for your time. And a full bottle of whiskey."

"Much obliged!" he said with a smile, swapping the money for a bottle.

By the time they made it back outside, Jane peeled the paper wrapper off with her teeth and popped the stopper out. Albert hurried toward the inn. She took a swig from her fresh bottle before jogging after him.

Albert stood at the corner of the building and peered into one of the windows. Before Jane got too close, Albert ran back to her on the dirt-packed street. She took one more sip and asked, "Well?"

"The gang is most certainly in there, and our friends are in danger. If we assume that everyone is in the main barroom area, then we might be able to take them by surprise if we sneak around back."

Jane followed Albert as best she could, fighting both gravity and the twisting terrain, navigating bumps and dips in the dirt. A mild sense of accomplishment swept through her as they slipped behind the building, and she neither fell nor dropped her bottle. However, that was replaced by anger and disappointment when she saw that there were no first story windows. There was a row of four windows on the second floor; only one was open.

Albert cursed in German, and Jane took another swig. While fighting the spin of the Earth, Jane spied a ladder against a balcony two buildings down. She elbowed her beleaguered partner and said, "Hey, Albie. Go get that ladder."

Albert grumbled to himself as he went to fetch the ladder. With a wobbling step, he returned, balancing the long ladder over his head, while Jane supervised, "C'mon, Albie. We gotta move faster. Get a move on."

He rested the top of the ladder under the opened window, and then stepped back and looked up to assess the situation. A deep inhale through his nose, a puffy cheeked exhale through pursed lips. Jane grew impatient and smacked his rump. "Come on, Albie. Up ya go."

Satchel slung over his shoulder, Albert scooted up the ladder, glaring at Jane until he reached halfway and turned his attention to the inherent peril of his actions. With every step, the ladder bowed and creaked. Reaching the top rungs, the ladder quivered nonstop.

"Get them spindly arms a-movin'," Jane encouraged, holding the ladder as steady as she could with her right hand, the bottle in her left. Doing as she suggested, Albert gripped the windowsill and pulled himself up. Legs churning, his feet slid along the wall as he searched for any kind of purchase. In a blink, he disappeared through the window.

"Well?" Jane shouted at the window.

Albert poked his head out and said, "The room is empty, but I doubt it will stay that way if you don't lower your voice."

"Blah, blah, blah," Jane mumbled to herself as she stoppered the whiskey bottle and tucked it into her belt. Even though the bottle's neck dug into her ribs, she loathed the idea of leaving it behind. As she started up the ladder, she complained, "That man bitches more than a princess on her period."

Once she had climbed as far as physics would allow, she reached for Albert as he reached for her. Their heads bumped as hands grabbed for arms, adding to the wobble of the shaking ladder. Jane jerked, her hips twisting. She kicked her feet, connecting with the ladder and sending it toppling backward.

"Pull! Pull me up!" Jane demanded, squirming with two fistfuls of the back of Albert's shirt.

"I'm trying… it would help… if you stopped fighting me." Albert grabbed the bottom of her jacket and top of her pants. Digging his knees into the wall, he pulled back, bringing Jane through the window.

Flopping on the ground, Jane landed on top of Albert. Through a nebula of whiskey vapor, she asked, "So, is that a gun in your holster, or are you just happy to see me?"

More gentlemanly than Jane thought possible, Albert rolled her off of him and stood. Straightening his twisted and half-removed shirt, he said, "I believe that would be your whiskey bottle. Shall we continue with our search, or would you like to make more of a ruckus until we attract attention?"

Jane stood, shuffling her feet to keep from falling back to the floor. "For a German, you sure are a namby-pamby."

Albert walked to the door and whispered, "I'm not entirely sure what that means, but I will certainly accept that title if being a 'namby-pamby' allows us and our friends to get out of this predicament alive."

Jane snarled her lips, crossed her eyes, flicked her tongue in and out of her mouth while mumbling, "mluh mluh mluh mluh mluh mluh."

Albert didn't react to her taunt. He simply opened the door wide enough to poke his head through and look side to side. "No one," he whispered, "but there are voices coming from the first floor."

Drawing both of her guns, Jane crept to the doorway and paused to regain her equilibrium. She tried to hide her dizziness by furrowing her brows as if in deep concentration. After a moment of listening to the voices on the first floor, Albert drew his ray gun from his satchel, and nodded to Jane. Not entirely sure why he nodded at her, Jane simply nodded back, but not too hard, lest she start the room spinning. They crouched and slunk along the second floor walkway, Albert in the lead. He slid to the right, slowly inching his way to the banister.

Jane shuffled to the left, toward the stairs, but found it easier just to get on her hands and knees and crawl. Kneeling, she glanced around the corner banister post and gazed down the stairs. The first thing she saw was Annie's stupid miniature top hat set perfectly on top of her stupid fluffy hair. How did she even keep her hair like that? Jane tilted her head just to feel the dirt-matted locks of her greasy hair brush over her jacket collar. Fancy products found in upscale stores in big cities, Jane deduced. The thought of shooting that stupid little hat off her stupid little head crossed Jane's mind, until she realized that Annie, as well as Billy and Howard for that matter, were standing with their hands raised.

Dragging her gaze from Annie and the boys to the rest of the room was a struggle. When her vision cleared, there were three grungy men with guns. Jane decided she could do it, she could take all of them out. She also decided to add a little flair to prove her shooting skills were better than Annie's.

Focusing on her targets, she moved to a crouch and positioned herself in front of the stair railing. A few quick breaths and she jumped onto the railing, rump first. Sitting, she slid down the railing and let out a howling whoop, pistols blazing. Four shots and four perfect hits—three into the chests of the men with guns, the fourth right in the center of Annie's stupid little hat, blowing it right off her head without messing a strand of her stupid fluffy hair. Luckily for Jane, there was no banister decoration at the end of the railing, allowing her to slide right off and land on her feet.

Smiling from ear to ear, she faced Annie, Howard, and Billy. A warmth bloomed within her chest, more from the dropped jaws than the whiskey. She blew the smoke from her gun barrels and said, "How'd ya like that, prissy-missy? Think you could do that? Even after a third of a... a half a bottle... three-quarters of... even after a bit of whiskey? In fact, I don't think many men could even do that!"

Jane's smile faded when she noticed that the trio still held their hands in the air. She paused her gloating to ask, "Why you three still stickin' 'em up?"

All three nodded with their heads to something behind Jane. She turned, almost losing her balance, and saw Jesse James and five other gunmen, most of them under the alcove caused by the second floor walkway. Shaking his head and smiling, Jesse said, "Impressive. Mighty, mighty impressive. You're right, though. I know I couldn't have done that. But I also know I can plug ya from right here. So, how 'bout you drop those pistols of yours."

"Damn it!" Jane yelled. Frowning, she put her guns on the nearby table. Since he said nothing about not drinking, Jane yanked the bottle from her belt, popped the stopper, and pulled a big swig. Jesse and his gang laughed.

"Look, Jesse, we ain't here to turn you in or nothin' like that," Billy said. "All we want is that satchel you took from me."

Stepping forward, Jesse smirked. "Is that so? What might be in that satchel that you find so valuable?"

"Nothin' valuable. Just sentimental."

Through blurred visions, Jane watched the two or three Alberts maneuver along the second floor walkway. He stopped and pointed his gun at the floor.

Jesse turned to Annie and pointed his gun at her. "Let me rephrase my question. What. Is in. The satchel?"

Howard blurted, "A battery containing dark energy from an enigmatic dimension that could be capable of universal annihilation if used for nefarious purposes!"

Jesse reared back as if Howard tossed a rattlesnake at him. Even his men stopped chuckling. That was the distraction Albert needed. He pulled the trigger.

The first flash of green light blew a splintering hole into the second floor walkway, above the men hidden in the alcove. Albert took a second to aim and fired two more times. The second and third flashes of green light reduced the planks of the first floor into exploding tinder and blew the men into nearby walls. They flopped to the floor like discarded rag dolls.

Jesse spun toward the chaos. By the time he turned back, he found himself at the business end of seven guns, including a futuristic one capable of discharging green flashes of destruction.

As the dust settled, Jesse placed his gun on the floor and raised his hands over his head. Billy's face shifted to his natural smile as he sauntered to Jesse. Mere inches from the outlaw's face, Billy said, "Now, about that satchel of mine...."

Chapter 11

As the train chugged along, the passenger car developed a slight side-to-side wobble, a rhythmic rocking. If amenable, a person could use it to loll him or herself to sleep. Many of the passengers were indeed amenable to that idea. Not Annie, though.

Sitting alone, she watched the scenery outside the train, the horizon creeping along in the distance. She was certainly happy as the scenery changed, going from dreary prairie to full crops of all kinds to lush plots of grass to distant mountains and nearby forests. But majestic scenery was hardly enough to satisfy a restless soul, and she grew bored.

Looking around, she found little entertainment potential in the car. Most passengers leaned to the side, resting their heads on anything available to aid their slumber. Even her new companions; though it was a minor miracle that anyone could sleep through Jane's snoring. However, Billy was still awake.

Sitting by himself, Billy stared out the window closest to him. Needing some form of distraction to pass the time, Annie made her way to the seat across from Billy. Making a display, she ran her hands behind her dress, to wrangle the ruffles, and sat with the grace expected of a lady. As expected of a pugnacious young man, Billy greeted her with a leering smile.

Sitting prim and straight, she placed her hands, one atop the other, on the knee of her left leg, crossed over her right. Even though she knew she shouldn't, she felt a touch more than prideful that she could elicit such a twinkle in Billy's eye. Her heart strummed her ribs a bit faster as he shifted in his seat to give her his full attention. With a flirtatious mocking, he, too, placed his hands, one atop the other, on the knee of his left leg, crossed over his right. With an exaggerated shimmy, he straightened his back, signifying that he was ready to receive his guest.

"Do you believe in magic, William?" she asked, her words tinged with lasciviousness.

Eyebrows curving upward, his boyish grin held both innocence and experience. "I sure do like where this conversation is goin'."

Averting her eyes to the scenery outside the window, Annie chuckled, bemused that he, through his palpable cloud of lust, made it seem like *she* initiated some form of romantic inclination. "I'm afraid I wasn't referencing that type of magic, Billy. I mean the type that Howard wallows in and Albert seems to fear."

Billy chuckled as well. "I believe that *they* certainly believe in it. Unless you forgot about our 'meeting of the minds' a few days ago?"

Annie's lips twisted into a sympathetic grimace as she recalled the event. The "meeting of the minds" felt more like an inquisition to her. Although she never claimed to have a full grasp of the situation, she understood the direness. Yet she believed both Albert and Howard had treated Billy unfairly.

The owner of the inn had been so grateful to the five for extricating the likes of Jesse James and his gang from his establishment, despite the damage they caused, that he let them use the back parlor free of charge after the sheriff and his posse wrangled the surviving members. The owner gave them two free rooms as well, one for the men, one for the women. Despite Annie's protests that Jane was more of a man, the two did indeed bunk together for their time in town.

The parlor had minimal frills, simply a round table large enough to seat eight, with a single door in. Annie assumed that she was the only one to notice the lovely silk tablecloth and matching napkins swaddling silver utensils. She also assumed she was the only one to notice the uneasy juxtaposition of the tetrahedron and the silk table cloth it rested upon, the unholy black and green liquids swirling about against pure heavenly whiteness. All those sitting at the table looked at anything other than the pyramidal abomination or each other. Howard didn't even sit, opting to pace fitfully about the room.

"William," Albert started with a tone that already added to the paternal feeling Annie got from him. Judging from the slight slump in Billy's shoulders, she assumed he shared similar feelings. "You had this the whole time?"

To answer Albert's question, Billy gave a shrug, eyes still solemnly downward.

"But... why did you keep this from us?" Albert asked, the patience in his voice forced.

A rare time when Billy's face showed earnestness, he looked up to Albert. "Why should I have brought it to you?"

"Because Howard and I are the experts on this. We know what this is."

"So says you, Albert. All I knew about you two is the night we met you came fallin' out of a hole in the sky behind Szilveszter. A hole! In the sky!"

"We explained to you what happened."

"Exactly. You. Your side of the story, minutes after we happened upon each other. That night, how was I supposed to believe you over the other guy who popped out of a hole in the sky? I didn't trust you."

Howard commanded everyone's attention with a derisive snort. Arms crossed, brows furrowed between sullen eyes, he looked like a judge wishing to be executioner. "I'd sooner trust a monkey with an incendiary device than trust this in your possession. I'd sooner trust Jane with this."

"Hey!" Jane barked.

"No need to be insulting," Annie said to Howard. Jane regarded Annie with glazed eyes, obviously trying to determine whom Annie meant to defend by that statement.

Howard looked at Billy and said, "Well, there is no need to hide dangerous weapons. Or be troglodytic. Yet, Billy does both rather deftly."

Billy slapped the table. "Do you want my help or not?"

Howard and Albert glanced at each other, their expressions softening from anger to nervousness. Neither could muster a response. Billy continued, "I decided to tag along for shits and giggles, gentlemen. 'Cause I was bored. 'Cause I thought a little adventure and a change of scenery could clear my mind. And to tell you what, I was more'n a little curious about what was goin' on with you and that whack job you're chasin'. Then I meet up with Calamity Jane and Annie Oakley and think to myself, 'What could be more fun than that?' Well, guess what? I don't need to be here. So, I'm gonna head off to bed and you let me know tomorrow mornin' if you want me along or not. Just remember—I was more'n willin' to sling iron for you at the carnival *and* against Jesse James with no want of reward."

The next morning, all five of them sat around the same table for breakfast, once more compliments of the inn owner. They ate in silence, all of them either staring furtively at their plates or longingly out the window. Nothing spoken, apologies were implied and inferred by everyone simply by being there. The closest thing to an apology came when Howard snatched Billy's satchel and opened the flap. Before Billy could say anything, Howard placed the pyramid inside and handed the satchel back to Billy. The rogue accepted it with a nod, but went back to his bacon and eggs. However, Annie opted not to get caught up in the awkwardness or brooding, and decided that she was going to make the best of the situation, since they were going to be in this town for most of the day, until the next train arrived.

Even though it hardly possessed the amenities of a city, such as her home of Cincinnati, Annie resigned herself to enjoy what this town had to offer. The clothing stores were bereft of the finest linens, but she shopped nonetheless, and stumbled upon a soft dress of blue that had intricately woven lace patterns at the ends of the sleeves, which she purchased for a pittance and a smile. A trip to the local cobbler yielded a pair of sturdy boots that bordered on stylish. After a much-needed jaunt to the haberdasher, Annie added three hatboxes to her collection as well as one miniature top hat, carefully pinned to her hair, to replace the one that Jane had shot.

She offered to purchase a change of clothes for everyone else in her cadre as well, but they all declined: Billy stating that he needed no other debts in his life; Albert stating that he was quite comfortable in what he had, but Annie knew he declined due to his gentlemanly code; Jane grunted and spat at Annie's feet upon hearing the offer; and Howard went on a longwinded tirade, one of quiet voice and clipped tone, but a tirade still, filled with superfluous words about how he despised this time period and would rather not dress himself in it. However, they all accepted her offer to pay the inn to draw a bath for each of them and wash their clothes. Jane said no to the clothes cleaning, but Annie had the inn clean them anyway while Jane soaked in the tub for the first time. Since the sourness of old sweat, stale whiskey, and prairie grime refused to take leave of Jane, Annie waited two hours and tricked Jane into taking a second soak in the bathtub, convincing her that the first soak was merely an alcohol-induced daydream.

The members of the ragtag group began to converse with each other again, but it was done with emotional distance or suspicion. Howard conversed with Billy through snorts; Billy in kind to Howard with grunts. Annie no longer questioned why men were often analogous to pigs. But neither Howard nor Albert were as loquacious as they once were. If they weren't talking, then Annie wasn't going to get any information about the future, information that she craved. To get everyone comfortable with conversing again, she knew she had to make the young man who sat in front of her on the train feel less ostracized.

Annie shifted in the train's seat and said to Billy, "Well, the minds have been met, and it is high time we move on from that."

"I would certainly like that, but I do believe I have lost everyone's trust."

"Well, I doubt Howard trusts anyone."

Billy laughed. "That might be a truth. Plus, I can't imagine me gainin' his trust becomin' a high priority in my life. Albert on the other hand… I do feel bad about that."

"Albert is a good man. I'm sure you will be back in his good graces soon enough."

"Yeah. I know." Smarm now dripped from Billy's smile. "How 'bout you? Do you trust me?"

Annie's erubescent cheeks gave her answer, her words merely details. "With my life? Yes. With my money? Maybe. With keeping my honor intact with my betrothed? Absolutely not."

Billy's eyes narrowed, a predator hunting prey that had evaded capture before. "So… where might this betrothed one be?"

"As I had stated before, he is back home working deals for our traveling show."

"Uh-huh." The disbelief in his words obvious. "So, tell me more about this betrothed of yours. What might he be like?"

"He might be like no man I've ever met."

"You didn't say he was *better* than any man you've ever met."

Annie laughed and shook her head. "I certainly meant to imply that he was. Let's just say he has many of the best qualities between you and Howard."

"Mostly the qualities I possess, I assume."

A shift in expression and shoulder shrug was Annie's purposefully ambiguous answer.

Even though he still maintained his smile, Billy scowled. "You cannot prefer a dandy like Howard over a fella like me."

"He is far more intelligent and capable of discussing a wide variety of topics. There is a subtle poetry about him, the way he talks."

"All the poetry I ever heard is about flowers and sunshine. His world is a dark and distrustful place, filled with monsters lurkin' in the shadows of shadows. He's happier walkin' through a nightmare than strollin' through a field of roses."

Annie gave a sharp exhale, a mixture of sigh and chuckle. "Well, that very well might be true, but that may be a sign of caution, a sign he that he knows consequences could be dangerous. A sign of maturity."

"Maturity? I doubt that boy has ever known the finer points of a woman. Probably too afraid of what demons lurk in the crevice of a woman's spread legs."

Despite the crudeness of Billy's comment, Annie found it impossible not to laugh. "Well, I cannot attest to the truth behind that statement, but... is the train slowing?"

No sooner did she finish the question then it was answered, the slowing momentum caused her to shift in her seat, but the subsequent lurch yanked her from her seat into Billy's lap. Some passengers yelped or shouted, surprised from the sudden shift, while others lost their balance and slid from their seats, a few landing in the aisle way. During a heartbeat of clarity, Annie silently commended Billy for not only resisting the urge to make a lascivious comment about her current position on him, but also by the way he protectively held her. She needed it as the train tipped sideways.

Chapter 12

The train car erupted with screams, quickly blending with the sounds of twisting metal. Billy thanked God that even though the train car tilted, it did so slow enough for him to wrap his arms around Annie and brace for impact. As their side of the train left the ground, Billy flopped onto the floor, landing on his backside. One arm around Annie's waist, the other hugged her shoulders and protected her head. Arms pulled against her body, she held two fistfuls of Billy's shirt while burying her face in his chest. He sat upright as best he could, waiting for gravity to take over.

With the yawning groan of a dying beast, the train continued to tilt. Billy and Annie slid across the floor to the wall on the other side as it became the new floor of the train. Billy tightened his grip on Annie. He didn't care who trusted him or where her betrothed might be, Annie was a woman worth protecting, and he was going to do just that, no matter what the consequences to his own body. These were not quite as dire as he had imagined, though they did hurt as his back slammed against the wall, now on the ground, a bag of luggage that had been thrown earlier softening the blow. He had plenty of time to protect his own face from the shards of glass falling from the shattering window now above him. Some of the larger pieces pierced the cloth cushioning of the seats, but the smaller slivers rained upon him harmlessly.

The train car continued to topple, and Billy tightened his muscles, but he was completely uncertain how to handle the new tumble. He tried to speculate what he should do, how to twist or turn. But the train car rocked back, settling on its side.

As the train's moans subsided, the passengers' screams intensified. Half a dozen families called out to various members, assessing the well-being of their fold. Husbands and wives stumbled about to find each other; fathers and mothers focused on their children. The healthy tended to the wounded. The aware looked for the lost.

The dull squeeze of torqued muscle burned through Billy's back as he shifted, trying to make assessments himself. Before he could get his bearings, or even form a coherent thought, Howard's face appeared, yelling, "Annie! Annie! Is she okay?"

Using the top of the seat, now perpendicular to the ground, for support, Howard stood tilted on the upper part of the car's wall, now on the ground. Annie stirred and tried to sit up, wobbling and disoriented. Still gripping the seat, Howard used his other hand to help Annie to her feet. "Annie? Are you injured?"

Blinking rapidly, she looked around the devastation and took a few deep breaths. "I'm... I... I believe I am uninjured, thanks to Billy."

Assisting Annie, Howard guided her away from her landing spot and toward the other end of the tipped train car. "Here. This way. The door may have relocated to the ceiling, but we can still use it to escape." Howard then looked over his shoulder to Billy, still on the ground, and mumbled, "Thank you for doing the right thing. Now, come on. There is chaos we need to disentangle."

Billy couldn't help but laugh at Howard's attitude, until the stabbing pain in his ribs told him to stop. He exhaled and stretched; the pain subsided. He got to his feet and stretched some more, twisting his body to determine the extent of his injuries. Nothing major, he decided. Soreness and throbbing could be cured with a night of whiskey at a brothel. Not everyone came out of this quite so lucky.

Billy aimed for the door Howard had mentioned, indeed part of the new ceiling. A few healthy men had climbed out and then reached down to help pull others through. Jane escorted a shirtless boy toward the way out, his garment now a blood-soaked cloth around his arm. Albert carried a preteen girl with tear-streaked cheeks clutching her arm, while her mother, crying as well, followed closely behind.

Walking to the far end of the car, Billy checked every nook along the way for stray survivors. It also afforded him the opportunity to collect his satchel as well as Howard's. Not sure of the ramifications of uncontained "dark energy," he peered into his satchel to evaluate the condition of the pyramid. Still intact. Satisfied that he did all he could do, he ambled to the exit.

"Are you injured, William?" Albert asked, his head poking through the door on the ceiling.

"Nah. Few bumps and bruises. Here," Billy said, handing the satchels to Albert. "Nothin' inside of them seems broken."

Albert leaned back in to assist Billy out of the train car. Stepping up on the nearest seat, Billy grabbed Albert's hand and hoisted himself out.

Astounding and sprawling, the wreckage rendered Billy speechless, like he just took a sucker punch to the gut. He stood on one of the half dozen passenger cars on their sides, survivors helping each other out of and away from the train. Another half dozen cargo cars had toppled over as well, industrial contents ranging from coal to nails scattered and spread as if seeping from wounds. The few cars at the end and the caboose remained upright and on the track, including those with the livestock. Billy breathed a sigh of relief—Annie's horses would be spooked, but unharmed. The engine and the passenger car behind it were upright as well. Billy was surprised that any part of the train remained upright when he saw what had caused the accident.

Beyond the locomotive, gray swirls of smoke flowed upward from a charred hole in the ground where the track should be. Thick forest lined both sides of the tracks, but fortunately the trees were too far away to catch fire from the explosion that had caused the hole in the tracks. Albert called to him from the ground, breaking the spell.

Billy joined Albert and the others by the edge of the forest. "We need to thank the conductor for saving our lives," Albert said. "From what the other passengers are saying, he saw the flash of light from the explosion and immediately started to slow the train down. It was still too close for a smooth stop, but it could have been worse."

"No doubt," Billy said. Thick smoke billowed from the still-smoldering hole. Dozens of people milled about, forming small groups. "So, we help who we can? Maybe get our bearings and find a town for assistance?"

"Good plan," Jane said, sounding the most sober Billy had ever heard her.

"No," Howard said. "We simply do not have that kind of time to waste."

"Now, look here, ya snit," Jane started. Albert put a hand on her shoulder and said, "What he meant was that even though we all would like to help out, time is not on our side. There are plenty of capable people here."

Both Jane and Billy looked at the other passengers scurrying around, helping with injuries or assessing the damage, or rummaging through bags and cargo. Billy said, "Right. We got ten good hands to lend, so I think we should."

"William, *who* do you think did this?" Albert asked.

Billy paused. "Are you suggestin' that Szilveszter did this?"

"Yes, absolutely. Helping these people will not stop Szilveszter from doing this again. It will not stop him from completing his mission. We need to stick to ours, especially since Szilveszter is close by."

"Why do you reckon that?" Billy asked.

"Because Szilveszter is a sadistic soul, one fascinated by the suffering of others. He must be close by not only to detonate the explosives, but to revel in… the… aftermath.…" Albert's words lost weight until they floated away on the slight breeze. He became enraptured with the forest. The others turned to see what demanded his attention. Indians.

Three hid among the trees, all as black as if they had wallowed in pitch. A fourth one appeared from behind another tree, as if the tree itself bled tar and pooled into a humanoid form. Then a fifth Indian materialized in the same ink oozing fashion.

Worms squirmed about in Billy's gut. What was he seeing? He had plenty of experience dealing with Indians, but with tribes of the southwest. Were all eastern tribes this intense? The practice of body painting was common, he knew, but for hunting, war or special ceremonies. He had never heard of any tribe drenching themselves from head to toe in coal black. That was not what unnerved him, though.

Giant bat heads and pelts adorned each of the Indians like cowl and cloak. Rows of needle-like teeth ringed around the natives' heads, protecting their eyes. Leathery ears stood straight up in a permanent state of attention. Even though the animals were dead, their eyes remained opened and glossy, mimicking life and awareness. Billy had never seen a bat large enough to clothe a man, and the sight of them chilled his fingers and toes.

Two more Indians seeped out from behind the trees, and that was when Billy noticed their hands and feet—only three fingers on each hand and three toes per foot, the missing digits the same for each Indian. Billy assumed that they removed the digits on purpose. What kind of tribe would do that?

Jane had dealt with Indian tribes before, so Billy turned to her to ask if she had any experience with a tribe like this one. Her wide-eyed expression of confusion and fear was all the answer he needed. Annie looked as nervous as a rabbit staring at a pack of wolves. Howard seemed uneasy, but inquisitive, his attention bouncing from one Indian to another, examining them while he slipped his hand under the flap of his satchel.

"Howard," Billy whispered. "What are you doin'?"

Howard offered his usual response to Billy—a begrudging look implying Billy's lack of intellect. He whispered back, "What does it look like?"

"It looks like you're tryin' to get us in a world of hurt."

"On the contrary. I am simply preparing to defend myself against any form of unwarranted acts of aggression from these savages."

"Well, genius, callin' 'em savages and pullin' out a gun could give them warrant to act aggressively."

"Howard," Annie whispered. "I... I think Billy might be right. We don't know anything about them."

"Listen to her, Howard," Billy added. "What do you think, Jane?"

Jane patted her hands on her jacket, close to her holstered revolvers. "I ain't never seen Indians like these before. If they was the friendly kind, then they wouldn't look like they got puked up from the pits of Hell. Ol' squirrelly Howard might be right on this one."

"They're just standing there," Annie whispered to no one. "Just looking at us."

Billy put his hand on her shoulder and said, "Well, we just need to find out what they want. Ain't that right, Albert?"

Billy hoped for support from the group's calm voice of reason. However, he received no response. "Albert?"

"Oh my God," Annie said, covering her mouth with one hand and pointing with the other. "Albert!"

Albert had already left them, striding deeper into the woods, toward the Indians.

Chapter 13

Howard had been so caught up within the cyclone of history and legend swirling together that he forgot he was in a time period where there remained pockets of unrest between the natives and the American government. Savages, as was anyone not of British background, but unlike many of the other peoples he found contempt in, these individuals held no compunction in ignoring societal rules about killing a fellow human. With that knowledge in the forefront of his mind, he focused on every spear and axe and arrow. The feral stares glaring from behind the teeth of gargantuan bat heads and the severed stumps of missing digits only added to the natives' truculent demeanor.

Howard eased his hand toward his gun until the ignoramus Billy found fault with that action. As they engaged in yet another senseless bicker, Howard failed to keep aware of the situation around him, until Annie gasped about Albert.

Astonished, Howard watched his partner, and one of the few human beings he would consider a friend, walk toward a perceived threat. "Albert? Albert, stop!"

Albert stopped and turned to show the clear mental acuity within his eyes. "I can't explain why, Howard, but I know we need to follow them. It's like a suggestion repeating itself in my head."

Albert continued farther into the woods, and Howard followed, his gait uneven as he struggled with the rough forest floor while trying to keep all of the Indians in his sight. The closest natives returned to hiding behind the trees, but did so as if the shadows had cast them, instead of the other way around, and bid reclamation. Seconds later the same number of natives appeared from behind trees deeper in the forest. One savage would disappear; one would appear farther away, oozing forth as if the trees leaked tar instead of sap. Or were they the same ones? The black body paint and bat pelts made them all look the same. Albert followed them, nonetheless, and Howard followed him.

Billy hollered from behind, "What in the hell are you doing?"

Howard glanced over his shoulder to regard his companions, all three with their arms crossed and displaying a variety of emotions upon their faces. Confusion cloaked Billy, while disappointment clung to Annie, and anger etched itself into Jane's face. "Following Albert, of course."

"Are you crazy?"

"Sanity is all perspective. My definition clearly differs from yours."

Billy threw his hands to the sky and shook his head, turning his back to Howard in frustration.

"Howard?" Annie asked, her eyes pleading more than her words. "Do you think this is a good idea? It seems very, very dangerous."

Looking upon her lovely countenance, patience washed away his disdain for Billy, and his voice went from curt to calm. "No emotion permeates my being other than fear regarding this situation. But not only do I trust Albert and his motivations, I am bound by that trust to do all within my power to protect him should the situation demand such action."

Annie looked to Billy and Jane, then back to Howard. She walked into the forest.

"Girlie, you are stupid," Jane mumbled.

"Well, I reckon in case Albert or Howard need my superior shooting skills, I best ought to provide them," Annie replied.

Jane spat on the ground, but followed anyway.

Billy huffed, "What about your whole usin' time we can't afford speech?"

Shifting his tone back to irritation with ease, Howard replied, "That was in regards to the mission. Even though this exercise may take us from direct chase of Szilveszter, I find the appearance of these savages beyond coincidental. Albert believes this to be paramount, and I believe Albert."

"You just said you don't believe in coincidence, and yet you haven't asked why they suddenly appeared now? This could be a trap!"

"Then I suggest that you remain vigilant and keep your guns at the ready."

Grousing to himself much in the same manner as Jane, Billy strode into the forest with the rest of his companions. Never considering himself a master of persuasion, Howard allowed himself an internal smirk for being able to convince Billy to come along. Howard still disliked him and viewed him as an unsophisticated lout, barely one step above the primitives they now pursued, but he was undeniably a good shot and if nothing else, served as another target if the savages turned dangerous.

Everyone maintained Albert's pace, only a few steps behind him, constantly looking over their shoulders. Even though Albert seemed to respond coherently when anyone talked to him, he remained monomaniacal in following the tar-colored Indians.

The natives continued to maneuver through the forest as if the trees were doorways. Howard focused on one of the savages, scrutinizing his every movement. As before, he flowed from behind the tree—or *from* the tree?—and then vanished in the same fashion. After the native disappeared, Howard ran to the exact spot to find nothing, no trace that the native was ever there. No inky residue, no sooty film, not even a stray hand print. As he and the rest of his group continued to tread through the woods following the enigmatic natives who moved as if by mysticism, Howard discreetly retrieved his notebook and pen from his satchel.

Billy caught up with Howard and whispered, "Way to protect your friend."

Howard scowled. "If the details of the situation are outside of your grasp, allow me to explain. Even though you share many qualities of these uncivilized savages, they are displaying that they are, or at least know how to use, the supernatural. Whenever such a phenomenon occurs, I feel it is my duty to record the details."

"Will you two shut the hell up and look," Jane growled, and pointed to a small clearing ahead.

Once out of the forest, Howard noticed that the ground terminated, a swift and rock-filled plummet awaited those who strayed too close to the edge. The stark upward slope of the mountain bordered the rest of the clearing, making the only form of egress either the way they had come or through the cave in the mountain. When Howard saw the cave, he froze. He debated about dropping his pen for his gun.

A roiling black liquid flowed from the cave, as if the mountain itself vomited ink. The stream of gooey pitch forked in many places, bubbling tendrils reaching into the forest. Howard noticed that each stream flowed to a tree where a native stood.

"Voormis." The word floated on the air like a feather plucked from the wing of a dark bird delivering a message of death. It came from nowhere, yet everyone heard it, turning their heads and shifting their eyes, trying to ascertain the source. Unable to articulate why, Howard knew the word referred to the natives as he wrote it in his notebook. He then furiously scribbled notes, scrawling erratic shorthand meaningful only to him. Detailing every movement, every flow of tarry blackness, every swirl of liquid coal, he recorded it all. His mind raced with possibilities and realizations. Maybe Albert and he were not the first ones to open portals to other dark dimensions? Have these doorways always existed in this plane of reality among mortals? Or were there others like Szilveszter, base enough to shred the fabric between the dimensions?

Scratching questions and concerns on the pages as fast as his hand would allow, Howard kept glancing from notebook to cave, until the cave's maw rippled.

Much like the portal in the warehouse that led Howard and Albert to this time period, the darkness of the cave danced. Undulating and pulsating, the blackness gave way to light and formed a scene populated with images. A young couple, beaming smiles exuding happiness. Albert gasped and whispered, *"Mutter? Vater?"*

Why the Voormis lured Albert to an enigmatic cave to show him his parents, Howard couldn't guess, but he wrote it down anyway. The image rippled again, this time depicting Albert's parents with a baby. Albert's mother cradled the swaddled infant with both arms while his father stood behind her, peering over her shoulder, his smile nothing but pride and joy.

"Albie?" Jane asked, walking toward Albert while keeping an eye on the Voormis. "Who are those people we're lookin' at?"

"My parents," Albert replied, voice cracking. "And me as an infant."

"But why?" Annie asked.

"I… I don't know."

Fulfilling Annie's request, the image flickered and folded in upon itself, changing once more. The swirling stopped and showed Albert's parents with Albert, still as a bundled baby. The images moved this time, Albert's parents reacting to a man approaching them. The man was Szilveszter Matuska.

Annie gasped. Billy and Jane tensed. Albert clenched his fists. Howard kept writing. They were all powerless to do anything other than watch.

Szilveszter spoke with Albert's parents, but there was no sound. Noiselessly, the new parents listened to Szilveszter. As he talked, their expressions changed; hers slid to fear and disgust while his hardened to anger. Szilveszter's eyes grew maniacal while the fervor of his hand gestures heightened. Albert's mother turned her back while his father stepped between her and the madman. Now angered, Szilveszter pulled a wavy bladed knife from his robes and sliced through the belly of the man standing between him and his goal. With no hesitation or remorse, he sliced the mother's neck mid-scream; her blood splashing over the crying infant. With a tenderness unbefitting his most recent action, Szilveszter pulled the infant from his mother's limp arms and coddled it. The scene swirled to black.

Tears flowed over Albert's cheeks. "No!"

Howard put his pad and pen away and ran to his friend. Placing a hand on Albert's shoulder, Howard said, "I believe we are watching what *could* happen, what Szilveszter is planning to do."

"But why?" Albert whispered, his voice quivering.

Again, the swirling darkness came alive with movement. This time still images flashed, one at a time. Szilveszter and a preteen Albert cavorting with shadows shaped like monsters. An adult Albert laughing with glee while covered in blood and viscera. Albert standing before blooming clouds that bloomed into shapes of mushrooms with his arms extended as if exulting divinity. Albert commanding armies of the undead, legion after legion marching across the world. Albert lording over millions from a balcony jutting from a tower in the shape of a mad god with mighty wings sprouting from its back and tentacles spilling from its horrible face.

The images faded to black.

Wide-eyed, Albert muttered, "No… no… no… no.…"

"What the hell did we just see?" Billy asked.

"The future, if Szilveszter's plans come to fruition," Howard answered. "It's clear now what he wants to do. We just need to figure out how."

The cave's darkness came alive to show two images this time; one of a warehouse dominating two full city blocks, the second a massive Cape Cod styled house on a large tract of land with a young woman standing in front of it, a maniacal zeal in her eyes.

Howard did his best to retain the details of the images. Even though he had never seen them before, he had suspicions. But he was more curious about the cave's resident. Having every question answered to this point, Howard asked the cave, "Who are you?"

A single word floated upon a whisper eerie enough to raise the hair on the back of Howard's neck. "Tsathoggua."

The darkness shifted again, but in a different way this time. The happening in the cave was not some mystically conjured image, but rather the reality of the moment, the source of the images. A face appeared in the cave opening, as if the abyss was expelling a poison. Round and flat, almost like a diabolical amphibian, the face possessed the pointed nose and ears of a bat. Black sputum dripped from rows of tiny, needle-like teeth. Matted fur sprouted from the darkness, but the monstrosity stopped before reaching the edge, preventing more light from touching its body.

Everyone reeled back. Billy said, "I think it's time to go now."

"This may be the only time I agree with you," Howard replied. He then tugged on Albert's shirt. "Come, Albert. We should leave this place."

Eyes wide, Albert turned from where he stood and trudged toward the forest whence they came, Howard guiding him. Billy and Jane backed away with their guns drawn. Annie tried to join them, but couldn't.

"My feet!" Annie yelled, ankle deep in a pool of tar. The pool coalesced, forming a black fist, and pulled.

Hard enough to drop her face first to the ground, the grip of Hell yanked Annie toward the cave. Albert dove and caught her hands. He struggled to halt her capture as they both slid along the ground. Billy shot at the Voormis; his bullets having no affect, simply passing through the human-shaped creatures. Jane unloaded both of her six-shooters into the cave creature, again with no affect. The monster simply smiled, hungry eyes watching Annie. His fifth appendage twitched and grew erect, festering black goo dripping from it. Howard would not allow this hell to befall upon anyone, let alone a soul that would grace even Heaven's gates. He drew his gun and fired.

The green flash of energy blasted the tendril between Annie and the cave. A squeal pierced the air, shrill enough to make everyone wince. Howard shot again, hitting the same spot on the tentacle. The inky tentacle deliquesced, relinquishing Annie as its stump retreated into the cave.

The Voormis lurched forward, brandishing their weapons and bearing sharp teeth. Jane and Billy continued to shoot them with zero effect. Scowling, Howard aimed at the closest attacker and squeezed the trigger. A direct hit to its chest caused all the Voormis to screech and flee to the cave.

Albert stood and helped Annie to her feet. Crying, she clutched him and pressed her face against his shoulder. Jane and Billy jerked about, aiming their guns at anything that moved. Howard asked, "Are you harmed?"

She stepped away from Albert and brushed the back of her hand across her cheeks. "No. No, I'm unharmed. Thanks to you."

If not for the potential of imminent danger, Howard would have cherished his heroism. Instead, he said, "I believe it is time to go."

"I agree," Albert replied.

"Where to?" Billy asked.

"To our original destination. New Jersey."

Chapter 14

Thomas Edison sat in his small wooden chair and watched the light bulb on the work desk. The light dimmed, slowly shifting from bright yellow to dull orange. Then, unceremoniously, the filament cooled to a dull gray, allowing the early evening to cast a pall over the room.

Thirteen hours. Thomas would have written the results down, but they had been maddeningly the same every time. He leaned forward in his chair, elbows on the table, and brought his face closer to the bulb. The filament. The filament was the problem, and he knew it.

Frustrated, he threw himself back into his chair and slouched. He rubbed the heels of his hands against his temples, hoping for the ache to go away. Or for some inspiration, a new idea to try. He had come too far to lose this race.

The world had light, manmade light. The power to turn night into day with the mere flip of a switch—God at the tip of man's finger. But that power was limited. Few had access to it, and the manmade daylight lasted the same number of hours as nature made daylight. The masses… the masses wanted their due, wanted the ability to walk into a dark room and light it without the aid of match and candle. And the race was on.

Thomas intended Menlo Park to be the genesis point for the future of mankind, to drag humanity out of the mud and give the people something better than sticks and stones. He wanted to be Prometheus. But so did others.

Joseph Swan was Thomas' closest competition, and the Brit was also experimenting with filaments. So, they joined forces to ward off the others trying to cross the finish line first. Especially the mainland Europeans, for only the Almighty knew what those madmen were doing!

Thomas heaved one last sigh while staring at the burnt-out light bulb. He'd been inspired to use a filament, now all that was necessary was the perspiration to make it work. Despite being tired and frustrated, he stood to see what was currently at his disposal. In Menlo Park, that was everything.

Two city blocks long, Thomas stocked his laboratory with every known everything he could think of. Whole walls devoted themselves to banks of tiny drawers filled with screws and nails, wads and tangles of hairs from mammals, chips of stones and minerals, and all forms of miscellaneous bits and pieces. Bottles of dusts and powders rested upon endless shelves, as well as jars filled with every liquid containable by glass ranging in natural colors found in a rainbow to more exotic shades few humans have laid eyes upon, let alone labeled with a name. Spools of wire, from hair thin to finger thick, jutted from the walls, next to bolts of every form of cloth from around the globe. He even had a special section more akin to sorcery, stocked with containers of bird talons and jars of floating eyeballs and dainty vials filled with disinterred organs. A million pieces available, but only one would complete this puzzle.

Wandering around the hairs and fibers, Thomas imagined how well each would last in a gas infused glass bulb. Maybe wrapping a specific hair or fiber around a twist of metal? Maybe... Maybe... Maybe... Thomas thought he smelled an unusual odor, but it was hard to distinguish "unusual" from "normal" in his fortress of oddities.

Losing his train of thought, Thomas blinked rapidly, his vision was blurring as his mind felt like it was being ground by pestle and mortar. He looked at hairs and fibers because... because... why? He couldn't remember. He felt that he should be more concerned, to the point of possible anxiety, but he simply couldn't muster those emotions. Water. A glass of water would help.

Thomas turned away from the shelving and pulled up with a start, greeted by five figures. Even in his suddenly lethargic condition, he didn't like the idea of strangers in his laboratory. Especially odd ones such as these.

"Greetings," said the young man in the front of the small group. His smile was charming, albeit tinted with overzealousness, and disarming enough to keep Thomas from becoming unnerved by the black robes piped with green. *Is it the young man's smile that placates me?* Thomas wondered. *Or the enigmatic odor?* Those questions quickly slipped away like water in a sieve, "My name is Szilveszter Matuska, and I'm here to help you."

"Help me?" Thomas asked, finding the sound of his voice muffled, as if speaking into a pillow.

"Yes. Actually, we can help each other."

Thomas wanted to be suspicious of Szilveszter and his companions, but his mind refused such a notion. A motley bunch, one Thomas knew he should deem dangerous: a garishly dressed carnival magician, holding a stoppered glass vile containing a lime colored liquid and similarly shaded vapors; two women, one wearing head to toe veils while the other... the other Thomas swore was a bipedal lizard with a sleeveless brown work-shirt and brown workpants, completely hairless and covered in thick scales.

The curiosity behind them, however, was what really caught Thomas's attention. It had the large, muscled stature of a circus strongman, but between its shoulders rested a jar with a brain and two eyes stalks floating about in liquid. Even in his muddled state of mind, Thomas so wanted to examine the creature further. First, he needed to find out more about Szilveszter's proposition. "Help each other?"

With a politician's smile, Szilveszter approached Thomas, his long robes creating the illusion of floating. Offering a piece of paper to Thomas, he said, "This. This is the secret to the incandescent light bulb. The material for your filament. The key to unlocking humanity's future."

Thomas unfolded the paper. What he read made sense, but no matter how hard he tried to get excited, to become exuberant, this mysterious dullness inhibited those feelings as well. He asked, "What do you want in return?"

"The same," Szilveszter replied. "Information. I have heard many tales told in the shadows of the underground that you have theories about reanimation."

Thomas's heart pumped ice, skin chilling from cold sweat. However, he could not react to this fear the way he should, could not express his indignation. But he knew what to say. "No."

Fingers intertwined in front of his chest, Szilveszter slowly walked back and forth in front of Thomas, his slow pacing hypnotic. "Mr. Edison, do you intend to act upon these theories and designs of reanimation that you have?"

"No," Thomas whispered.

"Then why even keep them? Why allow these ideas to clutter your mind? I'm here to liberate you from them so you may focus on what is more important. Wouldn't you like that? Wouldn't you like to usher in a new future?"

Fumes. The fumes from the concoction in the vial held by the man in the ridiculous top hat. Thomas' mind cleared just enough to understand how it became fogged in the first place. He needed to stall, buy time to gather his wits and wade through the muddiness. In a few minutes, he could certainly think his way out of this complication. He tried to think of questions, conversational threads to keep the young man occupied, but then the veiled woman stepped forward.

She approached and used one hand to part the veil from half of her face, exposing the soft features of a beautiful, young brunette. For an instant, Thomas thought he saw the features of a withered old crone peeking from under the left side of the veil but found that notion ludicrous as he regarded the sparkle in the maiden's emerald eye. Smiling, she glided the fingertips of her other hand over his cheek. Voice sounding like a lover's whisper gliding over a tombstone, her words seeped into his body, his soul. "Behold your future."

Behind her flawless countenance, the interior of Menlo Park rippled, giving way to wavy images. Colors coalesced into throngs of people cheering, applauding the good name of Thomas Edison. A growing home and thriving businesses appeared, made possible by his gift of light to society. Wealth. Admiration. Immortality the likes of which few had known. The mists of these visions dissipated to reveal that Thomas had never strayed from the interior of Menlo Park. The beautiful maiden stroked his cheek once more and asked, "Isn't the sacrifice of notes with scribbles and theories that you will never test, never use, an adequate price to pay for what awaits you?"

The effects of the vapors were wearing off, but Thomas felt the effects of the vision taking hold, gripping his heart and soul. Even if produced by some sleight of hand, smoke and mirrors parlor trick, he knew that what he saw awaited him. All he needed to do was follow the instructions on the paper in his hand and give away a few useless theories and sketches. "Yes."

Szilveszter clapped his hands together, looking more exuberant than a child discovering a tannenbaum choked with presents on Christmas morning. "Excellent decision, Thomas! Excellent indeed. The world will thank you."

A torrent of emotions surged through Thomas. Fear of this lunatic and his minions. Anger that he was being manipulated. Shame that he had accepted the reward offered to him. Eagerness to get started, as he fingered the edges of the paper in his hand.

Szilveszter continued, "Now, Mr. Edison, if you please. Your notes on reanimation?"

Guts tying themselves into knots, Thomas upheld his end of the bargain. Sitting back down at his desk, he opened a drawer filled with files. His hands trembled as his fingers glided over the contents, to the one in question. He rationalized that he was saving the world by, literally, pulling it from the dark ages. At what cost? Grabbing the file, he felt a tinge of foolishness for thinking he was turning over dangerous secrets. Even though papers overflowed the file and threatened to burst its crease, Thomas felt—no, knew—there was nothing of value in them. But this transaction was demand driven. If Szilveszter wanted the files, then there must be value to them.

With one last final push, his desire to be the man who could light the world shoved the potential consequences from his mind—even if this young man could reanimate flesh, what practical use would he have of it? Even if he did experiments in the most clandestine of ways, the authorities would discover his blasphemy against nature and bring a stop to it. Thomas made his choice, the reward outweighed the risk.

He handed the files to Szilveszter.

Chapter 15

Dusk took its turn with the sky, getting ready to give way to twilight. Albert and company moved about the streets with alacrity, obtaining directions from the adolescents lighting the gas streetlights. Rounding one last corner, Menlo Park stood before them.

"Whoa," William whispered.

"Agreed," Howard whispered back.

Following Albert's lead, everyone ran across the street and remained close to the body of the building while trying not to draw the attention of any passersby. Coming to the first window available, Albert peeked in. He saw Thomas Edison standing alone.

A slight smile played across Albert's lips. It seemed as if Thomas wrestled with a problem. Albert sympathized. Countless times he, too, flirted with evening, nights, and even the wee hours of the morning to wrestle with a formula or theory. Even though Howard had shared his tales of pacing his room at midnight struggling to cogitate the perfect word he needed to complete a story, Albert regarded Thomas Edison as a fellow scientist, and felt a bit more kinship with him. Albert's heart shriveled when he saw Szilveszter and his cabal enter the room with Thomas.

He turned to his associates and whispered, "Szilveszter is here with four others."

"Five of us, five of them," Jane whispered as she pulled her six-shooter from her holster.

"Well, look at that," Howard mumbled as he rummaged through his satchel. "The drunkard can count.

"Six bullets. After I plug the five of them, there's still one left for you," she replied, checking the revolver's cylinder.

Howard paused his search long enough to reply with a deep-browed scowl.

Annie softly cleared her throat and whispered, "What's our plan?"

"Guns a blazin' always works for me," William suggested as he unholstered both of his revolvers.

"Really?" Howard replied. Even though his voice was soft, his contempt was strong. "*Always* works for you? Never once did impulse control failure and rash decision-making lead to an outcome less desirable than you had anticipated?"

Albert intervened. "Now is not the time, Howard. William, your zeal may do more harm than good in this situation. We have an opportunity to capture Szilveszter and figure a way to get the three of us back to our own time."

"I say we just put a hole in his head, right between those buggie eyes of his," Jane mumbled, peeking through one of the windows.

"Despite the argument needed to disentangle the knot of moral ambiguity about that action, Howard and I might not be able to figure out how to use the pyramid to return us to our home. Plus, we need to know what his plans are and what he has accomplished in both this time period and ours."

William said, "How about you three go in through the front while Annie and I sneak in from the back?"

"You certainly are trying, aren't you?" Howard mumbled, pulling the ray guns from his satchel. He kept one for himself and gave the other to Albert. "Since you seem to favor a full-frontal assault, you may be one of those who burst through the front door, while Annie and I use stealth."

Albert never considered himself a leader, especially in any form of combat situation, but he had assumed the role immediately after his visions in the forest. The mysterious Tsathoggua, the vile creature worshiped by the Voormis, unnerved him to the core, but dealing with those emotions would have to wait. What Tsathoggua had showed him in the visions was the future Szilveszter wanted. During the rest of the train ride to New Jersey, Jane and William challenged the motivations of this creature. "Why should we trust it? Why do you believe what it showed you?" they had asked Albert. He believed because he felt it, felt his heart wither like a salted slug as he watched himself become Szilveszter's protégé. He didn't know why Tsathoggua wished to foil Szilveszter's plans, but the visions imbued Albert with a renewed sense of purpose. He could not allow those glimpses of possibility to come true. "Howard, William, and I will confront Szilveszter and his cadre while the women will attempt to sneak behind them to find a tactical position. The simple fact is if Howard and I do not confront him together, Szilveszter will find this suspicious and expect an ambush. Undoubtedly from the circus assault, he knows that we have enlisted the help of William, but he might not know about Annie or Jane."

The women hustled along the wall and around the corner of the building, in search of a way in. Albert led Howard and William in the opposite direction, thankful and a bit surprised that they both kept their respective mouths closed for the duration of the trip to the door. Once inside, the men did their best to maneuver through the expansive laboratory via shadows, made darker by the waning outside light.

They found an adequate vantage point from behind a wall-to-ceiling bookshelf, filled from edge to edge with science books that tugged at Albert's sense of jealousy. A little farther into the room, and he had a clear view of the five figures standing in front of Edison. Too far away to hear specifics, Albert could make out a few words, and recognized that Thomas was impaired. "He seems to be in a stupor," Albert whispered. "Almost... ensorcelled?"

"I think it's the circus geek in the dandy top hat," William whispered back. He shifted his weight, readying himself to rush into the room. Howard stopped him.

"Please tell me you do not intend to do what your body language suggests," Howard whispered.

Looking over his shoulder, William shrugged. "Why not? I was gonna shoot him and that freaky lookin' jar brain. That'll break the spell, and we can keep the other three under control with our guns. Simple enough."

"First of all, unless you became an expert in the dark arts of sorcery in the past few days, you have no reason to believe your actions would 'break the spell.' Second of all, do you not realize that this is the laboratory of Thomas Edison, one of the greatest minds on the planet, with accomplishments that will resonate throughout the world? One stray bullet could alter the course of history."

William sneered. "Sure. Tell me that this guy is important to the future, but keep me in the dark about me and my future."

"Despite stoking your frustrations, William, I must agree with Howard. Prudence could be the proper course of action today," Albert whispered.

William offered a soft snort, but returned to a crouch. He then nodded toward the scene playing out before them and whispered, "If he's one of the greatest minds on the planet, then why's he makin' a deal with Szilveszter?"

To that, Albert had no answer, just the suspicion of mystical interference. He could only watch as Szilveszter handed Edison a single slip of paper. In return, Thomas gave a folder chock-full of notes. Albert and his companions had to act now.

Smiling as if holding gold, Szilveszter thumbed through the collection of loose papers. Satisfied, he turned to leave and said, "Perfect. On to Massachusetts." His contingent followed his lead, until Albert stepped out from the shadows.

"Szilveszter!" echoed mechanically through the speaker emended in the muscled chest of the mobile brain in a jar.

Making his way farther into the laboratory, Albert aimed his gun at Szilveszter. Howard and William emerged from the shadows, adding three more guns. "I'm afraid we cannot allow you to leave."

Albert certainly didn't want it to come down to gun-play, but he could not allow this personification of evil to roam free with a folder of information he deemed to be valuable. The emotions of his younger companions behind him were palpable; Howard's apprehension and William's excitement.

Szilveszter spoke with a conceit reserved for deities. "I'm afraid that you cannot stop me."

No older than either Howard or William, Szilveszter's eyes held centuries of experience. The eyes of a man who had snuffed dozens of lives, if not more, and relished every single kill. They held the purity and sparkle of madness, the likes of which made Albert's soul twitch with discomfort. "I know what your plan is, Szilveszter. I will not allow any harm to come to my parents."

Szilveszter's eyes widened as he cocked his head, his smile twisting to one of admiration. "So, you truly do know a part of my plan. Very impressive. Unfortunately, you cannot kill me, for fear of stranding yourself in an altered timeline."

Albert adjusted his stance, now aiming for the center of Szilveszter's forehead. "Killing you is my last resort, but I will if I must. I would just have to make this timeline my own."

As if on cue, the crack of gunfire split the air, followed by the sudden hole in Zarkahn's garish top hat. The magician gripped his hat with both hands and squealed, a disturbing and haunting noise. Jane laughed as a smoke trail wafted from her revolver, a satisfied look plastered upon her face. "Ha! I got it!"

Jaw hanging as if it no longer served a purpose, Annie said to Jane, "You were aiming for it?"

Keeping her gun trained on the magician, Jane strode out from her hiding spot. "Absolutely! Our boys got in a stalemate. I wanted to get the attention of these idjits to let them know that they're now outnumbered."

Annie followed Jane; her gun pointed at Szilveszter. "You thoroughly ruined our element of surprise!"

Jane shrugged a shoulder and said, "Meh. They look plenty surprised to me."

If Albert even had a shred of a plan, Jane's actions weren't a part of it, but he took advantage of the opportunity and addressed Szilveszter. "You're outgunned. Let us end this nonsense and figure out a way to get back to our time period where we belong."

Szilveszter glanced to his companions. An evil smile slid across the lips of all their faces; even the brain floating in the jar seemed to express mirth as well. Then they all turned their backs to Albert and friends and started walking toward the exit, except for the veiled woman. Szilveszter strolled past Madame Sulola and slid his hand from her chin to her scalp, revealing the left side of her face. For a brief glimpse, Albert thought he saw the countenance of a strikingly beautiful woman but swore that to be impossible as he was now looking at the left half of a withered crone's face.

Albert tried to shout at Szilveszter to halt, tried to tell his companions to stop the villainous man. Even Jane's or William's misguided need to solve the problem with their revolvers would have been acceptable. Something, anything, to keep him from escaping again! But Albert found himself powerless to pull his gaze away from the wrinkled woman.

With her at the center, Albert's focus on the world around him rippled. Tunnel vision encroached, shifting him from where he stood in the laboratory to the outside, but not anywhere familiar. A balcony with banisters of rusting and flaking metal. The sky was the color of dried blood. Fearing what he would find, Albert stepped closer to the edge and peered over.

Sensory overload threatened his tenuous grasp on sanity. Huddled masses of what he assumed to be people flocked together in pockets, around broken and ruined structures. From this distance, Albert could hardly tell what hung from the emaciated figures below, clothing or skin. Others swarmed around giant machines, operating them and maintaining them, fueling them. Metal geared legs trounced the ground as they crept along the barren lands, belching smoke the color of festering skin.

Unable to stand this vision any longer, Albert turned from the sight and hoped the illusion would disappear. Instead, he spun to see a man standing there, smile warm and inviting. Despite the onset of wrinkles and gray hair, Albert recognized him immediately—it was Szilveszter. He was older now, about two decades Albert's senior.

Albert knew immediately what he was witnessing—his greatest fear after glimpsing it at the cave of the Tsathoggua. This was how the world would look if Szilveszter succeeded.

Szilveszter approached with open arms, and Albert tried to dispel this vision, awaken from this nightmare. Heart-racing panic set in as his attempts failed. He screamed. He shook his head. He dug his fingernails into the palm of his hand. Szilveszter walked closer. But salvation came before he succumbed to madness or fright.

Szilveszter stood with extended arms, beckoning Albert to take his hands. Albert refused, but the image remained frozen in time. An abnormal hue enveloped the immobile Szilveszter, starting at a pale green, then glowing in intensity until it became a familiar shade of emerald. A vertical blade of green light sliced through Szilveszter, splitting him in twain.

As easily as striding through a portrait painted on tissue paper, William advanced through the tearing image of Szilveszter. The surreal, outside landscape fell asunder quickly, leaving Albert disoriented now that he found himself back in Edison's laboratory. He tried to walk, but was too drained, using a nearby table for support to ease himself down to one knee.

William helped Albert back to his feet. His wits and strength returned, albeit slowly. Albert whispered, "Szilveszter…?"

"Gone," William answered. "He flipped the veil off that freaky woman and y'all went into some weird trance. Everyone seemed frozen. Before I knew what was going on, they skedaddled."

Everyone? Albert thought as he looked around the lab. A pang of guilt rushed through him, failing to consider that his companions might have also fallen under the same strange mysticism that befell him. Just as confused and unsteady, the others bore no signs of physical injury, but shaking their heads to regain their composure. He asked William, "You were not affected?"

William held the pyramid, a pulsing green glow emanating from it. The throb of light slowed, and eventually stopped, returning to its state of swirling clouds of inky greens and black. "No. I think this protected me. My bag started glowin' when the gypsy lady did whatever it is that she did, so I grabbed it."

Albert had misgivings about William keeping the pyramid, but despite not knowing its potential, he was thankful that it had released him from that living nightmare. "Put it back in your satchel and let's help the others. We cannot let Szilveszter get too far ahead of us."

William nodded and did what Albert had asked.

Albert walked over to Edison, now slumped in his chair, weary from the day's ordeals. Clearing his throat first, Albert said, "Mr. Edison. I have no time to explain who those people were, or who we are, or what our mission is. We will be leaving very soon, I assure you. But first, I need to know what you gave to Szilveszter."

Voice hoarse, it cracked as he answered, "Notes. Just some useless, silly notes."

"Notes about what?" Howard asked, coming up from behind Albert.

"Re-animation."

Howard and Albert exchanged frightful looks. Edison continued, "They're just scribbles of ideas, possible theories. Barely doodles. I tested none of them... none. I believe there to be nothing of value in them."

Knowing he had to extricate himself and his companions before Edison's curiosity took over and it became his turn to ask questions, Albert simply said, "Thank you. I do apologize for this... inconvenience."

Glancing to the scrap of paper in his hand, Edison mumbled, "I believe I will come out of this as a better man."

Albert rushed everyone through the nearest door. He took one last look into Menlo Park, a mix of emotions swirled through him as he desperately tried to remind himself the amount of good that the owner of this laboratory did for the world, and those deeds should not be sullied by a lone dealing with Szilveszter. The thought was there, though, a splinter embedded too deep as he wondered about what potential Hell Edison had given Szilveszter. Sighing, he exited and joined the others.

"Anyone have any ideas as to what or who he might seek in Massachusetts?" Albert asked.

"Actually, I do," Howard replied as the group made their way back to the train station.

Chapter 16

The coach rocked to and fro, a smooth gentle rhythm. Coupled with the plush cushions lining the backs and bottoms of the two bench seats, the ride was meant to lull the passengers into a nice slumber for their journey. A trip from New Jersey to Massachusetts left little to do other than sleep. Yet, Billy did not sleep. No one did.

Their recent encounter with Szilveszter, specifically the enigmatic gypsy woman of veils, left them all spooked and unnerved. Using her mysticisms, she had pulled them all into realms of unfathomable nightmares and horrors. Each different. Each personal. Except for Billy, but he could empathize. If he had experienced his deepest fears with all five senses, it would be some time before he could trust closing his eyes and surrendering to the darkness of sleep. As time passed and the trip moved forward, Billy felt that there was more to the tension and silence and furtive glances and far-away stares than just witnessing a few illusions. It was a matter of trust.

Billy knew he never had it from Howard. Not that he should have made any claims to it in the first place, though. All but from their first meeting, they antagonized each other. Frustrated by Howard's snobbery and prejudice, Billy couldn't help but knock him off his high horse whenever he could.

In the seat across from Billy, Howard sat with shoulders rounded in a slouch, protective of what he scribbled in his notebook. Rough words and crude drawings of dreadful things with tentacles and fangs and wings and scales and claws. As if Billy's gaze was as tangible as a tap on the shoulder, Howard paused and looked up. He cocked his head and gave a slight sneer, an obvious question as to why Billy looked at him. Billy shrugged a shoulder and smirked. Nonplussed, Howard rolled his eyes and turned his attention back to his notebook.

Billy never paid much mind to his nickname "the kid." However, "Billy the Kid" had flowed from Howard's mouth with such ease, that he knew that reference had been made—or will be made—often enough to make it a part of his name. But how? Was it William McCarty, perceived rube and uncultured hick that grated on Howard? Or did the name "Billy the Kid" serve as a justified source of contempt? What was to become of him that would make his name mean something more than it did now? Billy grunted to himself, frustrated that the future could scrutinize the past with ease while the only thing the past knew about the future was its name.

"Something wrong?" Albert asked in a hushed tone.

Billy looked across to the man who had been sharing the same window for the past few hours. "I am untrusted."

"Well, William, you do have an item of great power in your possession. We gave it to you to carry and you used it to free each of us from our own personal hells. Even though we are grateful, that kind of power can make people nervous."

Billy squinted, thinking about what he had yet to contemplate. He drew his lips thin as he said, "Nah. I don't think that's it."

Albert tilted his head, obviously curious. "Then what do you think it is?"

"What did I do?" Billy asked, gaze steeled. "Or should I be askin' what will I do?"

Albert leaned back in his seat, not masking his disappointment. "You know very well that we cannot tell you that."

"You had no issues tellin' us that Thomas Edison is important."

"I think it's reasonable to assume that everyone in this carriage has heard of him by now."

Billy shrugged. "That's a heck of an assumption. I'm guessin' he does more than what he's already done. And I'm guessin' soon."

Albert's eyebrows knitted as he tried to choose his words wisely. Before he could answer, though, Howard blurted out, "The light bulb."

Albert whipped his head around and glared at his young partner sitting next to him. Howard paused from his drawing and sat straight. With all eyes upon him, he said, "At the end of this year, he unveils the incandescent light bulb."

"Howard…?" Albert started.

Howard sighed, then continued, "Even if by some miracle we wrap up our mission and return to our time period within the next few weeks, no one in this carriage has enough time to use this information to alter their fates or anyone else's." Face pinched into its usual expression of contempt, Howard looked at Billy and continued, "Thomas Edison is a very important figure in this world's history. Far more important than you."

"That implies that I am a figure in history. All I wanna know is why."

"Don't matter none," Jane mumbled, voice gravelly from lack of use. "We're all gonna die anyway. Broken. Alone. Desperate."

"Well, I guess we now have an idea of what she saw," Howard said to no one.

"Howard!" Annie scolded. "That was very rude, bordering on unkind."

Hunching his shoulders, Howard retreated back to his notebook and continued to work on an image of a grotesque creature. "You are correct. I apologize."

Jane showed no signs of peeling her gaze from the window to acknowledge Howard. Sitting straight and prim, Annie turned back to Howard and said, "Well, it seems that Jane is preoccupied with other matters, so I shall accept your apology on her behalf."

Billy chuckled to himself as Howard relaxed his posture a bit, clearly affected by Annie's opinion. He begged the fates to somehow, someway finagle a situation where he could find himself in a high stakes game of poker with Howard, since it seemed that his body betrayed his every thought and emotion. Billy then remembered a previous rumination from earlier, about how he goaded Howard. He determined that he simply couldn't help himself. With an intonation sweeter than honey, Billy said to Annie, "My, ain't you the angel, concerned about everyone's feelings."

"I try."

Billy sat straighter and smiled, his eyes sparkling. "Well, you succeed. You certainly make me want to try harder as well."

"Well, I for one would never discourage a gentleman from trying to improve himself," Annie said, flirtatiously running her hands over his shirt sleeve in a perceived attempt to shoo away wrinkles. A few quick strokes, she then brought her hand to his cheek and patted it three times; the third offered enough force to give an audible slap. "It's refreshing to see someone aspire to be more than he is."

There was a mutual attraction, an instinct Annie refused to act upon. Judging from Howard's solemn glare and Albert's look of disapproval, Billy wasn't the only one of this opinion. Billy relished the effect of stoking Howard's jealousy. He winked at Annie and then turned to face Howard and Albert. "I do aspire, darlin'. However, I find some mighty frustratin' obstacles bein' set before my path."

Annie placed her hand on Billy's shoulder and leaned closer to him. While looking at Howard and Albert as well, she spoke to Billy the way two actors would ignore the audience for the sake of the performance, "Billy, they can't tell us. This, I understand."

"Don't you want to know if the fears that the veiled woman showed you come true?"

Inhaling deeply, then letting out a slow, controlled exhale, Annie replied, "What I saw was failure. Trying everything I could try, being as smart as I could possibly be, calculating out every decision, but still failing. Working hard, working long, working smart, and all of it didn't amount to a hill of beans. That was the fear she exposed me to, the fear she made me live through. But it is not going to come true."

Her confidence threw off Billy's sense of indignant entitlement. "How can you be so sure?"

"Simple," she said, voice bold and soothing. "I do believe Howard and Albert are from the future. A future that recognizes Billy the Kid, Calamity Jane, and Annie Oakley. We are history to them. History rewards success."

Annie's usual knowing smirk returned. She never looked away from Howard and Albert, both now wearing expressions of concern. She continued, "I know what the veiled woman showed me will not come true by the mere fact that they know who I am."

Billy delighted that for the first time on this journey, Howard and Albert seemed to have been one-upped. His smirk faded as his nagging thoughts returned. "Little good that does me. I still ain't gotta clue if they distrust me because of what Albert said is true about me havin' that green do-hicky, or because of some future history about me."

"Now, William," Annie said placing her hand on his lap. "If you were truly evil, do you honestly believe they would have accepted your help in the first place?"

Billy mulled it over, her words turning as if they were a flipped coin. "Well, I guess when you put it that way."

"Exactly. I'm sure your exploits and adventures are what you're known for."

"Is that true?" Billy asked his carriage mates sitting across from him. They responded with expressionless faces, the demeanor of stone.

"See?" Billy said, leaning closer to Annie as he pointed to Albert and Howard. "See, right there. To me, those are looks of mistrust."

"Oh, William," Annie cooed. "You are far from being an angel."

"True. But what I'm wonderin' is how far? I'm also wonderin' if that ain't why I didn't have a vision like everyone else."

"Well, like Albert suggested, maybe it was because of the pyramid."

"If not?"

"It seems to me that we all experienced some of our deepest fears within those visions. Maybe you simply don't have any fears?"

"I have fears."

Annie smiled like a lioness ready to pounce, and purred, "I'm sure you do, William, and I'd be willing to wager those fears are an empty bed, an empty beer glass, or an empty gun chamber."

Billy wondered how serous she was. The smirk on her face told him that she was proud of her words. The dour mood within the carriage was oppressive and needed to ease. So, Billy laughed, a guffaw that cleansed the impurities from his soul. This caused Annie to laugh as well, and Albert quickly followed. The levity seemed to break depression's morose grip of Jane. She smiled and shook her head while eyeing Billy. Howard returned to scrawling in his notebook, but it wasn't before he cracked a smile.

The laughter faded and all but Howard—raptly focused on his drawings and writings—returned to gazing out the windows and letting their minds drift. However, they now did so with smiles and smirks tugging at the corners of their mouths.

Billy found comfort in Annie's logic. He, like Albert, had assumed the reason why he did not see a morbid and twisted future was because the pyramid protected him from such a spell. However, a different thought shattered his contentment like a stone through a window—what if he had no future to see? It was now his turn to avoid all eye contact as he pondered that thought for the remainder of the trip.

Chapter 17

Lizzie Andrew Borden sat in her chair and regarded herself in her handheld mirror, a small rectangular piece a half-foot in length. The sun began its descent for the day, but there was plenty of light pouring through her bedroom window to allow her full regard of her countenance. Oval faced, her cinnamon colored locks chased each other to her shoulders. Her cheeks still held a fullness that men found alluring, and a perky nose that usually went neither noticed nor dismissed. With subtle shifts of her expression, she could sell her eyes as bored, or attentive, or wit-filled, or dull, whichever message she needed for the circumstance. For now, home alone, she could relax and let them be.

She turned the mirror over, and undid the clasps, setting the frame aside. Watching her own reflection, a slight giggle escaped as she held the mirror over the candle on her reading desk. After a moment of patience, the mirror began to change the way she expected; the shimmering surface warped causing a frozen ripple. Lizzie giggled again, slowly moving the mirror, quickly learning how to warp it the ways she wished. Little by little, she altered her appearance without once touching her face.

Creating concentric and lopsided circles, she stretched her features. Her eyes disappeared into dark streaks that dripped along the edges. Her nose smeared into an afterthought. The focal point being her mouth, the rest of her face became folds of skins around the center, her hair the new frame. Pursing her lips, then parting them slowly, she stopped when her reflection looked like a vagina in the full bloom of arousal.

This was how she saw herself.

As did her father.

And she loved him for it.

Lizzie squealed with glee as she opened and closed her mouth while gazing in her newly created aberration. Soon enough, she became bored, placed the mirror on her desk, and looked at her wrists. Her skin held the discoloration of yarn burns, causing a spark of excitement to dance from thigh to thigh. Being the daughter of a textile and twine manufacturer, it was easy to pass them off as part of the business.

But she knew how the rope burns really got there.

As did her father.

And she loved him for it.

Thoughts of taking a moment to squelch the heat forming between her legs occupied her mind, until she heard a noise downstairs. The rattle of a windowpane. Someone was trying to get into her house. At first, she thought it was one of her father's sometime business partners, but remembered that she had no such meetings scheduled for today. Interest piqued, she exited her room and glided down the stairs. She hurried across the foyer into the sitting room, and an excited gasp pulled over her quivering lips. A young woman crawled through an opened window.

A young woman covered in scales.

The interloper tensed, ready to react to whatever Lizzie might do. However, her expression changed to that of confusion when Lizzie ran to her with arms extended. Wiggling fingers probing this new creature, Lizzie ran her hands over the scaled woman's face and exposed arms. She laughed with rapt glee. Pure joy flowed through her as her fingers danced with the various twists and crevices of the woman's skin. The more she touched this woman, the more she wanted to do this forever, explore this new discovery. But the woman grabbed Lizzie's wrists, making her gasp again with tantalizing expectation.

The woman's eyes held sorrow, pain. She whispered, "Stop."

Confused, Lizzie asked, "Why?"

"I'm grotesque."

Snorting with disgust that this beautiful creature believed such falsehoods, Lizzie pulled away from the woman's grasp, then placed her fingers on cheeks, thumbs on her lips, and whispered, "No. You're beautiful."

"Impossible."

Lizzie caressed the woman's rough skin, her face, her hairless head. She guided the woman closer with every tender stroke. "No. Normal is grotesque. Every day is grotesque. Walking among people who look alike, feel the same, and make no attempt to be anything other than everybody else. That is grotesque. You are… *extraordinary….*"

Her words faded, attention shifting to the woman's jaw shifting from side to side. Lizzie said, "Let me see it."

With a slight reluctance, the lizard woman did as requested, allowing her forked tongue to snake from her mouth. As it wiggled, Lizzie watched it with great interest, her own mouth opening wider, drawing nearer. She whispered, "Beautiful."

With a slurp, the lizard woman retracted her tongue and pulled away. "I'm not alone."

Lizzie stepped back, but not before tracing her finger along the lizard woman's chin. She purred, "Sounds fun."

"We shall see," the lizard woman said as she walked to the door and opened it. Szilveszter strode in, his cadre in tow.

With a politician's smile, Szilveszter placed his hands together and offered a slight bow. "Please, Miss Borden, allow me to introduce myself. My name is Szilveszter Matuska. I have an urgent matter to discuss with you."

Lizzie cocked her head. "How do you know my name? Has my father sent you?"

Szilveszter made his way farther into her house. "This may be hard to fathom, but I am a prophet from the future, sent here by one of The Great Old Ones to usher in a glorious new era. He will tear this word asunder and recreate in his image, one of chaos and insanity with a place of power and control for those who help. We need your help."

Dubious from such outrageous proclamations, Lizzie looked to the lizard woman, who shifted her gaze to the floor. She turned back to Szilveszter, now strolling in a lazy circle about the living room. Matching Szilveszter's pace, Lizzie walked around as well, keeping a constant distance between herself and the intruder. "If this god of yours is so powerful, what do you need of me?"

"Well, my companions and I seek passage to Europe. We find ourselves at the mercy of capitalism's hunger with no means to sate it."

"Money? This is about money?"

"As loathe as I am to admit it. I apologize for such an inelegant request."

"Any proof of your wild claims, support of your fancies of grandeur?"

Szilveszter stopped walking and smiled. "Unlike any of the other pedestrian gods that man insists on worshiping, mine is always willing to make himself known." He gestured to his companions.

Lizzie stopped walking as well and regarded each of his other companions. She found the circus magician gaudy and unappealing. The brain and eyes in a jar atop a man's body certainly fascinated her, but was nowhere near as beautiful or enticing as the lizard woman. Then the other woman, the one who wore veils from head to toe, stepped forward and stroked Lizzie's cheek.

Squinting, Lizzie tried to make out the face behind the veils. What little she could see offered no help. The veils played tricks on her eyes—from one angle the woman seemed youthful, the other she seemed haggard. Standing before Lizzie, she removed the veils from only the right side of her face. Behind the woman, Lizzie's world rippled and distorted like her flame-warped mirror. Small at first, the size of an open window, but growing in size, engulfing everything around her. Lizzie saw a new world. It swirled around her as if she stood in the center of a cyclone of color or sound. It stopped to show Szilveszter's ancient god, one of tentacled face and winged back, leaving a trail of fire and death in its wake as it strode across the lands. The world around her swirled again, this time stopping on a scene of people screaming and writhing in pain, thousands of them twisting and bending together like a flowing river of agony. Her vision blurred once again, and then came into focus on a new scene, one where she found herself in the middle of an orgy, populated by the disfigured and deformed. Some had scarred and burnt flesh, others had malformed features, and all were missing limbs. The world around her swirled one final time, bringing her back to reality, the one place she found herself not wanting to be.

Sweat beading along her hairline while lustful wetness formed between her legs, Lizzie looked to the veiled woman. "Why do you torment me so? Whisking me away to such beautiful worlds, only to yank me away, bringing me back here?"

The veiled woman remained silent as she walked away, her veils floating on a nonexistent breeze. Angered, Lizzie turned back to Szilveszter. She was too worked up to demand answers, but he happily gave them anyway. "Miss Borden, what you saw was one possible future. A grand and glorious future, where you could have everything you have ever dreamed of and more. But that future is only possible if you are willing to help our Lord ascend."

So excited by the prospect of her vision becoming a reality, Lizzie licked away the saliva forming at the corners of her mouth. "What is it that you say you wanted?"

"Only the simplest of things, Miss Borden. The one god that all humanity worships, for now—money to fund our excursion."

Lizzie chuckled, finding it amusing to think of herself as the patron of such a great expedition. The notion flowed through her all the way to her tingling nether parts. Not sure how much longer she could keep from satisfying her yearnings, she turned back to the lizard woman. Hungry from anticipation, she walked to the woman, looking every bit the prey caught in a predator's gaze. Lizzie stroked the woman's face, causing an expression of both fear and desire. Lizzie said to Szilveszter, "My immediate payment shall be her."

"Done," Szilveszter said gleefully, clapping his hands.

Lizzie licked her lips and ran her fingers over her new prize. The lizard woman's breath hitched. "Perfect. My father's wall safe is in the study behind the portrait of me. The combination is 8-6-0-4. Help yourself to the money, but do leave everything else in this house untouched. I trust you can see yourself out."

Without another word, Lizzie took the lizard woman's hand in hers, and led her up the stairs to her bedroom.

Chapter 18

The house stood atop a hill, silhouetted against the crepuscule sky, strips of clouds muting the traditional oranges of twilight to dull grays. Howard and his associates followed the worn dirt path to the house. He did not like this house. Dark. Silent. Dread skittered through his chest like scattering insects, burrowing into various alcoves of his heart. The house was devoid of any light, not even a single candle flame to battle the impending darkness. Closer. Closer they walked toward this abysmal structure, this wallowing blackness encased in wood and window. From the corner of his eye, he noticed something amiss. Billy had stopped.

Fifty feet from the house, Billy stood, causing everyone else to stop walking and congregate into a tight circle.

"Is something wrong, William?" Albert asked.

"Please tell me you aren't too afraid to go any further," Howard said, hoping to educate Annie about the scoundrel he knew Billy to be. His statement garnered no reaction from her. As stoic as an army general absorbing information, her face remained calm, yet aware.

The fresh memories of the carriage ride gnawed at him like a famished rat; how Billy unabashedly flirted with Annie. The lasciviousness of his advances was broken up by a period of silent introspection on Billy's part lasting the better part of a day. The following morning, though, after a good night's sleep, Billy was all smiles and sappy words. Annie ate up the attention while leaving a trail of titillating morsels of her own. Shameful for a betrothed woman to act that way! Howard was no longer sure whom he was mad at.

Either ignoring Howard's sarcastic barb, or not understanding that one had been thrown at him, Billy asked, "So, what's the plan?"

"We discussed this on the way here," Albert replied. "The Borden family has affluence, which is why Szilveszter is probably targeting them. I'm sure Mr. Borden is a prudent and logical businessman, so he undoubtedly refused Szilveszter. We just need to meet with him, find out what he and Szilveszter discussed, and if there was any mention of where the unholy cabal are off to next."

Gesturing to the house with the flair of a stage-performer, Billy asked, "Really? We're stickin' with that plan? Just mosey on up to that house and knock on the door?"

The other four looked at the house. Fighting back the bile caused by the slightest implication that he agreed with Billy, Howard said, "The Borden abode does seem rather ominous."

This was their secret house, one Howard and company had to ferret out by piecing together fragments of information from the Borden neighbors and denizens of the local community. No one was home at the Borden house in town, so they made inquiries, Annie's charm leading the way.

"So. It's a creepy ol' house," Jane said. "Ain't you got those where you come from? You kinda remind me of someone who'd love to live in a house like that."

"That is not the point I was trying to make," Howard growled.

Chiming in, Annie said, "I think what he means is since the house is pitch black with night coming, it's reasonable to assume that no one is home."

Jane shrugged. "Then we wait. Ain't nothin'."

"If they truly ain't home, then that means Szilveszter and his posse are waitin' around, too," Billy said.

Albert continued to study the house as he whispered, "A possible ambush."

"Do we think they might be back at the other house?" Howard asked.

Billy shook his head. "They've been ahead of us every step of the trip. So, if they ain't waitin' for an ambush, that means they've already been here. Maybe even got what they needed."

Concern grew in Howard's gut with every throb of his heartbeat. "What if Szilveszter harmed them?"

"The potential travesty to the time continuum is limitless," Albert replied.

"Or…," Billy interrupted, "… they willingly gave Szilveszter what he needed."

Both Albert and Howard winced at his words. Albert said, "I cannot imagine why a businessman would agree to assist—"

Once again, Billy interrupted, "I ain't talkin' about him. I'm talkin' about the daughter."

Howard turned to Albert, willing to follow his lead with this situation. Albert said, "What do you mean?"

"The way you two got all twitchy when you thought about Szilveszter hurtin' the Bordens. You got that way in the carriage when the daughter was mentioned. What was her name? Lizzie? Yeah, Lizzie. Obviously, she's another character on some future stage. What made her so famous? You two are tight lipped, but you got bad poker faces. I'm thinkin' she's famous for reasons that ain't good."

Howard hated to admit it, but Billy was very good at reading people; just as he was poor at keeping himself from being read. He reached into his satchel and procured guns for Albert and himself, "If what was said about her was true, she could be dangerous. Be vigilant, but no harm can come to her or her parents."

Jane frowned and drew her own firearm. "Why? Din't you just say she was dangerous? If she does do somethin' so bad, like Billy's speculatin', wouldn't we be doin' the world, and history, a favor by offin' her?"

Howard's frown deepened. "Despite trudging through a moral quagmire of whether it's right or not to punish someone before they commit a crime, what you're suggesting is murder. I won't lecture you again about the ramifications of altering the timeline so drastically. Even though history has been pock-marked by evil, it is necessary, no matter how great or small. Tyranny creates altruistic ideals, wars create innovation. Whatever Miss Borden will do, we need to allow it to be done."

Jane grunted and rolled her eyes. Starting back toward the house, she grumbled, "I think you're just too big a pussy to do what needs doin'."

Wielding one of his revolvers and following, Billy looked to Howard and Albert and shrugged his shoulders. Howard had no doubt that Billy agreed with Jane.

Annie gently grabbed Howard by his arm and leaned close to whisper, "I understand what you're saying, Howard. You have nothing to worry from me. I'll try to stay close to Jane and make sure she doesn't get too trigger happy." With a wink, she hurried to catch up with Jane.

Howard appreciated Annie's intelligence; happy she wasn't as small-minded as her contemporaries. He also appreciated the tingling about his neck and the gooseflesh along his arms from when her warm breath tickled his ear.

"What are your thoughts about the situation?" Albert asked as he started toward the house.

"Dire, at best," Howard replied. He matched Albert's pace stride for stride, although he felt that he now aimed for the sashay of Annie's skirts rather than house. "Given the personalities of our allies, we must find time to discuss the further ramifications of our actions. I'm not entirely certain we can make it out of this without Jane or Billy altering the course of history, especially considering how they handled Jesse James and his gang."

"I agree. If we have to do any more traveling before our mission's end, we will talk about it then. For now…," Albert's words trailed off as he and Howard joined the others on the porch of the house. During their brief journey, the roiling clouds had multiplied, replacing the last of the setting sun's rays with flashes of scalding white followed by heavenly rumbles.

Howard tried not to wince at the lightning flashes, but at least he reacted. Jane didn't flinch, her eyes half shut. He wondered how much she had had to drink today, and if she even knew that an impending storm drew nearer. His belief that Annie could keep Jane from doing whatever Jane wanted to do waned. Albert reached for the doorknob, but stopped short.

The door was ajar.

And the nearest window had been shattered.

Szilveszter was here, or had been recently. Everyone looked to Albert for a plan of what to do next. Mouthing words and using pointed hand gestures, he instructed Howard and Billy to go through the front door while Annie, Jane, and he would go around back. Lightning flashed, and the ensuing rumble followed more quickly than before.

Once the other three rounded the corner of the house, Billy readied his pistol in one hand and placed his other on the door. The door opened with ease, nary a creak.

Howard poked his head in and allowed a moment for his eyes to adjust to the encroaching darkness. Lightning flashed again, exposing what potential terrors might be lurking in the shadowed corners. Satisfied with what he saw in the brief glimpse of light, he gestured for Billy to go first. With zero contention, Billy entered, and Howard followed.

The foyer led to a wooden staircase and a hallway stretching to the back of the house, mostly ensconced in shadow. On either side were rooms. Billy gestured at Howard to look in one while he'd look into the other. Howard wasn't fond of the idea, but he complied, nonetheless.

The room he entered was large and had one other egress in the far corner, leading deeper into the house. Howard's eyes had yet to adjust to the brutal darkness, the thick drapes drawn closed over the many windows. Even the lightning flashes were muted to insignificant flickers.

Howard's heartbeat hammered within his ears in a rhythmic throb. He tried to control his breathing and banish thoughts of lurking creatures with broken teeth and gnarled claws; creatures the veiled woman had revealed to him in his vision. With deliberate movements, he crept farther into the room. Slowly. One step at a time, cautious not to cause any creaks. Until something wrapped around his ankle, hindering his next step.

Startled, Howard yanked his foot away, but that caused the tendril to wrap tighter. Jerking his leg again, he spun around, just in time to ready himself for the impact of a figure lurching toward him. Yelping upon collision, he used its momentum to twist his fall into a tackle, causing a noisy commotion among the furniture hidden in the darkness.

Bouncing from chair to floor, Howard kicked and punched, trying to fight off the thin filaments the creature covered him with. Before succumbing to the desire to use his gun, Howard noticed a familiar green glow emanating from the entrance of the room. Billy, gun at the ready in his right hand, the emerald and black pyramid in his left. His face went from concern and readiness to a look of disappointment and condemnation. Billy looked at Howard the same way he usually looked at Billy. Thanks to the light from the pyramid, Howard could now see what he had been wrestling with.

A dress form.

Limbless and headless, a torso constructed of muslin over framed wire lay next to him. Ropes of wool that had wrapped around him reached from a half-finished sweater over the partial mannequin.

"Quit playin' with that judy, and let's get movin'," Billy whispered in hushed anger.

Indignant that Billy was scolding him, Howard stood and disentangled himself from the wool spider web. With a tone just as annoyed, he whispered back, "One could hardly blame me for my actions, given the circumstances."

"Well, your actions caused quite a clamor. Probably alerted the whole county that we're here. Shall we get movin', or would you like to stay and make some more noise?"

"I must point out that a green light bright enough to light up a room is not going to go unnoticed."

Scowling, Billy put the pyramid in his satchel, the light ceasing as soon as he lost contact with the object. "Ain't no how it's worse than you—"

A thump from above cut Billy short. Soft, quick squeaks from floorboards moved across the ceiling. Keeping his gun at the ready, Billy gestured with his head and mouthed the word, "Stairs."

The men slipped into the foyer, their focus on what might be lurking beyond the darkness at the top of the staircase. Something made that noise.

Billy started up the right side of the stairs, his back against the wall. Howard allowed him to get a few steps, and then followed up the left side of the stairs, his lower back sliding against the railing. One step at a time, the men moved upward without so much as a creak of wood, nor breath of air. They paused when the darkness at the top of the stairs hissed at them.

The noise made Howard's mouth go dry; his tongue ran over lips, chapped and begging for moisture. Wrapped in this new silence, he cursed his heart for beating so loudly, worried that he might miss a subtle noise or give away his position. It was best to wait and see what Billy would do.

As if the stairs were made of brittle glass, Billy lifted his back foot and brought it to the next step. No sooner had he put it down than a screeching figure slammed into him, sending him toppling down the stairs.

Howard tensed; this was no dress form. Unable to discharge his gun fast enough, he had only enough time to raise his arms up to protect his face from gnashing teeth. The force of impact was too great and knocked him off balance; both he and his attacker went over the railing.

Gun slipping from his hand, the fall knocked the wind out of him. He lay on the floor, his mind screaming commands to his reluctant body. Fighting past the aches and pains, he turned on his side and tried to make sense of his surroundings. Billy's rumpled body was at the bottom of the stairs.

His attacker stumbled as she got to her feet and staggered toward Howard. Human. A human woman. Naked. Her skin had a scaly look to it and Howard recognized her as the "snake woman" from Szilveszter's carnival troupe. Forked tongue skimming over her lips, she hissed as she drew closer.

Howard tried to get to his feet, but could only skitter backwards. Gun nowhere close to him, and not moving fast enough to flee from his pursuer, Howard stopped retreating and drew his legs close to his chest, ready to kick the woman the instant she struck. But he didn't have to resort to that tactic.

After three sharp cracks of gun fire, the snake woman stopped; her countenance of surprise twisted into agony. She fell to her knees, then flopped face first on the floor, landing mere inches from Howard. Blood seeped from the middle of her back over her callused and gnarled skin, the imperfections looking less like scales as the blood flowed over them to the floor.

Jane looked satisfied as she stormed into the room. Behind her, Annie and Albert looked shocked and appalled. With more glee than appropriate, Jane yelled, "Got 'er!"

"What have you done?" Howard asked, voice barely audible to his own ears, his mind racing through the different implications of Jane's actions. A shriek suddenly filled the house as if from an irate banshee. "Noooooo!"

A young woman, naked with blemish-free skin, ran down the stairs. She slid to a stop on her knees next to the fallen carnival sideshow attraction. Sobbing, she rolled the snake woman over, resting her scaled head on her lap. "No. No. No. No."

Shaking his head to clear his vision, Howard made his way to his feet. Billy did so as well, but wobbled and held both hands against his head. Howard found his gun while the young woman—whom he assumed to be Lizzie—continued to yowl.

Her crying eventually slowed to the point where she gazed upon Jane with a hate-fueled scowl. "Why? Why did you do this?"

Jane frowned and said, "Why? Look at her! She's a freaky snake woman. An' when a freaky snake woman attacks one of my friends, I shoot."

"She's not a freak!" Lizzie yelled, a mist spraying from her mouth with every word. "She was my gift!"

"Gift?" Albert asked, stepping forward next to Jane. "Gift from whom?"

"From my new master. The dark messiah who will awaken the Eternal Great One and make *you pay!*"

That was all the information Howard needed. Szilveszter had been here and Lizzie had given him the necessary means to continue his journey. By her own volition or by some other means of manipulation, it didn't matter. What mattered was Szilveszter could now easily make his way to Europe.

"Miss Borden," Albert started, voice soft and nonthreatening. "That man is no messiah. He—"

"Brought me happiness! Brought me this gift. This beautiful, beautiful gift. That you took from me. He brought me happiness. You took it from me!"

"I understand that you—"

"No! No more words. My father uses words to make me do things. My mother uses words to make me enjoy those things. And you two," Lizzie emphasized her statement by pointing a finger at Albert and Jane, "You two remind me of my parents! Look like them. Play with my emotions like them. Use words like them. Now look what you've done." Tears flowed from her eyes as she looked down to her broken gift on her lap. "Leave. Leave me with my sorrow."

"We only wanted—"

"Go!" Lizzie screamed, jumping to her feet; the snake woman's body slapping the floor like a slab of meat. Blood smeared the front of Lizzie's bare legs and dripped from her clenched fists as she screamed with such passion, her eyes shut. "Go! Go!"

Without so much as another word, or even eye contact with each other, the five complied. The anguish in the young girl's wailing would never cease to haunt Howard.

Chapter 19

Annie watched. After the events she had experienced with the others, she decided observation would be the best course of action for her. Watch. Study. Learn. And when the opportunity presented itself—manipulate.

Considering herself to be an upstanding and moral person, she thought the word "manipulate" might be too harsh, but that was what she did as an entertainer. Despite her considerable talent, every time she graced the stage, she would manipulate the scene that the crowds witnessed to her advantage and manipulate their emotions, which ultimately led to manipulating them out of their money. Now she found herself in a situation where a little manipulation could certainly benefit her position in life. First, she needed to observe. And there was plenty to observe on the docks of Boston.

She had little trouble finding a bank in Boston to withdraw the necessary funds to purchase five tickets for the next outgoing ocean liner for France. She even took the opportunity to withdraw more cash and convert it to pounds, francs, and marks. Wherever this little adventure took her, she wanted to be prepared.

During her brief stay in the city, she found some time to do a little shopping. As with before, she offered to buy new clothes for her companions, but they all declined. They all stated that they would take advantage of the ocean liner's water services and launder their clothes aboard the ship. That certainly didn't deter her from buying a few items for herself, though. Assuming this leg of their trip would involve at least as much activity, she opted for a pair of black, durable pants with matching black boots. To counteract the masculine effect of the pants, she found a white blouse with frilly ruffles down the center, and topped it off with a jacket made from crushed velvet dyed a deep purple. She found another lovely dress as well, but had that sent to her house as a future reward for soon saving the world. She took another moment to pen a letter to her betrothed, Frank Butler, letting him know that she would be leaving for Europe to investigate the entertainment market abroad. She did her best to send a post to him whenever the opportunity presented itself, even though she doubted that he received many of them, since he was involved with travels of his own to promote their show. Excited about going to Europe, even if danger and peril were certainties, she looked forward to seeing the latest fashion trends.

Clasping only the bottom fastens of her jacket created a pucker, and the exposed ruffles of her blouse gave the illusion that her bosom was more substantial than what she truly had to offer. Men's heads turned as she made her way to the docks. She wondered if it was because a woman wore slacks, or that those slacks flattered her feminine curves. Why didn't more modern women wear pants as an everyday style? Would they in the future? A question she'd have to ask Howard at a later time. He was too busy being persnickety to ask at the moment.

Sticking close to him meant she'd have a better chance of ferreting out the information she sought. Albert was far too disciplined to give away knowledge of the future willingly. The price she paid for maintaining such a close proximity to Howard was that she had to endure his fastidiousness and outbursts. As well as his constant feuding with Billy.

"Madness and damnation!" Howard cried as a low-flying seagull relived itself on his shoulder. "Infernal winged devil creature!"

Billy and Jane laughed. Brows bent from scorn weighing heavy upon them, Howard spat, "Just because you two crave to wallow in such fetid surroundings hardly means that any other decent human being shares such desires."

Still chuckling, Billy shook his head and walked over to Howard. He procured a handkerchief from his back pocket and used it to wipe away the mess. "Ya need to lighten up. Learn to laugh at yourself. And learn the benefits of a handkerchief."

"I do not own a handkerchief," Howard said.

After Billy finished wiping Howard's shoulder, he wadded up the handkerchief and pressed it into Howard's left hand. He said with a smile, "You do now!"

Howard immediately released the cloth, letting it fall and remain on the boarded walkway, and yelled, "Bastard child of the devil himself!"

He and Jane walked toward the ocean liner, laughing again. As Jane strolled by Albert, she hooked his arm and hooted, "Come on, Albie! Let's say we get us a drink."

Despite his protests, Jane dragged Albert to the boarding ramp as Billy followed behind. "Save some for me, will ya?"

Pulling at his sleeve and tilting his head at awkward angles, Howard did his best to examine his shoulder. "I am beginning to doubt that the benefits of allowing him to join our mission are still outweighing his exasperating personality."

Hooking her right arm through his left, Annie led him toward the ocean liner. "Come now, Howard. You've been saying that every day since we met. We all know he's been invaluable to this mission."

Annie hypothesized she could get Howard to do anything by simply showing him some attention. This situation seemed a perfect test for her theory. Glancing down to where their arms hooked, he blushed. Guiding him through the boarding process proved no challenge, especially since their close proximity to each other flustered him to the point of speechlessness.

Onboard, the passengers milled about as the vessel sailed, their excitement palpable. Most wandered about the wooden deck, marveling at the massive sails and the great stacks that allowed steam from the engines to escape. Smiles and pleasantries passed from one passenger to the next. Annie confessed that the experience was nothing less than grand as she indulged in the magnificence of the vessel. Without needing any more provocation, Billy and Jane slipped right in with the camaraderie of the other passengers, taking Albert with them. Despite keeping his sentences short and his words deliberate, Albert appeared to be enjoying himself. Only one person on the ship was not.

"You don't find this ocean liner a testament to what mankind can achieve?" Annie asked Howard over the din of cheers as the vessel slipped away from the docks.

"I come from a period in time where science is dispelling the mysticism of the world around us. To move our boats across the waters, we use... well, we no longer use sails for larger crafts such as this."

"Oh my," Annie purred. "You are quite generous with information about the future."

"I have divulged nothing. We are standing upon a boat being powered by steam and sail. You are a very intelligent woman; I find it difficult to believe that you would not be able to surmise that one of those modes of propulsion loses favor in the future."

"Well, I do believe you are correct in your assumptions," Annie chuckled as she patted his arm.

They continued to mill about topside as the crowds began to dwindle; undoubtedly, to prepare for their dinners and other social activities. Annie was not going to let Howard's disinterest in what was happening around them squelch her curiosity.

Toward the area of the deck where the bow became the port side of the ship, cargo was being moved and jostled into place. Most noticeable was an older man with a bit of girth and a well-kept, full-faced beard who fussed over a few pieces of cargo while barking orders in French to half a dozen hired hands. He wore utilitarian clothing like Albert—woolen turtleneck, pants of thick material, and boots—it was very clear to Annie by his posture and stance that he was usually seen in far fancier clothing.

She watched as he fretted over the men handling his cargo, a large contraption as big as a stagecoach covered by thick canvas. By the way the covering draped, Annie guessed that the bulky item came to a point, but she had no idea what it might be. Once stowed to the bearded Frenchman's liking, his helpers immediately set about positioning wooden crates, each as long as a man is tall, around the larger piece of cargo.

"What do you suppose they are transporting?" Annie asked, more to herself.

Howard answered, "If they wanted us to know, then they would not have bothered to cover it."

Annie smiled. "For a writer and adventurer, you don't seem very curious."

Howard offered a chuckle, an uneasy thing for him to do, Annie knew, and something that she assumed he did only for her benefit. "Sometimes I am *too* curious. However, as this evening approaches, my curiosities and energy wane. Even though I do enjoy your company, I believe it would behoove me to try to get a good night's sleep."

With a bow and a kiss to the back of her hand, Howard left, leaving Annie to ponder any number of things.

Annie awoke the next morning to Jane's snoring, and was thankful she hadn't heard the woman currently sprawled across the floor return to the room last night. One leg was out of her pants, while she wore her coat backward. Drool and snot coated the bottom half of her face, a bubble by her nostril inflating and deflating with every breath.

Unable to stay in the same room, Annie decided to dress quickly and make a hasty exit. She'd rather throw ice at the devil himself than awaken Jane from an alcohol-induced slumber.

She ventured back to the main deck, back to where she and Howard had parted ways last evening. Much to her surprise, Howard was already there, looking very much like he'd had none of the sleep he had sought. As she approached, she saw that he furiously scratched away in his notebook.

Not wanting to startle him, she announced her presence from ten feet away. "Good morning, Howard."

He offered a slight smile, as if too tired to form a full one. The vibrancy of his bloodshot eyes made hers sting and water in sympathy. "Good morning. You are a much welcome sight, I must confess."

Annie gave him a slight curtsy. "Much obliged. So... you didn't sleep well?"

Howard's bitter expression returned as he went back to sketching. "No. I fear this adventure of ours may be too taxing for my sanity."

Annie placed a hand on his arm and peered over his shoulder at his drawings. He turned the page to show her the newest illustrations. Various forms of humanoid shaped fish men filled both sides of the book. Many wore long coats with upturned collars and top hats. With their hands tucked into pockets, some looked positively human. It was their eyes that looked alien. Lidless and round, black beads shoved into the sides of smooth heads. A few drawings were renderings of them with no clothes, gills cutting into their necks, fins poking from skin, lipless mouths wide and agape. She assumed since there were question marks around them that Howard drew these fish things' anatomy out of pure speculation. "You saw these... creatures... last night?"

"Indeed, I did," Howard sighed. "Madness, no?"

"No," Annie replied.

Howard stopped drawing and looked at Annie, who stared at his notebook. "Really?"

Annie pitied him for his lack of sleep, but if he had been chasing monsters like these, or any of the others in his notebook, then she pitied him even more, for his reality held more horrors than most people's nightmares. "Really. Let us not forget that recently you saved me from a vile and wretched creature lurking within a cave whose followers seemed to have been cast out of the great abyss itself. You do not need to convince me that monsters exist, Howard. I have seen them with my own eyes. I am on this mission to help ensure the rest of world never has to see them."

Even though she emphasized certain parts of her speech to manipulate Howard's feelings, to garner his trust, her words held truth.

So caught up in attempting to offer some form of comfort to Howard, neither he nor she saw the man amble up behind them and peek over their shoulders. "Fascinating drawings. I, too, fancy the fascinating."

The stranger's words weighed as heavy as his thick French accent, and caused Howard to jump. The man smiled and stood with his hands behind his back. Annie instantly recognized him as the one commanding the helpers to handle his cargo with care yesterday. He was still dressed in the same clothes. Once he had their attention, he extended a hand and introduced himself. "Greetings and salutations, good people. Please allow me to make acquaintance. I am Jules Verne."

Howard gasped, and Annie swore he made a slight squeaking noise. She knew of Jules Verne, had even read some of his works. But the awe found in Howard's face told her that Verne would be something more than he already was. Something she wished for herself—celebrity.

Not blinking once, Howard slipped his hand into Verne's grasp and shook it. Knowing that the shock of meeting someone of such influence further hindered his sleep-deficient senses, Annie decided to assist. "My friend's name is Howard, Howard Lovecraft."

Chuckling, Verne said, "Is Howard, Howard Lovecraft incapable of speech?"

"A restless night mixed with meeting someone of your celebrity seems to have left him temporarily mute. He, too, is a writer."

Verne's smile widened; a glint flashed in his eye. "Ah, fantastic! What might he have published?"

Annie smirked as she said, "He has yet to be discovered."

Verne's countenance shifted to one of sympathy as he said, "Don't fret. I have been in that position as well. Writing is the art, while publishing is the business."

Finally pulling his hand from Verne's grasp, Howard muttered, "Thank you for your words of encouragement."

"Ha! He does speak! Very good. Maybe sometime during our voyage, you will allow me the honor of reading some of your works." Verne then turned to Annie and took an exaggerated step toward her. His wide smile returning, he extended his hand and said, "And who might this lovely creature be, who enchants all of my senses?"

Placing her hand in his, Annie smiled as well. "Her name might be Annie Oakley."

"Charmed, indeed." Annie stifled a giggle as Verne leaned forward to kiss the back of her hand. "I am very pleased to make your acquaintance, Miss Oakley. Or is it Missus?" He punctuated his question by looking at Howard.

"It is still Miss," Annie said, causing Verne to turn his attention back to her. Even though she didn't feel threatened by the hunger in his eyes—more akin to a husky child standing before a mound of candy as opposed to a wolf stalking a wounded rabbit—Annie still felt compelled to finish with, "But I am betrothed."

In one fluid motion, Verne released her hand and spun to clap Howard's back hard enough to almost topple him. "Well done, my boy. Well done. The heart of a charming and witty beauty is a most elusive prize to capture indeed."

Annie winked at Howard, now looking perplexed. Not only was it simpler to allow Verne to believe that Howard was her betrothed, there was an element of comedy in Howard's confusion that she could not deny herself. Verne did not recognize her name, and that rekindled her motivation to get every bit of information of her future from Howard. For now, she decided to have fun with what fate threw at her. "So, Mr. Verne. We couldn't help but notice yesterday that some of the cargo over yonder belongs to you," she said, glancing slowly to the stack of crates and still covered object sitting at the edge of the cargo area. "I find myself curious as to what a writer could be transporting. A copy of your latest manuscript, maybe?"

"Ha!" Verne laughed. "Such a fabulous sense of humor! She'll make a fine wife, indeed!"

"Much obliged," Annie replied, smiling. "Maybe we can take a peek under that tarp and solve the mystery?"

Before Verne could answer, the ocean liner lurched, and then slowed to a stop. The sudden change in speed caused many people on the deck to lose balance. Those less nimble fell, Verne being one of them.

"Did we strike something?" Annie asked as she and Howard assisted Verne back to his feet.

"I do not believe so," Howard said, looking around. "I think our stopping would have been even more abrupt. It's as if something ensnared us."

"Miss Oakley, I believe you will get the opportunity to peek under the tarp after all," Verne said as he pointed to the starboard side of the ship. Accompanying a chorus of screams from the fleeing passengers, a massive tentacle squirmed its way onto the deck.

Chapter 20

Albert awoke with a jolt, and immediately wished that he hadn't. A rope twisted behind his eyes, tightening in his head. The pain made worse by the sunlight pouring in through the porthole. An unpleasant paste formed as he tried to use his tongue to do something about his dry mouth. He didn't understand how he could possibly be both drenched in sweat and shuddering with a chill. It had been a long time since he had a hangover, and he hoped that it would be an even longer time between now and the next one.

Sitting up, Albert noticed a metal pitcher of water on the small table next to his bed. The very panacea he sought, he grabbed it and brought it to his lips. Before he indulged, though, images of William deciding to be a rapscallion and filling the pitcher with something far less desirable than water danced through his throbbing head, so he sniffed the liquid. Nothing but a minimal metallic smell. Albert gulped the water down.

After draining half of the pitcher, he held it against his forehead, the coolness of the metal aided with his headache. Another sip of water, and he looked for his roommates. He was alone. Howard's sheets were in a twisted state of disarray, while the pristine quality of William's suggested that his bunk had not even been touched.

As he got dressed, Albert traversed through the fog of memory, looking for any clues as to the whereabouts of either of his partners. Before being dragged away by William and Jane, Albert recalled Howard accompanying Annie for a stroll about the deck. Albert had a vague recollection of returning to his cabin drunk and finding it empty, but not caring because all he sought was the comfort of his bed. Clearly, Howard had returned later in the dark beginning hours of the morning. Either he did not sleep well, or had an errand to run, forcing him to leave before Albert had awakened. William on the other hand....

Taking another swig from the pitcher, Albert remembered the party, remembered Jane and William coercing him to relax and have fun. Albert had asked every crewmember he could find about Szilveszter and his cadre, then surmised that they had found alternate travel. Many mentioned that the day before, a zeppelin had left for Europe with far fewer passengers than it could accommodate. Dismayed that evidence pointed to Albert and his companions arriving eight to ten days after Szilveszter and his minions, Albert partook in a libation. Then another. Then more, taking less time to savor each newer drink than the previous one.

Once he got to the point of the room spinning, he decided to turn in. Neither of his associates took notice to his departure; Jane was busy ballyhooing with a contingent of off-duty cargo men, and William had been pouring sugary words over two Mexican beauties. Were they twins? Albert couldn't quite produce a clear enough image in his mind, and chuckled to himself about William's audacity if they had been.

No longer sweating, Albert finished the pitcher to wash away more of his aches and pains. Satisfied that he could now move about the ocean liner without forfeiting the contents of his stomach, he opened his cabin door and stepped into the hallway. Before he could close the door and begin his quest for William and Howard, he found one of them. Half naked, William walked toward him.

William's bare feet poked out from the bottom of his long johns as he tiptoed down the hallway. The top half of his long johns draped around his waist, leaving him bare-chested. He carried the rest of his clothing and boots, while his ever-present hat sat atop his head. With twenty feet to go, a door opened behind him and two raven-haired beauties—identical in every detail—poked their heads out, giggled, and as loudly as possible said, "Goodbye, Billy!"

As their door shut, other doors along the hallway opened, some with gasping women covering the eyes of their children while others were elderly couples. All wore expressions of disapproval and disgust as William sauntered by greeting them with, "Good mornin'," except for one cloud-haired, toothless crone who winked and smiled at William. With hastened pace, William scurried past her, then past Albert and into the cabin.

As William dressed, Albert shook his head. "I almost wish Howard were here, because he would never believe that I find myself speechless."

"What?" William asked with a beaming smile. "I ain't married."

"But twins?"

"Jealous?"

If nothing else, Albert certainly envied the vigor of youth. He was about to say as much, but the ocean liner slowed, then stopped. The shifting wood and twisting metal groaned.

Buttoning his pants, William said, "That sure don't sound good, does it?"

"No, William, it does not," Albert replied as he stepped back into the hallway. Once again, other doors opened, members of curious and concerned families asking each other if they knew what caused the sudden stop of the ocean liner. A scream, so primal and steeped in fear that it was indistinguishable as a man's or a woman's, erupted from one of the cabins as a family of three stumbled from their room. The mother, arms wrapped around a girl toddler, fell into the hallway. The father fled from the room with such zeal, he slammed into the hallway wall. Getting their feet under them, they ran away. Witnessing such a display, everyone else followed suit.

Shouts and hollers echoed as the passengers pushed and shoved each other down the hallway, even though Albert was confident that they had no idea what they were running from. He thought about investigating the cabin that started this commotion until William yelled, "Albert!"

William used his drawn gun to point to the porthole. Outside, a slick tentacle slowly ascended, the underside cups sucked and massaged the hull wall, seeking purchase. Slime dripping, the tentacle grew in thickness as it climbed.

Albert reached under his bunk and thanked the heavens that Howard's satchel was there. Grabbing it, he ran from the room and started down the now emptied hallway. "We need to find the others."

"Ain't gotta tell me twice," William said as he slung his own satchel over his shoulder and followed, a gun in each hand.

They made their way through pockets of people who were confused and panicked. As they climbed the stairs to the outside, they fought against a barrage of people trying to get back inside. Stewards and crewmembers of the ocean liner blew whistles and waved people back into the bowels of the vessel, ordering everyone to the mess hall. Water dripped from most of the passengers as they pushed and shoved; all wore blanched expressions of eye-bulging fear.

Squirming their way through the waves of humanity, Albert and William finally made it to the deck. A scene from the theater of insanity played out before them. Half a dozen tentacles were wrapped around the bow or thrashed about ten, twenty, forty feet above the deck. No longer spectators to the action, Albert and William realized they were upon the stage as well when they had to dodge one of the tentacles as it slapped the deck close enough to spray them with sea mist and slime. More tentacles smacked the deck, one crushing a fleeing passenger beneath it. As it lifted, the underside suction cups gripped the man it had crushed, his lifeless body emptying of blood like a ruptured water skin.

William shot a tentacle that slithered along the deck; the bullets did little damage—tiny blood-blotched holes, mere pinpricks. Albert procured a gun from his satchel and fired at the same tentacle with better results. Too much better, though.

The green ray from the weapon burned the indigo tentacle with a hiss, the stench of cooking meat immediate. The tentacle lashed out toward the source, connecting with Albert's hip and knocking him to the ground. His gun slid away, and he fought against the water-slicked deck to get to his feet. He chased after the gun, the tentacle slapping the deck behind him. Two others joined in swatting at Albert, each strike getting closer. His gun in sight, he dove as all three tentacles lifted high for one crushing blow. He prayed. He was surprised to see his prayer answered in the form of a barb-tipped harpoon embedding itself into one of the tentacles.

A second harpoon speared the same tentacle, the sickening smack of punching meat. A third harpoon missed, but four more followed, all sinking deeply into the other two tentacles.

Albert rolled toward his gun. Grabbing it, he got back to his feet and found the source of the harpoons. This spectacle was no less unfathomable to behold than any of the others he had witnessed since coming topside. A rather husky fellow operated a weapon akin to a massive cannon with an eight chamber, rotating barrel. It was large enough that the back end held a seat for the man so he could crank a wheel, rapidly launching the projectiles. What truly stunned Albert was seeing Howard and Annie next to the weapon, assisting in loading the harpoons from a wooden crate into the machine.

Blasting any tentacle that wriggled too close, Albert made his way to William, and the two joined their partners next to the large rapid-fire harpoon gun. William holstered his guns and ousted Howard from the task he been doing. "You're doin' it too slow!"

Howard wore his indignation like a mask, but he acquiesced. Albert clapped Howard's back and said, "It appears that the calamari does not agree with us."

Howard's face puckered as if biting into a lemon. "What has happened to you, man? Clearly the time spent with Billy has reduced your intelligence to that of a gnat, if you feel the need to trivialize this situation!"

Howard's words rang with the possibility of truth. Perhaps Albert was changing due to this mission? However, now was not the time for such introspection. Now was the time for survival. He pointed to the husky man in the chair turning the wheel on the harpoon gun. "Who might this be?"

"Jules Verne," Annie replied. She grinned while Jules laughed and hooted while firing his weapon.

Albert looked at Howard and asked the unspoken question of how they continued to find themselves in the company of individuals many would consider architects of history. Deciding it best not to give voice to it, Albert instead asked, "Has anyone seen Jane?"

As if she were an actress merely awaiting her cue to enter the stage, Jane burst from one of the doors onto the deck holding an exceedingly long rifle. Judging from the four stout men in pith helms and khaki clothing also carrying such guns, Albert assumed that Jane had befriended a group of large game hunters en route to see what sport the Dark Continent had to offer.

Albert almost laughed at her ability to insert herself into the situation. With a throaty war-cry, she charged toward a mess of tentacles and pulled the trigger. If not for the slickness of the deck, the kickback of the gun would have surely knocked her down; instead she slid backward as the muzzle of her gun released a controlled conflagration. Her aim was true, and the heavy ordinance severed the tip of the tentacle. A slab of charred meat fell to the deck while the limb it had come from retreated back to into the ocean.

As Jane stepped back to reload, her new friends stepped forward, each displaying the same level of bloodlust while waxing poetic, calling upon the gods for victory. Most of them successfully hit their targets, each wounded tentacle withdrawing. Their cheers of celebration were short lived as the cries of the wounded beast emanated from the deep, reverberating through the ocean liner and all on it.

More tentacles appeared, even those that were injured returned. But they were longer and thicker than before. Albert was certain that the body that owned them was now closer, and that there would be a mouth involved soon enough. He also presumed that the mouth would be big enough to rend the ship to tinder, or the creature would not have attacked it in the first place. Unless this was an elaborate trap set by Szilveszter. Did he have the power to call forth such a monster? If this was some form of wicked mysticism, then Albert knew how to stop it. "William! The pyramid!"

William pointed to Howard, and then to the open box of harpoons, indicating that he needed to take over helping Verne with his weapon. Howard nodded and did what was needed. William procured the pyramid from his satchel. Albert didn't know why it responded the way that it did for William, but if the young man could garner favorable results, then knowing why was of little consequence at this moment. With both hands, William held it out in front of him, toward the closest mass of squirming tentacles.

Nothing.

Frowning, William brought the pyramid close to his face, then held it out again. Still nothing. He shook it and tried again with the same result. The black and green colors barely flowed. No energy emissions. No glowing. "Albert! It's not working!"

"I don't understand," Albert said to himself. "It comes alive any time magic is involved."

"Magic? Ha!" Verne yelled. "The Architeuthis may seem like it escaped from the pits of hell, but it is as much a part of God's world as you or I; a sick, twisted joke from God, but one of His creatures nonetheless. Ten degrees counterclockwise, boys!"

It took four cargo men to do so, but they rotated Verne's weapon. He whooped and cheered as four out of his next ten harpoons struck their target.

William returned the pyramid to his satchel and asked Albert, "Now what? Should we stay here? Or try to help Jane?"

Albert turned to Howard for his thoughts, but got none. The younger man simply stood and stared off as if unaware of the chaos around him.

Two figures in top hats and long coats stood by the port side railing. Why Howard stared at them with such rapt fascination, Albert couldn't fathom. Before he could ask, though, Howard started to walk toward the figures.

Annie called out, "Howard!"

Albert yelled over his shoulder, "It's okay, Annie. I'll follow him. You and William do what you can to help Mr. Verne."

Howard walked faster, and Albert hastened his pace to keep up, while remaining vigilant of the flailing tentacles. Albert could not ascertain any further detail of the men Howard followed, other than their height. Then, without provocation, the strange men ran.

Sprinting, both Howard and Albert fought to keep from slipping on the water-soaked boards. The men they chased had unusual gaits, as if swimming through the air rather than running along the deck. For the entire length of the boat, Howard and Albert gave chase, but gained no ground. Closer to the stern, Albert heard voices. Not conversation, but many voices combining to make one—a low chant of a single word, "Dagon!"

Albert wondered what it meant and how many voices there were, the deck of the stern obscured by the walls on his left. Once Howard and he made it past the walls, at least one question was answered, but it led to many more.

The two figures they pursued slipped out of their coats and dropped their hats, exposing themselves for what they truly were, and joining two dozen others that looked exactly like them. Humanoid in shape, the creatures were more fish than man, their shimmering scales the color of the ocean. Onyx eyes moved independent of each other on either side of their heads, while their gawping mouths opened and closed in rhythm of their chant.

"Dagon!"

The ship listed to the port side, throwing Howard and Albert against the railing. Albert gasped, staring over the edge at the great beast latched to the vessel. Past the giant squid, deeper into the choppy water, a darkness formed.

Watery shadows moved and shifted, coalescing to create a shape. As the blackness moved toward the surface, the first detail Albert saw was an eye. Almond shaped and alert, it held intelligence despite being embedded in the head of a beast. Skin and scale the same hue as the fish creatures, bony ridges flared away from the great eye, forming a rigid cowl that crowned the leviathan's head.

"Dagon!"

The beast stopped ascending, exposing no more of its head, but slowly reached up with one massive claw, its shape a hybrid of a hand and a talon, and grabbed the giant squid. As if squeezing an over-ripened tomato, viscera exploded from the cephalopod. The Architeuthis offered a muffled bellow of pain; its tentacles fell limp and slowly slid from the vessel as the great ocean monster pulled it into the abyss of the depths.

Rocking from the momentum of being released, the ocean liner righted itself. The fish creatures all jumped over the railing, back into the only part of the world where they belonged.

Albert looked around. Howard stood in wide-eyed amazement, then shook his head as if waking from a dream. He pulled out his notebook and flipped through the pages. Albert noted all of the drawings of the fish creatures, and understood why Howard had spent so little time in their cabin.

Turning to a page that only had one word written on it—Tsathoggua—Howard added a second.

Dagon.

Chapter 21

Nikola Tesla adjusted the prongs sticking out of the frog's brain. A little jiggle, nothing more. Eyes mere inches away, Nikola scrutinized the positioning of all four prongs. One in the front, one in the back, one on either side. Perfect.

Stepping back, he rubbed his hands together as he examined his experiment in full. Splayed, the frog lay with legs spread wide and pinned down, its belly sliced open from throat to groin, giving access to all of its inner workings. Copper wires led from the prongs in its brain to the pulse generator, a small box of components attached to a modified Gramme dynamo, one he had modified himself to add efficiency to the machine.

Licking his lips in rapt anticipation, he cranked the dynamo. Electricity flowed into the pulse generator. When there was enough of a charge, the generator released the pent-up electricity in rhythmic bursts. Caught up in his excitement, he cranked faster, but the electric pulses to the frog's brain remained constant.

A leg twitched.

Even though its foot was pinned to the board beneath it, the leg jerked with a spasm. Two other legs soon joined in the frozen dance. Then, its heart beat. Once. Twice. On the third beat, the lungs expanded.

Nikola's own heart sped up as he cranked faster and faster. His experiment was working! Alas, no sooner had that thought skittered through his mind, than it was quashed. The lungs stopped. The heart stopped. Not a single twitch more from any of the legs.

"No," Nikola moaned, haphazardly adjusting the prongs. "No. No. No. No."

"You cannot have success without failure," a voice came from behind Nikola.

Startled, he spun around. At the bottom of the stone stairs of his basement laboratory stood a smiling young man wearing a thin black robe piped with green.

Nikola found the young man to be odd, but not nearly as odd as the trio behind him. The woman in head-to-toe veils failed to tickle his curiosity, as did the garishly attired fellow with a handlebar mustache and equally tacky top hat. However, the large man with a jar for a head and a brass-grated speaker embedded in his overly muscular chest was spectacular.

Fear flickered through Nikola—though his height surpassed most people, including three of these four strangers, his width was certainly lacking—but his desire for knowledge quickly shooed away any notions of danger. He needed to learn more about the large fellow. Ignoring everyone else and forgetting about his recently failed experiment, Nikola made his way to the large man. Marvel of marvels! As Nikola strode closer, he got a much better look at what bobbled about in the jar—two independently moving eyeballs attached to a brain! "Fascinating."

"He certainly is. My name is Szilveszter Matu—"

"Tell me more about this automaton. What propels it? Are its internal workings clockwork? How—?"

"I assure you; I am no mere piece of machinery," the hollow, metallic voice emanated from the modified man's chest. "My name is Dr. Sivkas, and I am just as human as you. Albeit, a bit more modified."

Nikola reeled back. "Human, you say? Then, how do you hear my words with no ears?"

"The instrument in my chest is used for more than just speaking. It captures sound as well."

Nikola leaned in, close enough to create a temporary fog on the brass with his breath, and spoke with increased volume, "What a fantastic substitute!"

Dr. Sivkas took a step back and covered the speaker with his hands. "No need for that!"

"Interesting," Nikola said as he stood straight and reduced the distance between himself and Dr. Sivkas to mere inches. As he brought his face closer to the jar, he studied every cerebral fold and twist, noting the wires flowing from the brain to the top of the spinal column. The floating eyeballs scrutinized Nikola's every move, especially when Nikola brought his index finger up to the jar, ready to tap the glass.

This time Dr. Sivkas did not step backward. Instead, he folded his arms, thicker than Nikola's thighs, and flexed to the point of prodigious muscle attempting to push veins through skin. His hollow voice declared, "I highly recommend that you do not do that."

Nikola paused, finger still poised for tapping, and considered the warning. He heeded it and withdrew his hand, placing it with the other one behind his back, lest they do something beyond his control that would lead to an untoward consequence. He even took one long step backward. "So, modified human, what is it that you do?"

"As I said before, my name is Dr. Sivkas, and I would certainly appreciate it if you addressed me by that name, title included."

Nikola smirked and nodded his acknowledgement. "My apologies."

"As for what I do, I am a scientist. I submit my services to Szilveszter Matuska so we may free the Chaos Bringer and usher in a new and momentous era for this world."

Nikola winced as if Dr. Sivkas struck him across the face. "Matuska? What's a Matuska"

"I am," Szilveszter said. Nikola turned to regard the young man in the black robe. He still offered Nikola a pleasant smile, but a bit more strained and forced this time. "As I began to mention earlier, my name is Szilveszter Matuska and we are here to recruit you for a wondrous cause."

"Recruit me? What might I have to offer you?"

"Your mind, Nikola. Your mind."

"What might you have to offer me?"

"The ability to be *recognized* for your mind."

Nikola sneered. "I'm sure time and patience will offer me the same thing."

Szilveszter sighed and folded his hands together, a preacher at prayer. "You believe when you help others it's mutually beneficial, but in reality they are using you as a stepping stone to traverse the quagmire of life. I could tell you this, but I think it more effective if I show you."

The veiled woman stepped closer to Nikola and exposed the old, withered side of her face. Before Nikola could muster a question, the world around him turned into a mist, as if every item and object lost molecular integrity, allowing the atoms to dissipate freely and reform. The swirl of colors stopped and showed Nikola a new scene of life, one outside of the basement walls, in a different land. The images rippled, as if they were projected on a backdrop of flowing water, but he could see them, understand them, feel the impact deep within himself, nonetheless. He felt ignored.

The image conjured Thomas Edison, visage pinched and folded, but smiling. Nikola saw himself. A bit older with a thin mustache, but it was the face he had seen in the mirror. Even though he was vaporous and blurred, he still noticed the sparkle in his own eyes, of promise and hope. The image changed; still of Edison and himself, but now he was in the background and frowning. Edison waved and nodded, smiling from ear to ear as he moved closer to the foreground with every step forward, the image of the older Nikola retreated into the background. Edison grew larger as did his smile, now open-mouthed and laughing, as camera flashes popped in the periphery of the scene; so real Nikola could smell the phosphorus. The image of Tesla vanished as Edison loomed closer, his laughing head the size of the room. Nikola shrunk back and raised his arm to shield himself as the open maw threatened to swallow him. "Illusion be gone!"

The face of Edison burst into sparkles, winking out of existence. Nikola relaxed and asked, "What is to become of me?"

The glowing motes swirled again and reformed, shaping into a man sitting in a chair. The seat was but a creaky, wooden contraption, threatening to give way from nothing more than a suggestion, but the man perched on it sat as if upon a throne. Stature tall and slender, but regal, Nikola recognized his aged and wrinkled countenance again, this time with a feral expression and insanity glazed eyes, a look that no person would trust even if the truth were spoken. This kind of hunger could only come from desperation, he knew. He wrapped his arms around himself to stifle a chill. "No more. Please, I beg you."

As soon as Nikola blinked his eyes, he found himself standing back in his laboratory with the assortment of motley guests. He inhaled deeply, gulping the air as if emerging from the ocean depths. He turned to the veiled woman, her face now hidden, and spat, "What hex did you place upon me, witch?"

"None," Szilveszter said. He stepped closer; his hands folded together. "She merely showed you the truth."

"The truth?" Nikola cried. "The truth? Are you meaning to tell me that I am to be used… betrayed… by one of the most influential inventors of our time?"

"Yes. Later this very year, Thomas Edison will unveil an incandescent light bulb that will pave the way for families to light their homes. You will travel to America to gain employment with him, study from him. Your ideas are better, but he will manipulate them, claim some as his own, discredit others he finds too threatening."

Horror tickled Nikola's spine with frozen fingers. "The world... the world will not know me?"

Szilveszter chuckled. "Oh, the world will know you, Nikola Tesla. As the crazed and maddened man you saw in your vision before awakening. A joke to some, a diabolical legend to others. Inventor? Yes. An engine of progress? No."

Nikola twisted his face tightly as he clenched his fists. Body shaking, he yelled, "Mad? Mad? That is preposterous!"

"Said the enraged fellow trying to reanimate a dissected frog." Szilveszter's simple act of slowly gazing at the experiment doused Nikola's internal fire faster than a splash of ice water.

Emotions still ran rampant through Nikola from the vision, but now embarrassment pushed its way to the surface. Trying to return life after death had claimed it was such a preposterous notion that it had always been reserved for witches and necromancers of medieval times. As a scientist, he felt shamed. "I was just... trying...."

"You were experimenting," Szilveszter said. "You are a scientist, even if you've terminated your scholastic career before earning a degree. Scientists experiment, especially when motivated."

Confused by that statement, Nikola offered a quizzical look. Szilveszter answered the unspoken question. "Your father passed on earlier this year. You two had never seen eye-to-eye. I'm sure that fact coupled with his untimely death must bear down on you, for there is no weight heavier than that of guilt."

"How do you know such things?" Nikola barked.

Still smiling, Szilveszter replied, "Simple. I am from the future. I know what you saw in the vision you had. To me, it is already history."

"How can that be? How are you here?"

"The great God of Chaos that I worship... that *we* worship," Szilveszter corrected himself with a sweeping arm gesture to his colleagues, "is imprisoned. During a ceremony, I almost freed him, but a pair of heretics stopped me, keeping me from freeing *our* god. With one last effort before his cell door slammed shut, he summoned enough power to propel me through time."

"You say you want me? My mind? What exactly do you wish of me?"

As if performing a parlor trick, Szilveszter reached into one of his sleeves and produced a folder. He handed it to Nikola and said, "Two things. First, we simply wish you to finish your experiment."

Nikola debated about the validity of Szilveszter's statement. A man from the future? A god of chaos? Preposterous! But the man-machination? A woman capable of warping the world around him with a single glance? Astounding! In his heart, his soul, he felt that his vision could come true, had already come true. Szilveszter courted him and Edison used him. The God of Chaos wished for Nikola to use his talents. The rest of the world did not.

Nikola opened the folder and examined its contents. What he saw amazed him. "This... this is... so... so simple."

"Indeed. We need you to use your incredible talents to make that device. Multiple times."

Despite being enraptured by the information that Szilveszter had given him, Nikola still had enough of his wits about him to ask, "You said you wished two things from me. The second thing being?"

"The use of that."

An archway stood against the back wall of the basement laboratory, its peak touched the ceiling. It was wide enough to fit two people shoulder-to-shoulder. Brass fittings were clamped on copper wires that spiraled around the iron piping on the archway. The copper vines led to and grew from random nodules poking from the underlying metal, making the contraption look like a twisted tree taken from a hellish jungle. Dozens of wires terminated at another Gramme Dynamo, half the size of a horse and on the floor by the left post of the archway. Also connected to the archway was a bronze globe wide enough to make one wonder how it fit through any doorway to reach its final destination in a basement laboratory. The globe had all of the continents etched into it, each country in meticulous detail and containing more cities than found on most maps. Rivers, mountains, deserts all included as well. It was mounted by its poles and tilted forty-five degrees. A pointer no wider than the tip of a pin dangled from a thin cross bar, connected to the archway by wires.

"My transportation doorway?" Nikola asked. "Nothing more than another frustration."

Szilveszter ran his fingers over the topography carved into the bronze. "Does it not work at all?"

"Therein lies the frustration. I used it once, but I had tapped into the town's electrical power. I traveled thirty kilometers by simply stepping through the doorway. However, the damage I did to the power source left the town without electricity for quite some time. Mercifully, the incident was not tracked back to me. To fix that problem, I crafted and attached a Gramme Dynamo. In my lust for success, I failed to take into consideration that it would take at least four men far stouter of chest than myself to turn the crank at sufficient speed to produce the necessary charge."

Smiling as if knowing the punch line to a half-finished joke, Szilveszter quirked an eyebrow and said, "Is that all?"

Dr. Sivkas strode to the Dynamo crank. With great strain he cranked the handle one rotation; turgid muscles testing the limits of his skin's elasticity. The second rotation was easier, as was the third. Once he converted momentum into rhythm, the Dynamo hummed, bristling with electricity. In less than a minute, the air within the archway rippled, colors shimmering and blurring.

Szilveszter spun the globe under the fixed pointer. With the delicacy of handling a soap bubble, he nudged until the pointer hovered above a region of Germany.

Colors formed and rippled together within the archway, mixing, then separating, forming a view of buildings on either side of darkened cobblestone road. With the dramatic flair of an actor upon a stage, Szilveszter gestured to the portal. "Shall we be going?"

Myriad thoughts collided with each other in Nikola's head as he stroked his stubbled chin. A stranger appeared, bringing with him a bizarre cabal. Speeches of gods and madness, visions of frustration and disappointment. The strange man offered Nikola much of what he sought, and promised that his greatest desires would be met. Nikola struggled with what was right and what was wrong. Ultimately, the thought of growing old and swaddled by nothing more than madness left his mouth bitter. "Let us go," he said. As he continued to run his hand over the growth upon his face. The various images of his mustachioed-self flitted through his head. He did, indeed, like that look. Much to the visible consternation of Szilveszter, Nikola said, "But before we go, I must shave."

Chapter 22

Billy was uncomfortable, but not with the carriage ride as it bounced over the worn cobblestones of the Parisian streets. Jules arranged for the carriage with his own funds, so the ride was as luxurious as money could buy. Sitting on pillowed seats and leaning against quilted seatbacks, Billy decided that if he made it back to the States, he would forgo ever riding a horse again and travel only by stagecoach.

If. Such a big word. If he had resisted temptation for one day longer, he would not be in such discomfort. Keeping the pyramid a secret from the group until it had been stolen had earned him no graces in anyone's mind. Now this.

The boat ride was unbearable. He had never been on one before, and was more than excited for the adventure to Europe. Being attacked by a giant squid had been confusing, especially since it was a problem that he couldn't solve with six-shooters or smooth talk. After the squid had released the vessel—a mystery to the passengers; another nightmare for Billy and his friends—the captain and crew interviewed all witnesses. By the following day, the captain had learned enough. Even though he couldn't piece together all the details, he had enough of the puzzle to know who was involved. Led by Albert, the group feigned ignorance and stated that they simply acted in an effort to help the whole ship. They witnessed nothing more than the squid releasing its grip of the boat. This was not good enough for the captain.

Having done nothing wrong, Billy and friends remained free from the brig, but not from suspicion. The captain assigned a set of crew members to watch them at all times, but it was the rampant rumors among the other passengers that segregated the group.

As the days progressed, the number of pleasant conversations with the other passengers diminished, while calloused leers laced with paranoia and anger rose dramatically. When the passive stares turned into snide remarks from the other passengers, Billy and his posse resigned themselves to quarantining in their quarters except to fetch necessities. Even then, they hurriedly purchased food and beverages in bulk and scuttled back to their rooms like unsociable hermits.

The remainder of the trip melted into droning conversations among Jules, Albert, and Howard, recapping and rehashing the events that occurred. Annie contributed as well, much to Billy's consternation. He had hoped to use the close quarters to woo Annie into more salacious activities. Instead, four voices formed one thrumming hum while he and Jane chose to drink away the rest of the journey.

Even though the boat pulled into port a day ahead of schedule, Billy could not have been happier to depart it—until the six gathered at the corner of the first street they came to. Jane winked at him. Astute, Annie noticed the gesture and asked, "Now what was that all about? A private joke of some sort that no longer wishes to remain that way?"

Cheeks aflame, Billy pondered the idea of running back to the docks and leaping right into the water. He avoided eye contact with Jane. He avoided eye contact with everyone, including strangers hustling and bustling around them along the streets.

Jane laughed. "Nah. Not a joke."

"Oh?" Annie pressed, smirking. Her smile faded as she turned her judging gaze to Billy. Slouching with his hands in his pockets, he could feel her suspicions form by how heavy her words became, adding weight to the albatross around his neck. "Please keep me in suspense no longer. Why is... William... acting so peculiarly?"

Jane honked out a laugh, barely able to control her glee. "I don't know. Maybe it's because he and I knocked boots last night?"

Everyone looked at Billy. Passersby within earshot of Jane looked at Billy. The whole city of Le Havre looked at Billy.

Keeping his head low, he peeked at the group from the corner of his eye and realized the truth—Jane had used him. Turning his shoulder away from Annie, he tried to use his back as a shield from her stern disappointment. No luck. Not needing to say a single word, her tightly drawn lips, clenched jaw, and knitted brows told a story of betrayal and disgust.

Jane laughed.

With a guffaw usually reserved for drunken sailors, Jane also conveyed her message without words. Slapping her knee, she didn't even look at Billy. Instead, Jane reacted to Annie's look of intense disapproval. He was simply a pawn in the chess game of brinksmanship between the two women, a game Jane clearly felt that she had won. Others had an opinion as well.

Before the carriage had arrived, Annie took a moment to "freshen up" and Jane had to "see a man about a horse." They went in different directions and left the men.

"How could you?" Albert snapped at Billy.

Trying to retain his confident and nonchalant image, Billy shrugged. Had he been back in the Sates, he'd simply wander away from this mess, maybe shoot a few bastards along the way for good measure. With no concept of which way the wind blew in this town, he tried to muster a whimsical smirk. "It happened."

"It certainly did, young man!"

Billy rolled his eyes.

Albert continued, "I cannot believe that you have no inclination of how grave the situation is. Howard, don't you agree?"

Howard's gaze lingered in the direction that Annie had gone. He, too, shrugged. "Why should I care if two filthy beasts can't deny their base desires to rut like the animals they are? We don't get mad at swine for frolicking in pools of mud, do we?"

Billy rarely understood half of what Howard said, but this time he knew the meaning of every hurtful word. He wondered, if Jane had been around to hear them, if they would have had the same painful impact, and then doubted it. She didn't care about what others thought of her.

Howard's statement had been so strong that it even softened Albert's attack. "Be that as it may, it was still disruptive, and the temptation should have been avoided."

With a jovial chuckle, Jules clapped Albert on the back. "My good man, I can hardly see why there should be a fuss. Billy's a young, virile man with needs. Jane is a… woman. I'm sure there are some attributes of youth still desperate to make themselves known. Let them have their fun, I say."

Albert sighed, one of exasperation. "Because of their 'fun,' they have changed their relationship, thusly changing the dynamic of this group."

Jules chuckled. "Their relationship is what they make it, and I hardly doubt that they will affect this group or our mission."

"Unfortunately, I've seen it happen all too often. Even in less exciting environments such as the college where I teach, the most outrageous dramas pull in innocent victims like a voracious whirlpool."

"Bah! You're talking about fops and suits. We're adventurers! Such folly would never slow us down."

"We're still human. As such, folly is within each and every one of us."

Billy didn't feel human as he stood around listening to others talk about him as if he were somewhere else, someone else. He didn't say another word, even when the women had returned, and the six "adventurers" waited in uncomfortable silence for the carriage to arrive. Now, sitting in the carriage, all he could do was replay past events and try to focus on the comfort of the ride.

The life of France happened outside the coach window. Billy didn't belong here. Nothing about this city, this country, appealed to him. Spending his whole life on the plains of the southwest territories and in towns barely large enough to support a sheriff's office and two saloons, he really didn't know what to expect from a city, let alone one in Europe. What he saw made him feel simultaneously unimpressed and overwhelmed.

Streets filled with horses and carriages similar to the one he was in now, some bigger, most smaller. Two- and three-story buildings shoved together like pieces of a puzzle that didn't fit, some freshly bricked, others barely ramshackle. The people on the sidewalks resembled what Billy saw in the city itself; new and old, pretty and ugly. Clean and fresh-faced families walked along hand-in-hand in their pristine clothes, colors bright enough to have been stolen from a rainbow. Businessmen in their suits. Fashionistas parading around. All of them scurrying about, paying no attention to the anyone other than themselves. Worn-out laborers scuttled about with blood-stained butchers, filth-covered beggars, and drab-clothed everybodies. The buildings. The roads. The markets. The people. People everywhere! No, Billy realized, he did not belong here, in a city, in Europe.

The horses drawing the carriage moved at a satisfactory clip, but Billy felt almost at a standstill. Another carriage was in front of this one, two men on horses behind it, and a constant stream of traffic raced along in the opposite direction. Billy went back to focusing on the luxury of the ride, and tried to settle his mind, ease the tension in his body. That seemed an unobtainable fantasy. Every time his muscles started to unknot, a snorting horse with a creaking carriage would zoom past, too close to his window for his preference.

Thankfully, a small break in the oncoming traffic allowed Billy a moment's peace, but even that was soon taken away. From behind the carriage, a team of horses pulling a coach of equal size trotted into the other lane. They sped up as if to pass.

Billy tensed as they pulled even. He silently cursed at how everyone needed to be other than where they were. A few days in the lazy prairie would do them all some good. But the other carriage did not pass. Instead, it matched their speed. And drifted closer. As the wheels of the two carriages touched, they both rocked.

"What the hell?" Jane snapped.

"What is going on over there?" Jules asked from the other side of the bench.

All Billy could see were the drawn curtains of the other carriage. Squinting, he drew his nose nearer to the window, trying to discern any of the shapes or movements from the other carriage. In a flash, the curtain flung aside to reveal a jaundiced and snarling face.

Billy jerked back, almost crawling onto Albert's lap. Albert placed his hands upon Billy's shoulders for support. "What's happening?"

Sitting on the same side of the carriage as Billy, Howard replied, "It appears that a man with the skin tone of oozing pus, and thick tendrils of dirty hair just as yellowed, is demanding that we pull over and stop the carriage. Curiously, both his iris and sclera have yellowed as well, albeit different shades. And his teeth... ugh!"

Twisting to reach the wall behind him, Jules slid a small door and yelled to the driver of the carriage, "My dear sir, please evade the carriage next to us."

The lurch forward from the carriage speeding up pinned Billy to the seat back. He wondered how they could find such speed on a busy street, then suddenly found himself pressed against the window, with Albert pushed up next to him as the carriage made a sharp right turn. After the carriage passengers righted themselves, Albert ripped open the curtain to the back window and said, "They're pursuing."

Billy reached for his guns, but grabbed only his own pants. He had forgotten that he had packed them away for the cruise, and never strapped them back on after the commotion that Jane had caused. Now, they were in his satchel, secured to the roof of the carriage.

The pursuers gained ground; their horses devouring the distance with their hooves. They drew even once again. The only thing Billy could do was brace himself when then carriage slammed against his side.

Everyone gasped and grunted from the jolt of the impact. Too shocked to do anything other than watch as one of the members of the other carriage leapt across the short divide and tossed aside their driver. Jane and Jules both grimaced as the driver fell to the ground, flopping about like a broken doll. Both carriages slowed.

Jules puffed out his chest as he said, "Once we come to a stop, we all must rush out this side as quickly as possible. I will bulrush as many as I can. Hopefully Billy and Albert will be able to join me in the fisticuffs while the others get the guns from the top of the carriage."

Howard frowned. Billy presumed it was from the indignation of Jules' plan relegating him to be with the women. He wanted to tell Howard, "No time for hurt feelin's," but decided against it. No time for petty sniping.

Hand on the carriage door, Jules looked around to make sure everyone was prepared for what was about to happen. Billy clenched his fists and pushed down the feelings of unease as he recalled the features of the yellowed face.

The horses brayed and the carriage slowed even more, finally stopping. Jules flung open the door.

Chapter 23

The carriage rocked and lumbered to a standstill. Howard inwardly groused. Jules had just offered a strategy that lumped Howard in with the women. The older writer had expressed his opinion of the younger one, and Howard was not sure that he appreciated it. He never prioritized "machismo" high on the list of qualities he wished to be remembered for, but there was a certain sting to his ego when Jules didn't include him with those in the carriage who should be involved with the impending skirmish. And Billy's reaction, albeit subtle, stoked his fire.

Howard shook his head as if the action would dislodge such meaningless and trivial thoughts. *Why would I even care about such insipidness during this dire moment in time*? he admonished himself as the carriage stopped.

As promised, Jules shoved open the door and leapt out, leading the way with some form of war cry mixed with laughter. Howard was the last one out.

The inside of the carriage offered no darkness, but the drawn curtains had offered enough shade from the noonday sun to make the sudden brightness sting Howard's eyes. He struggled to see, trying to blink away the sudden flood of tears. The watering distorted his vision, but Howard could see his companions tussling with those from the other carriage. They all possessed thick and wiry dreadlocks of urine yellow hair, their beards the same style and color. Howard had a difficult time distinguishing them from one another or getting an accurate count. He figured there were six of them that Jules, Billy, and Albert tangled with. Jane went against Jules' plan and chose to join in the fisticuffs. Annie used the ladder to scurry to the roof, but yellow hands yanked her down.

Fueled by anger, Howard knew that he couldn't wait for his full vision to return. He grabbed the ladder toward the rear of the carriage and climbed. Ignoring the frantic shouts and noises from the skirmish below, he reached the roof of the carriage and found his satchel. His vision cleared just in time to see the mangy and jaundiced face of one of his pursuers pop up from the other ladder. Prone, Howard worked the ties of his satchel faster as the yellowed man climbed onto the roof. Success! Howard pulled out his gun and targeted his attacker.

"Wait!" the man yelled as Howard tapped the trigger. The gun discharged a pellet sized burst of green and struck the man in the chest, knocking him from the roof. Howard knew that the energy blast was not enough to kill him, just enough to render him useless. Gun in hand, Howard scurried down the ladder, ready to neutralize the remaining assailants. But there was no more fighting, just eleven pairs of eyes looking at him.

"What is the meaning of this?" Howard asked, pointing his gun to two of the yellowed men helping the one that Howard had shot.

"Howard, please put the gun down," Albert said, approaching. He stopped when Howard turned and pointed the gun at him.

"No. Not until I can ascertain your sudden change in motivations. Have you been ensorcelled?"

"Are ya fuckin' serious?" Jane spat. "The first time you're not actin' like a pansy-assed sissy all trip, and you ruin it by talkin' like a pansy-ass sissy!"

Jane's reaction was all the proof Howard needed. He lowered his weapon. "My apologies. I just found it inconceivable that within the matter of seconds, we are no longer in quarrel with our adversaries."

"Pansy-ass," Jane mumbled.

"That's because they are not our adversaries," Albert said.

"It's okay, Howard," Annie said as she walked over to him and placed a hand on his arm. The act was far more comforting than he'd ever admit. "Albert's right. He would never lie to you. And neither would I."

Howard was deft enough to realize that Annie's words and actions acted as ways to spite Billy, but he didn't care, content to bask in her proximity. He glared at the yellowed men. "Continue."

"They are here to aid us," Albert said.

"Aid us?" Howard turned to the one he had shot, now standing on his own. "What do you know of our mission?"

"We know very little. The one we serve wishes for your success and has sent us to assist you." His voice held a limpness that made Howard wonder if the price of his servitude was his very soul itself.

"Who is your master?" Howard asked.

All six men bowed their heads and held out their hands as a form of genuflection. "The Yellow King. He Who Must Not Be Named."

Howard frowned. He knew of this creature, this "Yellow King." He pulled out his notebook and flipped to the page that had the two names of the supernatural creatures that he and his colleagues had encountered so far and added a third: Hastur.

As he returned it to his pocket, he noticed that Annie had watched him. Recalling her experience with Tsathoggua, he hoped that seeing the newest name didn't cause her any more undue stress. No one else spoke, wordlessly conveying that they trusted his authority regarding the topic at hand, so he continued, "In what ways were you instructed to assist us?"

The yellowed man answered, "In whatever way you see fit. We have a dozen more members gathered nearby at one of our many houses, waiting to serve you."

"A safe house? That may not be a bad idea," Jules said. He then patted his prodigious belly and continued, "I'm certain that I'm not the only one bitten by the bugs of hunger. We could use the time to formulate a plan more detailed than just aiming for Germany."

Not taking his eyes off the yellowed men, Howard replied, "There is always a price with the one they serve. I have yet to determine how he benefits from helping us, or if we will end up looking like these wretches if we accept his aid."

"We do not know the answer to those questions. We can only deliver the message given to us," the yellowed man said as he gave a deep bow. However, he lingered in that position, his face contorting as if he saw something that confused him.

Curious, Howard looked down as well. Around his feet, a thick fog rolled along the street as if being poured from a great container. It emanated from a nearby alleyway, and a dozen men shambled out, using the fog as an escort. As if they had been dipped in grease, their pallid skin had an unnatural shimmer, while their slimy hair matted to their faces. Eyes wide, yet undeniably lifeless, they walked toward those near the carriages while their gaping mouths were only used for breathing.

Howard and his cohort drew closer to the unnerving yellowed men, all facing this new menace. Annie stepped back, closer to Howard. "Are… are those… the circus hands? Oh, they are! Howard, what has become of them?"

Annie received an answer as two more figures emerged from the fog. With pounding steps and clenched fists, Dr. Sivkas lumbered behind the twelve shells of humanity. Zarkahn followed, the source of the fog. Plumes of smoke billowed from the sleeves of his outstretched arms. With a flick of his wrists the smoke stopped. Howard noticed something that seemed to glow deeper in the alley, but couldn't see the details through the lingering miasma.

"These are two of the men you have told me about, no?" Jules asked. "Then that means your adversary is near."

"Unfortunately, that ain't always the case," Billy said. "That varmint has a way of bein' right where he ain't wanted the most. No matter how far ahead of us or behind us he is, he seems to be everywhere."

Despite the ineloquent way of stating it, Howard was mildly impressed that Billy had been paying attention enough to make such an astute observation. He added, "Indubitably. From asking around on the docks, we confirmed a suspicion that we had on the ship. A zeppelin came eight days prior. It is doubtful that Szilveszter has remained in Le Havre this entire time."

"So now what?" Jules asked.

Before anyone could suggest a plan, Dr. Sivkas bellowed with his inhuman, metallic voice, "Attack!"

"Cover me while I get everyone else's guns," Billy yelled, smacking Howard on the back. Howard groused over Billy's necessity for the slap, but his plan was the best option available.

The mutated circus lackeys no longer possessed the speed of healthy human beings. With two long pulls of the trigger, Howard felled two of the oncoming minions, leaving bubbling patches in their chests, smoldering with green smoke. He was saddened by Annie's whimper.

Howard's aim was true, but it wasn't enough to stop the small horde. Jules and Jane were more than happy for fisticuffs; Jules using his size to add devastating power to his swing, while Jane used what Howard assumed to be the fury of some form of psychosis to fuel her punches. Albert tussled as well, but not with the same verve as the other two. He shoved and pushed, making an attempt to keep them away from the carriage while Billy climbed his way to the top. Annie stayed behind Howard and pointed to where he should shoot. All form of the soul in these minions had been poisoned beyond repair. These people were no longer human, and now Howard felt it almost a mercy to terminate the fleshy husks.

Those who served the Yellow King fought as well, all charging Dr. Sivkas and Zarkahn. The large body of Dr. Sivkas looked like an adult swatting toddlers. The garish magician waved his hands about with aplomb, calling forth arcs of lightning from his fingertips, striking three of the yellowed men. Howard couldn't tell if they were alive or not, nor did he care, perceiving the yellowed men to be as soulless as the minions he now shot at.

The creatures lacked any fighting skill, but possessed a monomaniacal drive to perform a specific task. Needful fingers reached for Albert no matter how many times he pushed or hit. Two others shoved their way to the carriage and started to climb.

Howard blasted at the ones grasping for Albert. As he trained his sights on the ones closest, one of the other creatures broke free from the small pack that Jules and Jane tangled with to reach for Annie. With gnarled fingers, the once-man grabbed Annie's sleeve. She screamed as he yanked her away from Howard. Trying to defend herself, she swung wildly, but her slaps couldn't free her as the creature used its other hand to grab her neck.

Howard spun and aimed at Annie's attacker, but a creature swatted him as he discharged his gun. A bolt of green energy shot impotently into the sky. Annie's screams were cut short as the hand tightened around her neck. Arm now pinned behind his back, Howard felt useless, needing as much help as the damsel he tried to rescue. Just as the minion started to drag Annie away, a small crack of thunder resounded above the ruckus, and crimson ooze exploded from the back of the once-man's skull. It relinquished Annie and fell limp.

Much like a storybook legend, Billy stood tall and proud atop the carriage. Backdropped by the sun, he looked like a rescuing god. With a smirk and wink, he tossed Annie's shotgun to her. She winked back and then trained her weapon on the once-man attacking Howard. A squeeze of the trigger later, she rescued Howard.

"Thank you," Howard forced himself to say. Fantasies of turning his gun on Billy danced through his head. In mere seconds, Billy managed to re-endear himself to Annie while simultaneously putting her in a position to emasculate Howard. Just as quickly, Howard again chided himself; this was neither the time nor place for such whimsy.

"Anytime, Sugar," Annie said. Billy leapt down from the carriage; one of his six-shooters in his right hand, Jane's gun belt and Albert's gun in his left. Landing right next to Annie, he and she shared a smile.

Howard wondered if the quality of those in power could be reflected in those who followed them—the followers of the Yellow King lay strewn about the streets while the followers of Szilveszter's nefarious chaos god still fought on. Even though Billy and Annie felled two attackers, the others still grappled with Jules and Jane. These followers were nothing more than pawns and exemplified their purpose—distract the opponent while positioning the more important pieces.

Dr. Sivkas and Zarkahn stayed behind the mindless drones. Billy shot at Zarkahn, but with a wave of the magician's hand, the bullets exploded as puffs of smoke. "That ain't good," Billy mumbled. "Jane! Albert! I gotchyer guns!"

Fist full of shirt, Jane held one of the minions with her left hand while delivering punch after punch with her right. She continued to punch him as she dragged him along with her, backing up to Billy. When his face looked like an over-ripened tomato that finally burst, Jane let go, allowing the body to flop to the ground. After using the side of her pants to wipe the blood off her hands, she took her gun belt from Billy. "Much obliged."

Howard sneered, and Jane sneered back, asking, "Ain't never gotten your hands dirty before?"

He had, but he would never purposely wipe them on his garments. The thought of Billy having carnal relations with such a brutish woman turned his stomach. His distractive thoughts came to a halt when Zarkahn ordered, "Followers, retrieve the targets!"

In one coordinated effort, the remaining minions swarmed on Albert. Annie trained her rifle at the squirming pack of twisted humanity, but it suddenly turned into a rattlesnake. Screaming, she dropped it. Billy no longer held guns either, instead two writhing black snakes.

Howard turned to shoot Zarkahn, but when he brought his hand up, there was nothing in it. Stunned, he could only stare at his empty hands like a dimwitted buffoon.

"What's wrong with you idjits?" Jane yelled in between her trigger squeezes. She dropped one of the attackers, the bullet shattering his skull and taking bits of brain with it, but her efforts did nothing to hinder the huddled mass. Cursing, she shot another one dead. Still not enough. The minions rendered Albert unconscious, and started dragging him toward the alleyway whence they came.

"Albert!" Howard cried. But before he could do anything else, Dr. Sivkas was on him with a speed unbefitting his bulk. With an effortless backhand, he cracked Howard along the side of his face.

Howard's world blurred into millions of radiant star bursts as his legs turned to silk strands. Dr. Sivkas caught him with ease and lifted him by his armpits. As Howard looked at his out-of-focus friends, he realized that Dr. Sivkas used him as a shield. He heard their voices, muffled as if he were under water.

"Get 'em, Jane!" Billy yelled.

"Shoot him!" Annie screamed. "What are you waiting for?"

Jane aimed, but did not pull the trigger. "I might hit Howard!"

Caught in the ambiguous state between conscious and unconscious where Howard found himself, he still got angry. How could she possibly miss when the target was a brain floating in a jar? He wanted to call her a worthless donkey, but all that came from his numbed lips was a slurred, "Shoot."

The image of his comrades faded away as Dr. Sivkas dragged him into the alley. Howard lolled his head to one side, feeling an unwarranted sense of comfort when he saw Albert. If they were dragging him away as well, that at least meant he was still alive.

Once within the alleyway, consciousness slipping from him, Howard saw what caused the glow. Blue arcs danced and spiraled into twisted strands of electricity forming an oval. Within the oval, Howard saw furniture and paintings hanging from walls. A portal.

Howard knew very well that he should be more frightened than fascinated, but as he slipped into the blackness of unconsciousness, he knew that he would have plenty to fear when he awoke.

Chapter 24

Annie wasn't thinking when she grabbed Jane's arm. There was no doubt in her mind that she could better Jane in any form of shooting competition. No one, not even herself, would ever speculate that Annie could beat Jane in one-on-one fisticuffs. Yet, she factored none of this as she gripped Jane's arm and yanked her around. "What the hell was that?"

Looking more surprised than angry, Jane pulled her arm from Annie's grip and yelled back, "I didn't wanna accidentally shoot Howard!"

"Bullshit!" Annie erupted with such vehemence that spittle sprayed from her mouth. "You froze!"

The initial shock wore off and Jane's countenance shifted to ire. "Did not! I didn't have a clear shot!"

"I find that hard to believe, coming from the person who has been bragging this whole time about how good of a shot she is!"

"You couldn't have made the shot neither!"

"I most certainly could have!"

"Then why in tarnation did you drop your gun?"

"Because the magician in their midst turned my gun into a snake!"

Screwing her face sour, Jane reeled back. "What in the blazes are you talking about, woman?"

"This!" Annie pointed to the ground, expecting to see a thick snake. Instead, it was her rifle. Stunned, her anger flowed out of her like acid being poured down a drain. She mumbled to herself, "But... but... I was holding a... a snake. It squirmed. I felt it squirm in my hands."

Billy placed a hand on her shoulder. "I saw it, too. My shooters turned to snakes as well."

"As baffling as it may be to comprehend," Jules interjected, walking closer and dusting himself off, "I witnessed the same trick."

"It was a snake," Annie whispered to herself as she retrieved her rifle. "A snake."

Jane snorted at Annie. "Whether you seen a snake or you was too chicken shit to shoot don't matter none. Szilveszter's goons got Albie and Howard. So now what are we gonna do?"

"Get them back, obviously," Annie snapped.

"Yeah, pretty girl? How you reckon we do that?"

One of the jaundiced men stepped forward. He placed his hands together and offered a courteous bow. He smiled; his teeth more akin to diseased toenails. "We can assist with that. Our master can offer more than just a safe place for respite."

"Yeah, we heard ya the first time," Billy said. "But it didn't seem like Howard trusted your master none too well."

Jules placed a hand on Billy's shoulder, and directed everyone's attention to a spot farther down the street. A crowd of onlookers had gathered, fearful enough to keep a very safe distance, but still curious enough to stay and piece together the mystery. Dozens of fingers pointed at the spectacle, while just as many voices speculated amongst themselves as to what was happening.

Whistles sounded, faint at first, but getting progressively louder. The police. They picked and pushed their way through the crowd, and once within earshot they yelled to everyone involved in the ruckus to halt. Annie knew very well that no one was going to follow that order.

"That could certainly be a problem," Billy said. "Looks like we gotta go."

Refusing to ride with her, Annie waited until Jane got in one of the carriages, and then chose to ride in the other. Billy and Jules exchanged looks, clearly confounded by the inner workings of the fairer sex, before choosing their carriages. Jules rode with Jane while Billy nuzzled up next to Annie on the bench seat. Within seconds, the yellowed men had both carriages moving away from the police, the crowd, and the city.

Seething, Annie rested her chin on a clenched fist and stared out the window. She offered no acknowledgment when Billy whispered to her, "We'll find 'em. We'll get 'em back."

The scenery went by and Annie started to feel guilty, as if she abandoned Billy, leaving him to the awkward silence and the hideous visages of the yellowed men riding in the carriage with them. Undoubtedly, he had no other recourse but to look at their weathered faces or the back of her head. If she knew Billy as well as she thought she did, he probably stared at the back of her head, desperately trying to string the right words together to make her feel better, to diminish her anger and elevate her hope.

The yellowed men must have known the most expeditious way out of the city; they were in the countryside before Annie noticed the stark change in scenery. There were no pursuers, for which Annie was thankful, but she was torn about the rest of the trip—she wished for some form of respite to collect her thoughts and gather the opinions of the others, but she loathed the idea of doing so in whatever lair these yellowed creatures called home. To her surprise, the last leg of the short trip took them to a well-maintained cobblestone path, flanked on either side by manicured shrubbery, which led to a rather large house. Annie was not one to know the exact qualifications that separated a "mansion" from a "large house," but this structure could be the subject of such debate.

As the carriages pulled up to the front, Annie imagined that a team of staff would be waiting to greet them. As much as it shamed her to feel this way considering the circumstance, she did feel a pang of disappointment when there was none to be seen. She felt quite a few darker emotions when she heard Jane call out from the other carriage, "Holy shit! Look at these digs!"

Billy placed a supportive hand on her shoulder. She wanted to thank him, but he was too busy gawking at the columned abode and the pristine lawn, an expansive plot of lush grass. She said, "It seems that we will be here for at least a night, so we should unpack. Especially your satchel."

Nodding in agreement, Billy climbed to the top of the carriage. Annie admired the estate's landscaping while pushing aside the reason to be viewing it. So caught up in its regality, she missed the rustling coming from the carriage top as Billy rummaged through their bags and supplies. He poked his head over the railing and said, "It ain't here."

Half from letting her mind drift, half from not believing his words, Annie replied, "Excuse me?"

"My satchel. It ain't here."

Both Jules and Jane gawked up at Billy as well. Jane spat, "What do ya mean it ain't there?"

"I mean I can find everyone else's bags except for mine. I found Howard's satchel, but not mine." To prove his point, he held it up.

"Check again!"

"I already checked three times!"

Jules looked to Annie. "Our adversaries must have taken it. I must confess that during the street brawl, I barely knew my whereabouts, let alone those of our ambushers."

"This situation just gets worse and worse," Annie moaned. She looked back up to the carriage roof and said, "It's okay, Billy. Grab the rest of the bags and come on down."

Billy did as directed. Once on the ground, one of the yellowed men came over and offered the best humble smile his gnarled teeth and cracked lips could offer. "Welcome to our master's home. My name is Skaag and I am your servant. Please, follow me."

Annie and the others did as requested. Skaag and his fellow yellowed men led them inside, the interior just as surprisingly immaculate as the lawn. The foyer had two sets of curved stairs leading to an opened second floor. Skaag asked that his guests leave their bags and instructed a few of the other yellowed men to take them to the guestrooms. He then escorted his guests to a great room.

With seating enough for everyone, Skaag offered his hospitality. Annie refused and walked around the room, feigning interest in the art upon the walls, or the fabric of the exquisite curtains, or the pristinely kept tomes on the bookshelves. She even shunned the wines and waters that Skaag's associates offered on silver platters. Skaag requested that they relax and free themselves from their burdens, even for just a fleeting moment.

The group did as asked, Jules being the only one to follow polite protocols. Billy would offer a dubious "thank you" now and again, while Jane simply grunted after accepting what was being offered. Annie would have shown more respect, but she had nothing but bad feelings about her jaundiced hosts and their enigmatic master. Jules took a sip of his wine and said, "Your master has quite a beautiful home. When should we expect him?"

"We who follow live here. He does not," Skaag said with a placating smile.

Annie scowled at Skaag upon hearing that. Both Jules and Billy shifted in their seats. Jane's countenance soured even more. Jules continued, "So, we will not be meeting your master?"

"You would not wish to. We, his servants, shall provide all necessary communications between you and him."

"Who is your master?" Jules asked.

"The Yellow King," Skaag replied.

"Who is the Yellow King?"

"Our master," Skaag said, accompanying his words with a slight bow.

Billy jumped up from the couch and approached Skaag with clenched fists. "Give a straight answer, unless your Yellow King is the Tooth Fairy and he's willin' to replace the teeth I'm about to knock out!"

The familiar click of a hammer being drawn back stopped Billy. Jane had drawn her gun and pointed it at Skaag's head. "He's gonna be missin' more than a few teeth if he don't give us a name."

"I cannot," Skaag said with a calm that implied he feared Jane's gun no more than a bouquet of flowers.

"Why?"

"None say his name, lest he be called. To say his name is to summon him."

"You need to do something to earn our trust," Jules said. "We need to know who owns this house, who wants to help us. We need to know why we should accept the aid of one who strikes such fear in those who follow him."

Annie stared at Skaag. He was a freak with discolored skin, malformed teeth, and nasty hair in the service of some mysterious lord. A lord so dreaded that his very name was a blight to the tongue and ear. Annie knew the name. She had seen Howard write it in his journal, and could see it as clearly as if she held the page in front of her right now. "Hastur," she said.

All of the followers shrieked, a sound that curdled Annie's blood, yet she smirked. She was right. Turning on her heel, she exited the great room and went into a small sitting room. "Hastur!" she cried again.

Skaag followed Annie into the room, but stopped short of actually touching her. He closed the door and begged, "Miss Oakley, I beg you. Do not do this."

"Hastur!"

Vaporous air distorted the far wall. The stripes of the wallpaper flowed like the surface of a pond after so many pebbles had been thrown into it. Half the size of the wall, a face emerged from the center, gray and gnarled, a ghoul arising from a forgotten grave. Distorted and shifting, part of the flowing image, glowing yellow eyes opened and locked onto

Annie. Even through the rippling, the perniciousness of the jagged teeth in the lipless mouth was not lost when it spoke. "Who dare call my name? What fool requests an audience with me?"

Flopping to a prostrate position, Skaag demonstrated complete subservience. "My Lord, I insisted that she stop. I insisted that she not call upon you."

The walls perpendicular to the face began to ripple as well, emanating tendrils of smoke, a horrid mix of yellows and grays, the hues of disease and fester. As the ribbons of smoke squirmed like worms through a fresh corpse, they elongated and thickened, forming gnarled fingers upon crooked hands. They moved to either side of Annie, strumming the air around her. Shifting eyes looked to her. In a deep, gurgling voice Hastur asked, "You insisted? Humans are so quick to wish to meet their demise."

Fear percolated within her, but Annie tamped it down and did not react to the smoky fingers grabbing at her. Instead, she trusted her deductions about this mad place and said, "I wish to speak to you. Alone." After her last word, she glanced at the sniveling man on the floor next to her.

The undulating face continued to stare at Annie. The rippling made it even more menacing, but Annie stood firm, never once flinching. Decayed flaps of skin around the mouth twisted into what Annie assumed to be a smile. The glowing eyes peered down at Skaag and said, "Be gone, minion. Go forth and remind the others never to disturb me again, or I will suck the marrow from your bones."

"Yes, master," Skaag replied. He leapt to his feet and rushed out of the room. Before he closed the door, Annie caught a glimpse of Billy and Jules watching, trying to see past Skaag as he fled. Even Jane seemed concerned. The door closed. Annie was alone with the Yellow King.

Annie turned back to the yellow eyes and rictus and grasping fingers. With mirth in his voice, the King asked, "What form of madness possesses you?"

Ignoring his question, Annie got to the point, "I wish to make a deal."

The thing laughed, the haunting sound of corpses spinning in their graves. "What could you possibly offer me?"

"My celebrity."

The thing laughed again. "Human affairs hold no interest to me."

"I disagree. My friends and I have adversaries. Those adversaries have kidnapped two of my friends. You know this. You know this and you know what our adversaries are attempting to do—release a fiend more powerful than *you* from whatever prison holds it."

"I do know this."

"You've gone so far as to lend us use of your servants to assist us in thwarting our adversaries' plans. Why?"

"The—fiend, as you put it—they wish to release does pose a threat to my position within this world. I wish him nothing but failure, and will sacrifice more than your paltry mind could ever conceive to see him suffer."

"You're jealous."

The cloudy hands turned to fists while the sickly smog of his face darkened. "What?"

Annie knew that her safety was no longer a commodity she could purchase. Every second alone in this room with this being jeopardized her escape. She pushed the limits of this thing's patience. But she did so with only one final outcome in mind. "Your antagonist is closer to walking about this world than you are. It seems to me that if you can't walk about this world, then you wish to make sure that he does not either, so you assign your servants to assist us."

"Your point being?"

"My point is that after we rescue our friends and stop our adversaries from helping your antagonist, I can offer you a way to influence this world without walking it."

"How?"

"My fealty. I offer it to you."

The face scowled, making it even more nightmarish. The hands moved in front of Annie, clawed fingers curled, ready to shred her to strips of meat. "Maybe I should just take it now!"

Reaching deep into the recesses of her soul that she rarely had need to explore, Annie found the courage she sought. As effortlessly as swatting away a fly, Annie waved her right hand through the threatening apparition. As she suspected, just smoke. "You cannot, or you would have done so already. More specifically, you would have done so centuries ago, or however long this jealousy of yours has existed."

The Yellow King parted his hands and glared at Annie. "I have a house full of minions."

Annie shrugged. "It's obvious you wish for more than a mere houseful. Many more, or else you wouldn't bother having any in the first place. None of your disciples can travel to the local market. I travel across the country, every season of every year, and maybe the world, should fame and fortune escort me. As long as you don't wish to alter my appearance to that of a diseased banana, then I can spread the word of Hastur, help you build your following, your army, your country, to be ready should your adversary find release from his prison."

The face in the yellow and gray smog scowled. "Clever girl. What do you wish in return?"

"Accelerated transportation to our friends. Immediate if within your power."

"Why not allow my followers to take you? I would tell them where your friends are. Eventually."

"Eventually is not soon enough, and conventional methods of travel would do us little good. Our adversaries fled through a glowing portal, caused by either science or magic. I assume you have similar capabilities at your disposal."

"I do." The face and hands flowed across the room with the roiling smoke, as if trying to get a better vantage of Annie, but she kept turning in time, never taking her eyes off the Yellow King's face. "You are a foolish girl to trust one such as myself."

"Maybe I am. But I'm confident that you will abide by the conditions of our agreement. I know nothing about you, but what I have gleaned over these past few minutes is that you are bound by a set of laws. I do not know what they are or how they are enforced. All I know is if you and this other creature have both been denied access to this world, then that means that there is something, some form of power stopping you. I'm trusting that if you break your deal with me, there is some form of punishment for you."

The Yellow King remained silent, his face rippling.

Annie was not happy with any part of this. However, she knew that Howard understood this world of mysticism and dark dimensions, knew the rules and workings better than she. It was a risky wager, one based on guesswork, but she deemed it necessary to get Howard and Albert back. Once the greater evil was thwarted, she would divulge to Howard her dealings with this creature, and he would then be able to devise a way out of it. Until then, she said, "Do we have a deal?"

"We have a deal," the Yellow King said. Pronounced waves rippled through his expanding face as he extended his billowy claws. His smoky features darkened like storm clouds ready to let loose. "But never forget, just because I cannot walk the earth does not mean I cannot hurt you!"

In a flash, his face and claws rushed toward Annie. Out of reflex, she brought her arms up to protect her face and screamed. A searing pain burned through her left hand. The panic passed, and she was alone in the small sitting room, the walls displaying nothing more than striped wallpaper.

Checking her left hand to make sure it was still there, she saw three faint lines across her palm, yellow scratch marks. She curled her fingers into a fist, knowing that the marks signified the bond of the contract, and immediately wondered how big of a mistake she had just made.

Chapter 25

Albert awoke, the pain in his head dulling his sense of urgency to open his eyes. They burned as he blinked, tearing up and distorting his surroundings. He went to wipe them, but could not bring either hand to his face. As his consciousness returned, his wits followed. He tried to move but found his attempts futile; his arms and legs bound to each extension of a rack that formed an "X." His shoulders burned and ached from supporting the full weight of his body. Pushing as best he could with his spread legs, he alleviated the pressure across his shoulders, but a burgeoning fire grew in his thighs and lower back. Any respite from pain was all too brief.

Head untethered, he looked around the room. He was positioned upright, and for that small convenience he was thankful. Howard was to his left, trussed up on an "X" shaped rack as well. The racks were angled to face each other, but not directly in front of each other. Howard looked at Albert with a pained and miserable twist to his face, more pained and miserable than usual. He moaned, almost as if disappointed, "Well, we're still alive."

"Szilveszter wouldn't be able to torment us if we weren't," Albert replied.

"Too true," Howard added, voice weary. "Judging from our surroundings, he certainly plans on that."

Albert craned his head from one side to the other. The large room held two more such contraptions as he found himself harnessed to, as well as a horizontal rack, a metal stockade, and what he assumed to be an iron maiden. "A torture dungeon."

"Torture yes, dungeon no," Howard said. "The walls are paneled, and the floors are planked. The wall behind you is half hidden by a bookshelf. Also, behind you is what I believe to be the grimmest feature of the room, a large writing desk with papers scattered about it. From what I can see, they appear to be drawings and diagrams of the internal workings of the human body. I also see more than a few tomes pertaining to dark and arcane subjects."

Shifting his weight to move the dull throb from the base of his neck to his right hip, Albert said, "Am I to assume that the subjects of the books are what we wish to keep arcane?"

"You should assume that, yes," a man's voice said. "But anyone not wishing to learn the secrets within those pages is a fool and a coward."

Standing in the doorway was a man wearing a uniform—blue jacket with two rows of golden button down the front, crisp white pants, and polished black shoes. His round face sported a head capped by the fuzz of closely cropped hair and a thick mustache long enough to escape the confines of his chin. He had the posture of a soldier and the air of a dignitary. His accent was thick and sounded similar to Albert's. "My name is Alois Hitler, and I am your host."

"Always a pleasure to meet another servant of Szilveszter," Howard mumbled.

Hands clasped behind his back, Alois stepped farther into the room. "I must correct you, boy. Szilveszter and I are allies, as we both serve the same master."

"One of lies and chaos."

Alois' smile made his mustache twitch. "There is no greater truth in one's self than when faced with chaos. I intend to see the greatest liars of all burned from this Earth."

"Dare I ask who that might be, other than Szilveszter?"

Alois laughed at Howard's comment. "My new friend Szilveszter, he is true to himself. He has his own motivations for bringing forth our master."

"Your motivations? To wipe away these great liars you speak of?"

Alois's expression went as cold as a tombstone in winter, his voice equally as chilled. "The Jews. They have been a pustule on history's skin for thousands of years. I will gladly serve any master who would cleanse this world of them."

Albert knew Howard's prejudices were many and ran deep, though he never wished to know the depth. He also knew that Howard would do nothing to jeopardize the mission. However, a tiny doubt scampered through Albert's mind, wondering how Howard would react to being in the presence of a like-minded individual. Relief washed through Albert when Howard said, "So you're willing to raze the entire planet and commit genocide for one group of unsavories?"

"I prefer to think of it as creating an opportunity for the strong to survive."

"You don't believe the Jews are strong?"

Alois offered a sneer, causing the left tip of his mustache to dangle lower than the right. "Hardly. And they willingly admit that themselves. Throughout history they have depicted themselves as sympathetic, persecuted. If that is how they wish to be seen, then I wonder why anyone would argue to the contrary. Well, that has certainly been my experience."

To punctuate his statement, Alois turned to the doorway and clapped his hands. In walked a servant, using slow steps to carry a silver platter. He was dressed as any other butler or houseman, but his fineries were oversized and disheveled, mussed as if hurriedly assembled, a deliberate mockery to the man the servant once was. Like those who attacked Albert and his friends, the servant had the slack jaw of a dullard while his eyes bulged like a slow child trying to learn the simplest of concepts. A film of grease covered the man, creating a glimmering sheen in the light. Albert wondered if it was caused from days of no bathing, or it was a part of the nefarious transformation process, like the gaudy scar running from his right temple to the base of his neck.

The servant carried one item on the tray, a crystal goblet half filled with an amber liquid. Alois took the goblet without so much as a recognition of the servant's existence. Never taking his eyes off Albert and Howard, Alois took his time sipping the liquid.

Even though the liquid was most certainly liquor, watching Alois imbibe reminded Albert of how thirsty he was. Gazing at the goblet, he craved a splash, no matter how painful the resulting sting upon his tongue and throat would be. He tried to hide his desire, but failed.

Alois returned the goblet to the tray and muttered something to the servant. The wide-eyed caricature replied with a slight bow deep enough to release a string of drool that had been collecting in the right corner of his mouth. As the servant shuffled from the room, Alois moved closer to his captives. Hands behind his back, he said, "You think of me as a monster."

"One who cavorts with monsters usually is," Howard said. Visibly pained, he twisted his body as best he could in his quest for relief.

"The lion is strong," Alois said, "Don't you think? A majestic creature that takes what he wants from the weak, yet I doubt either of you would consider the great beast to be a monster."

"A lion doesn't revel in what it has to do," Albert replied. "Nor does it sacrifice its fellow lions or the surrounding environment for a meal."

The servant returned, still carrying the silver tray, this time with a carafe of water and an empty glass on it. Despite the dread and anger and physical pain he felt, Albert could not stop himself from looking at the carafe.

Alois filled the glass with water and brought it to Albert. With no form of gentleness, because this man seemed to possess none, Alois brought the glass to Albert's lips and sluiced the liquid into his mouth without spilling so much as a drop. Finished, Albert looked away as Alois moved on to Howard.

"See?" Alois said. "I am no monster."

After emptying the glass, Howard remarked, "Offering prisoners basic life-giving needs is hardly the high mark of civility."

"Prisoners? No. You are not prisoners. You are an audience. You will be the first to see how we usher in our master. You will be the first to see the new world he creates."

"We will also be the first to see flesh rend from your body and your bones turned to dust. That is the reward from your master."

Alois smiled as he returned the emptied glass to the servant's tray. "One of us is right, but I hardly think it matters who. All that matters is releasing our master."

Before either Albert or Howard could speak again, another man walked into the room. A young man, about Howard's age Albert guessed, over six feet tall with a thin mustache drawn by nature upon his upper lip. He surmised that this young man was Nikola Tesla.

"Alois? The machine is set up. Szilveszter asked that you have your minions escort our guests into the other room."

"Very well, Nikola," Alois replied. "Give me a moment to gather some servants."

Alois left the room, the bulge-eyed, slack-jawed servant in tow.

Nikola stepped closer, standing between Albert and Howard and looking from one to the other. "You know who I am."

"We do," Albert said, not even attempting to try a gambit in a game that he was losing.

"So, what Szilveszter has said about you two, and himself as well, coming from the future is true."

Albert clenched his jaw. He refused to answer even though Nikola probably had accurate knowledge. Howard chose to stare with a look somewhere between anguish and anger.

Face holding no emotion, Nikola said, "Fascinating."

"You are young and foolish," Howard blurted.

Nikola stepped closer, examining Howard. "I believe you and I are contemporaries in age."

"I have dealt with people like the ones you're dealing with now. I have seen the monsters that they're attempting to conjure."

Nikola kept staring at Howard's face. Studying. "Your face is long, like a horse. With an under bite that puts you in perpetual pout. I'm curious if this is the reason why you're such a fussy little snit."

"Fussy—?"

"I think a full-face beard should help with that. A thick one, too. Not some bushy animal like those bristly Russians. No, something thick, but well maintained. You have the potential to be regal."

"What are you even talking—?"

"You see, I went with something elegant, sleek, cunning," Nikola said, using his right hand to present his mustache to Howard. "I believe faces for the most part are indistinct. If you huddle a thousand people together, what stands out? What is memorable? Eye color? A pleasant smile? Jaw line, forehead, nose? No, these are important for one-on-one. I mean what makes an individual stand apart from a crowd?"

Albert tried to garner his attention. "Nikola, please."

Nikola would have none of it until he was finished. "It is the facial hair that makes a man stand out from a crowd of a thousand. Women, for the most part, have none. It is rare for a Chinaman or a negro as well. Yes, a white man's face is different than a colored man's or a woman's. But in a crowd of a thousand, how does one stand out?"

Albert understood the allegory, understood why Nikola was helping Szilveszter. "Nikola, there are better ways to stand out, to rise above, than assisting a madman."

Nikola finally looked at Albert, like he was a puzzle to solve. Hands fiddling together behind his back, he walked over to Albert. "They say you are from the future. Is it true that I work with Thomas Edison, and he steals my ideas? Is it true that he profits greatly from this? Is it true that I do not escape from his shadow?"

Albert tried to lie, but the acting talent needed surpassed the skills he possessed. The moment of hesitation was enough, and before he could say anything, Nikola chuckled. "To mindlessly follow that fate, I would call that madness."

"There are other ways, Nikola," Albert said.

"None more direct than this way. Now, if you'll excuse me, I have my machine to prepare."

Nikola left the room, and Albert could only mutter, "This is madness."

"Madness begets madness. What perplexes me is this Alois Hitler," Howard said, shifting as best he could within his bindings.

"How so?"

"Most everyone we have encountered during our experience in this time period we have recognized as an architect of our history. Or at least the history that we know."

"This is true."

"Those who have aided us have been looked at kindly through history's eyes, other than Billy. Even so, he could be considered a rapscallion, but not evil. Those who have aided Szilveszter? You and I know them to have a tenuous grasp on sanity at best."

Albert understood the point that Howard wished to make. "We do not know of this Hitler fellow. Maybe he does not fit into history's tale?"

Howard mustered a feeble chuckle. "You surely don't believe that, do you?"

Albert sighed; the action caused a streak of pain down his back from the base of his neck. "No. Sadly, I do not."

Albert pushed as best he could with his legs, making the slight relief it brought to his shoulders seem like an angel's kiss. His contortions allowed him a better view of the room. "We should use this time alone to formulate an escape plan."

Howard looked at his four restraints, one at a time with exaggerated intensity, and then said, "Sorry, no means of escape here. Plus," he paused to nod toward the door, "I fear our time alone is over."

In walked the servant they had seen before, face still frozen in stupefaction. A dozen more trundled in behind him, all looking indistinguishable from one another—dark hair matted to their faces from sweat and grease, breathing through their mouths as if their noses no longer functioned, and no spark of life within their eyes despite the fact they all bulged from proptosis. Unlike the drone in front, the others wore workman's clothes, the thick pants and long-sleeved shirts stained and tattered.

With blind obedience and single-minded purpose, the minions made their way to Albert and Howard. Less than dexterous, but able to succeed because of the numbers, the drones lifted and carried the structures the two men were strapped to out of the room. Howard complained of the tipping and barked orders not to drop him or bang him against a wall or doorway.

After a trek through two rooms and a hallway, they were finally delivered and set upright in a great room. It looked like any other great room of any mansion: spacious, decorative ovals of carpeting upon a polished wooden floor, chairs and sofas dedicated to comforting those accustomed to luxury, fireplace of intricately carved stone. However, most of the furniture had been moved to one end of the room to make space for a circular archway constructed of metal and tubes and wires. The tallest person in the room was Dr. Sivkas, and he could walk through it without needing to duck.

The minions shifted Albert and Howard so they could have a clear view of the archway. A few milled about while others followed the commands of Nikola as he fiddled with a typewriter-sized control panel on a nearby table. Connected to it and emitting a pulsating green glow was the tetrahedron of dark energy.

Albert's eyes widened. He hadn't realized the pyramid had been in Szilveszter's possession. The situation was much more dire than originally suspected.

Nikola worked the control panel. Needles fluctuated, and he adjusted the dials accordingly. Szilveszter stood next to him with the soft smile of a madman. Once the minions finished positioning Albert and Howard, he addressed his guests. "Ahh. How good of you to join us!"

Howard replied with an icy glare. Albert, however, could not pull his gaze away from the pyramid. Szilveszter's smile broadened. "You've noticed my tetrahedron? I appreciate that you brought it back to me. I don't believe I could release the master without it."

Frustration boiled within Albert, scalding greater than the pain in his shoulders. Any attempts to talk reason with Szilveszter would be futile.

He instead called to Nikola one more time. "Nikola! Stop! Stop what you are doing. You don't realize the destruction that you are inviting into our world."

Szilveszter quickly moved to Albert, his thin robes flowing behind him like a trail of black mist. The young man stopped within a foot of Albert, his smile sinewy and lecherous, stretched beyond what should be possible for a human face. His hand moved to his crotch, and as he spoke, he adjusted and pulled. "Yes, Albert, we are inviting chaos into our world, and when that happens, it will become my master's world, and he shall allow me to be a conductor for an orchestra of agony. The angelic voices of pain and suffering shall sing from the oceans of blood to the mountains of corpses. Those screaming voices shall be so beautifully wretched that Heaven itself shall collapse and crumble. God will give up and surrender his almighty throne to my master! It... will... be... glorious!"

Szilveszter clenched his teeth and shook with the satisfaction of sexual release. Albert reeled back as best he could within his restraints, and looked away in utter disgust. This was the true reason why he felt the soul-weighing need to stop Szilveszter. Tyranny, the desire for power, the want of man to lord over fellow man were abhorrent motivations, but understandable ones. But the vile level to where Szilveszter took the quest for power frightened Albert. The arousal and sexual gratification that came from the unmitigated torment of others

After his eyelids stopped fluttering, Szilveszter continued. "But we will not be using my pyramid to call forth the master quite yet. We have other plans to fulfill first."

"Wretched bastard," came from Howard. Albert agreed with the sentiment, but could not lend voice to it. He could do nothing more than seethe.

Szilveszter laughed as he walked to the archway. "See, Mr. Tesla here has developed an amazing portal, one that anyone can step through and end up anywhere else, which was how we so deftly captured you in Le Havre. Mr. Zarkahn was able to fold dimensions a few times to move us along quickly." Szilveszter gestured to the garishly dressed carnival magician. Zarkahn gave a slight bow, his smile just as thin and curled as his handlebar mustache. "But his range was limited, and the energy expenditure was too great. However, Mr. Tesla has invented this magnificent machine. Alas, it, too, has is a limit to the distance traveled, and the might of Dr. Sivkas is needed to crank the motor to generate a charge. But now, thanks to the return of my pyramid, we can travel the globe as easily as stepping through a door."

Szilveszter extended his arm to the archway, and on cue, Nikola started the machine. The air buzzed and crackled, blue arcs of electricity danced along the archway as Dr. Sivkas cranked the dynamo. Within the arch, the world rippled, the colors spun into a whirlpool blending together faster and faster. Once the spiraling colors formed a dull brown, the chromatic cyclone slowed, giving way to a different scene, a different room. A room that Albert was very familiar with—a room within his parents' house.

Chapter 26

Billy felt helpless. So did Jules and Jane, he could tell.

Jules, a curious fellow, continued to ask questions that received no answers, or enigmatic ones at best, until he made the yellowed man he conversed with uncomfortable to the point of giving a nervous smile, followed by a hasty retreat from the great room. Jane, on the other hand, asked no questions, content to stare at the closed door of the room Annie had gone into, while pacing back and forth, drinking whatever wine the hosts had offered straight from the carafe. Billy neither paced nor interrogated. He simply leaned against one of the walls with his arms crossed over his chest. Waiting. Watching.

No one liked the idea of Annie talking to a "master" who wielded enough power to make those who follow him into such worrisome yellowed men. Skaag, the mouthpiece of the followers, also paced back and forth, muttering to himself while looking at the door as if he could see the happenings on the other side of it. Billy didn't like him, didn't like any of the yellow freaks one bit. But it was Skaag who really riled him. He hoped before this adventure was over, he would have an opportunity and necessity to shoot at least one of them.

The hosts allowed Billy to keep his six-shooters strapped on. Even though there was no sign of immediate need, they comforted him. Jane had hers on too, as well as that elephant blaster in the other room she had acquired during the boat ride from the States. She snatched her third carafe of wine from a yellowed freak as soon as he entered the room with it. Her aim had always been precise, even when Billy thought her to be skunk drunk, so he had no true worries about her at the moment. Plus, she provided the only source of mirth right now; her face twisting in soured disgust with every large gulp of wine, clearly too sweet for her whiskey palate. He debated about talking to her, but considered the dalliance on the ship and decided against it.

Annie screamed.

Billy rushed to the door. Skaag reached for the knob, but withdrew his hand quickly and cradled it, mewling like a simpering child as if the knob had burned him. Jane and Jules gathered around the door as well. Other yellowed men took notice, but none moved from the safety of the farther ends of the great room.

Billy went for the door, but Skaag moved to block him. "Please. Please, I beg you, do not go in there. Do not disturb the master."

"He's your master, not mine," Billy drew one of his guns, but didn't aim it. Instead, he held it low and cocked the trigger. "This is your only warnin'. Move out of my way. You should have a real good idea what the 'or else' will be."

Skaag still forced a smile, now quaking as a single tear rolled down his cheek. Before he could beseech anything more from Billy, the door opened.

Annie exited, showing no sign of muss or fuss, her expression the picture-perfect definition of control and grace. "Now, Billy, there is no need for such brutish threats. Even though I most certainly appreciate the concern, I can handle a simple conversation."

"Master!" The word burst from Skaag's mouth as if he had been holding it all day and could do so no longer. He ran into the room and shut the door behind him. No one paid any mind to his actions, all eyes on Annie.

Billy holstered his gun, but was still worried about Annie's so-called conversation. "We heard a scream. We heard you scream."

Annie smiled and made a shooing gesture with her hand. "The Yellow King gave me a start, nothing more."

Addressing the yellowed servants, Annie then said, "I'm parched. Could you be so kind as to fetch me some water? And some of those adorable little finger sandwiches, too, please."

The yellowed ones who had been milling about left the room, set out with a new purpose. No one spoke until all the yellowed men were out of the room. Jules was the first to do so. "My dear girl, are you certain you are unharmed?"

"Mr. Verne, I assure you that I am fine."

Despite Annie's glowing smile, Billy noticed that she twitched her left hand and casually moved it behind her leg. He didn't think it wise to address that now, so he let Jules continue with his questions. "What did you discover?"

"That with everything involving power, those who do not wield it are mere pawns."

"Huh?" Jane asked, twisting her face.

Billy caught the general gist of Annie's statement. He expected Annie to hurl a sharp-tongued insult at Jane, but with an even tone, she explained, "It appears that the master of our yellow hosts is at odds with Szilveszter's master."

"Ah. All kings are the same, no matter what shape, size, or dimension they are from," Jules said.

"So, what'd you two talk about?" Billy asked.

"Well, I deduced that this Yellow King cares very little about the happenings of man, or we would have seen his influence earlier. He wishes to disrupt the progress of Szilveszter's master. So, I implored his aid to help us locate Howard and Albert."

"At what expense?"

Annie smiled, but Billy caught a slight quiver in her chin. "In the grand scheme of things, very little."

The servants returned with the requested food and water. Annie accepted what they had to offer with a smile. "Thank you."

Billy watched her snack and drink. The air of bravado she displayed was false, proved by her sudden jerk when Skaag opened the door and reentered the room. As humble as ever, he said, "If you will please excuse us, my brethren and I must prepare the transportation that Miss Oakley has secured for you."

All the yellowed men bowed in unison and followed Skaag from the great room.

Jane took long pulls from the carafe and eyed the yellowed men until they all left. "I don't understand why they're so scared. The King in Yellow didn't seem to bother you none."

"Oh, I assure you the Yellow King is just as vile, if not more so, than the creature from the cave."

"Then how the hell are you remainin' so calm?"

Annie flashed a wicked smile and purred, "What? Are you worried about my well-being?"

Jane reeled back harder than if Annie had spat in her face. Billy was fairly confident that Jane would have preferred that, because she would know how to respond—a punch to the mouth. Words were a difficult weapon for Jane to wield, let alone parry. "I need to be drunker than this to step in your horse shit." With that, she turned and aimed for the kitchen.

Clearing his throat, Jules said, "I'm still a bit peckish. I think I'll join Jane in the kitchen."

After they left the room, Billy shook his head and turned to Annie. "You know, you can be awful mean to her."

Annie smacked her lips against her fingers, cleaning away any remains of the finger sandwiches. "She can be awfully mean to me. As can you."

"Me?" Billy asked, so surprised his voice almost cracked. "What'd I do?"

As the question fell from his lips, he immediately wished for some way to catch it. He swore he even heard the words thud on the ground. But there was no way to erase what he had said, nor ease the sting from Annie's follow up. "What'd you do? I mean, nothing, really, I suppose. Although, after disembarking from the ship until now, I'm a little surprised that I haven't seen more affections from the happy couple. Just out of curiosity, have you two decided on any particular pet names for each other yet? Perhaps wedding bells in the future?"

Billy put his hands in his pockets and looked to the floor for a comeback, or a way to change the conversation. What happened with Jane on the boat should have no bearing on Annie, but he could hardly say that. Or could he? He lifted his head and looked her square in the eye as he asked, "What should it matter to you anyway?"

For the first time during the conversation, Annie looked surprised. Upper hand potentially fleeting, Billy pressed on. "I am an unmarried adult. Jane is an unmarried adult. What we did, we did behind closed doors. If I ain't mistaken, you had mentioned that you are all but engaged to a fella back home. So, why is what happened on the boat so stuck in your craw?"

Annie crossed her arms over her chest, but more in the way of hugging herself. She lowered her eyes and turned away from Billy. "I'm not exactly as betrothed as I said I was."

"So, why do you say that you are when you ain't?" Billy asked.

Annie shrugged, still looking away. "Lots of reasons, I reckon. It makes me feel complete, less alone. It gives me a goal to work for. It reduces the number of advances I receive from suitors, yet there are those who still pursue and they…" Annie paused just long enough to look back to Billy and lock eyes, "… are usually more rakish. Exciting. Tantalizing. Offering the forbidden fruit that we all know to be the most delicious."

One. Two. Three. Billy's heart beat four times before he pulled her to him for a kiss. Their lips moved together with an outpouring of emotions churned up from their journey; their bodies pressed together with the desperation of two people trying to cling to what little sanity they had left. Despite being absorbed by the softness of her lips and the ferocity of her tongue, Billy felt all ten of her fingers dig into his back as her arms trembled. He pulled her tighter, hoping to convey that she was safe; that he would protect her, even though he knew fully well she was capable of protecting herself.

They both jumped and separated when a door squeaked open. The yellowed men entered the great room from one end while Jane and Jules entered from the other. Billy could tell by everyone's expressions that the yellowed men did not witness what had just happened, but Jules and Jane did. Jules wore a smile of rapt intrigue, as if caught up in the plot of a stage play, while Jane scowled at Annie. A soft blush colored Annie's cheeks as she gently, but poignantly, used her thumb to wipe her lips, while a smirk tugged at them.

Billy's stomach flopped. Had he been used again, just a token to be slid back and forth across a board set between two women playing some devious and enigmatic game of jealousy? Was this game—he, himself—proving to be a distraction to the greater mission at hand?

Skaag cleared his throat to garner everyone's attention. "Our master asked for us to prepare rides to take you to your friends. Now, if you please, follow me."

They did as asked, Jane and Annie ignoring each other, while Jules came up behind Billy and mirthfully whispered to him, "I admire the exuberance of youth, and yet so envy your ability to follow through with it."

Billy would have gladly switched places in life with the older man, preferring the comforts of wealth and stability over the torrent of adventures without a map, the whirlpool of uncertainty swirling his mind. Jane had used him, this he knew. It was a night of booze and urges, a type of night he had experienced many times back home. But Annie? He had a difficult time accepting the idea that she had used him. Her words were pure and truthful. She had clung to him like he was salvation. She was a woman, though, and a clever one at that. Billy could not fathom what fueled the inner mechanisms of women.

He bumped his elbow against a roughly hewn stone wall, and fissures of pain rippled through his arm. When did they start down a flight of stairs leading through cut rock? Skaag and a few of the other yellowed men carried lit torches. Billy admonished himself for his lack of concentration. When they reached the bottom of the stairs, he wished he could go back to being oblivious of his surroundings.

An expansive room of cut rock. Billy wondered how a room this large could exist underground, but then the odors of feces and urine, festering meat and rotten vegetables assaulted him, and he pulled his handkerchief from his back pocket. He was going to use it for himself, but instead gave it to Annie, draping it over the lower half of her face and tying two of the corners together behind her head. Both Jane and Jules had their own handkerchiefs and did the same thing. Billy pulled the top of his shirt over his nose. Not happy that he needed the smell of his own sweat to mask the other odors, but it would have to do. Now, if he could only do something to muffle the unnerving noises.

He and his associates huddled closer together, not straying by even a footstep from behind the yellowed men as they went deeper into the room, cleaving the darkness with their torches. Animal noises echoed in the blackness beyond the torch light, a mixture of grunts and snorts, groans and warbles. Bursts of shrieking excitement erupted to the left; a guttural yawn reverberated from the right. Billy tried to keep his eyes straight ahead, fighting against his perverse urge to look to either side. During the briefest of glimpses, he made out the rusted iron of evenly spaced bars and saw the movement of dark flesh—or scales or fur?—scraping against the other side.

"Almost there," Skaag said as an attempt to comfort, but the enthusiasm behind the statement made the situation all the more unsettling. But his words were true. After fewer than a dozen paces, the yellowed men split into different directions and rested their torches in sconces embedded into the stone walls, lighting the room.

The room was circular, with a dozen cages lining the walls. Ahead was one large gate, made of the same time-worn iron bars as the cages. As the other yellowed men worked the locks of a few cages or fussed with the gate, Skaag stood in the center of the room and addressed his guests. "These are our stables. Our master has ordered us to prepare your steeds."

"Steeds?" Annie asked. "Do you mean horses?"

Skaag gave an effeminate laugh akin to a titter. "No. Horses do not possess the speed or endurance necessary to take you where you need to go. Instead, you will be riding byakhee."

"Be what?" Jane asked.

The yellowed men answered her question by leading four of the creatures to the center of the room. Billy couldn't stop himself from trembling.

"No," Annie whimpered. "No. No. No. No. No."

"Good God in Heaven," fell from Jules' mouth.

Jane drew one of her guns and used two hands to aim it. "What the fuck are those?"

"No! Don't shoot!" Skaag pleaded as he jumped in front of Jane. "They are harmless. Steeds. Simple steeds, as I have said."

Billy looked at the byakhee and could not fathom how Skaag's words could be true. Over eight feet long, each byakhee was shaped like a giant stinging insect, a hornet or yellow jacket with leathery wings. Instead of mandibles, they had jaws that opened and closed to show a barbed tongue and jagged teeth. They walked upon thick, jointed legs with long talons jutting from the ends, looking too much like hands in Billy's mind. Horns for antennae, the byakhee also had animal eyes, black and inky, yet holding an intelligence unbefitting their appearance.

"No. No. No. No," Annie kept muttering.

Looking nervous, Skaag skittered over to her and whispered, "Miss Oakley, you made a deal with my master. This is his end of the bargain."

Billy overheard and turned to Annie. "Deal?"

Annie looked at Billy with an expression that begged for forgiveness, her eyes glistening with the start of tears. She then closed her eyes and trembled as she inhaled deeply. When she opened them, her stark focus returned, no threat of tears, not even the slightest shiver. She turned to Skaag and said, "They can get us to where we need to go? Quickly?"

Skaag smiled, pleased. "Yes. Yes, they can. Less than an hour."

"And you and your yellowed men are coming with us."

As coyly as if receiving an unexpected compliment, Skaag shook his head and said, "No. This is not our—"

"That was neither a question nor a request," Annie snapped, a forcefulness in her voice Billy hadn't heard before. "You said yourself that your master wished for you to do whatever it took to aid us. One can assume that the men we encountered earlier today will be there, and we need to meet them in kind with numbers. Your numbers."

Skaag's smile faded and he bowed. "My apologies. You are correct. We shall prepare more steeds."

The yellowed men opened more cages and added more saddles, simple in shape, designed to keep the rider mounted, but lacking any form to control the beast.

The squeal of aged metal against metal echoed through the room as two of the yellowed men winched open the large gate, revealing a ramp that led upward. A way to the outside world. Cool air rushed into the room and made the stench less oppressive. Billy let the top of his shirt fall and he took a few deep breaths, trying to come to terms with what he had to do. Annie pulled out Howard's notebook and after writing the word "byakhee," she proceeded to draw an illustration of the wretched beasts.

Chapter 27

Howard's shoulders hurt. As a relatively young man at twenty, and one who rarely subjected his body to the rigors of manual labor, he should have been much more limber and spryer. However, since he eschewed recreational exercise, opting to run or swim only when chased, and had no formal training from any kind of armed service, he was not physically prepared to be strapped to a rack

Sure, many people would prefer this form of torture over what Howard usually immersed himself in—ferreting out dark dimensions and consorting with the horrid creatures that inhabited them. Right now, he would take the mental abuse of a lost night of sleep due to chronicling the movements of fish people aboard a cruise ship to one more minute of this sheer agony.

Flexing the muscles in his legs and hips in hopes of taking some of the pressure off his shoulders, he looked around this new room. Large. Rectangular. Decorated with an homage to warfare: paintings of gory battles hung on the wall as did all types of swords and shields. The furniture was pushed to one end where a dozen of the gape-mouthed lackeys sat and assembled nodules of spooled copper wire, small batteries, and prongs. The nodules were half the size of a fist, and Howard estimated two hundred of them were lying about while the servants worked on making more. What were they? What purpose did they serve? Szilveszter's blathering offered no useful information.

Howard regarded him with a stare reserved for the most wretched and despicable. If Szilveszter had simply been a young man who ignorantly dabbled with things he did not understand, attempting to quench his thirst of curiosity, Howard would have been almost able to forgive him. But Szilveszter's evil belied his years, the atrocities he'd committed by such a young age, the same age as Howard, surpassed those of most ruthless tyrants. Even despots craved some form of order—only a scant few truly reveled in the suffering of others. Another human being's screams were an aphrodisiac to Szilveszter. Yet, he somehow convinced others to join his nefarious plans.

Nikola and Dr. Sivkas worked in tandem to bring electric life to a metal archway, and the cold hand of terror plucked at Howard's nerves like harp strings when Nikola started his machine. Szilveszter's plan was coming to fruition. As the world within the archway reduced to nothingness and reformed, Howard struggled against the ropes that bound him, hoping beyond hope to find failure in even one cord. No such weakness was there, and Szilveszter now had a doorway to Albert's childhood room, with unfettered access to the baby found within it.

Albert yelled at him in German, but his words, no matter the language spoken, fell impotent. Pontificating about the impending new world order, Szilveszter strolled to the edge of the portal, but before he could cross the threshold, a screeching noise caught the attention of everyone in the room.

A frayed thread of hope poked away from the tapestry of evil. Howard wished to pull on it, but dared not to yet, afraid of snapping it. The noise happened again, this time being more obvious that it came from an animal. The thread of hope seemed sturdier as Szilveszter and Alois looked to each other, both men clearly expecting the other to know the answer to the unasked question of, "What was that noise?"

It was Nikola who stated the obvious. "It sounds quite like an animal, doesn't it?" The screech happened again, and Nikola followed up with, "It sounds like it's getting closer."

"Yes, it does, doesn't it," Szilveszter said, his words laced with frustration. "Mr. Hitler?"

Alois turned to his minions. He snapped his fingers repeatedly as he yelled at them in German. Half of them jumped from where they sat, abandoning their projects, and rushed from the room toward the mysterious noises. Alois continued speaking to the remaining minions, their myopic expressions making them seem surprised and attentive. Their new task was packing the nodules into their burlap bags.

Szilveszter stood at the precipice of the nursery like a grim reaper, staring at the wooden crib and the child within. With a growl of frustration, Szilveszter turned away from the artificial doorway and snapped, "Dr. Sivkas! You and Tesla open a doorway to our secondary location. We will go to Turkey first and capture the baby later. Zarkahn! Go fetch Madame Sulola! If we need to flee, I want everyone to be prepared."

Szilveszter and Alois chattered about potential plans like two witches concocting a potion. Albert exhaled a sigh of relief. Indeed, Howard was pleased with the turn of events; any upheaval in Szilveszter's plans was fortuitous. However, monsters were needed to fight monsters. The harrowing screech from outside the room told him that whatever creature it came from was not born of this dimension. Was this new creature sent to aid them? If so, which monster sent it?

Something was vexing Szilveszter, and that would have to be good enough for now. A forlorn look fell upon Albert's face as the scene of his childhood room disappeared, simultaneously taking and preserving the memories found within it. Dr. Sivkas and Nikola operated the control panel of the archway while Szilveszter and Alois fussed at the mindless servants to move faster. The fussing stopped when a scream ripped through the mansion. A human scream.

The scream came from a man, and, even though one of agony, it still had a soullessness about it. These poor wretches not only played the part of slave, but cannon fodder as well. Alois barked orders to the remaining servants and they, too, left the room upon completing the task of packing the nodules.

Szilveszter scowled and looked to Alois. "Troops in battle need a battlefield commander. This is your house, after all."

The two men stood eye to eye, sharing the same stern expression. Alois finally folded. "You are correct, Herr Matuska." With a bow, Alois turned to leave the room, but not before arming himself with a saber he pulled from a wall mount.

Szilveszter turned to Howard and Albert, the fire in his eyes suggesting he believed they possessed knowledge of the happenings in the other room. Howard had no idea, but refused to let Szilveszter know that. Instead, he issued a slight smirk, and garnered the reaction he was hoping for—the lines in Szilveszter's face deepened. He began to approach his captives, but stopped short when gun shots rang out from the other room. He fidgeted with his robes as noises of a large skirmish filled the air. Howard liked that.

Szilveszter rushed to Dr. Sivkas and Nikola, joining them at the control panel. "Have you entered the coordinates?"

"Finishing that now," Nikola said, turning the dials, aligning arrows to numbers.

"We must hurry."

"Done." To prove the truth of his statement, he grasped the lever and pulled. The archway hummed as tiny arcs of electricity skittered over it.

The noises from the other room jumbled together. Shouts and moans and grunts and squeals. More animal shrieks, Szilveszter wincing after every one. Familiar voices rang within Howard's ears; both Jane and Billy could be heard, their typical raucous nature dominating. He heard the baritone of Jules' voice as well. Howard longed to hear one more voice. Even though he would wish her away from such a scenario if he had the means, hearing her voice meant that she was still alive, still healthy and capable of participating in such a maelstrom.

There! He heard her. Even though it was a shout of some sort, it was done with authority, and he now knew she was unharmed.

Zarkahn raced into the room followed by Madame Sulola. "It's them."

"Impossible," Szilveszter spat. "Impossible!"

"It's those yellowed abominations that helped them in Le Havre," Zarkahn said. "There are giant insect beasts with them."

"Bah!" Szilveszter said, looking toward the archway, now displaying a different room within its perimeter. "Byakhee. No doubt given to them by the so-called Yellow King."

Upon hearing those words, the marrow in Howard's bone froze as his veins now sluiced ice water. For the first time since waking up, his bindings no longer hurt.

Chapter 28

Jane fought with her steed. She knew the creature she had mounted was the furthest thing from a horse, but she thought of it as a steed nonetheless, needing some form of familiarity within this cyclone of strange. She wondered if it was really worth it, really worth the effort to prove that she was the best gunslinger, to leave her home—hell, her country—to follow her competitor across the ocean. Now she found herself riding a... a... thing... resembling a giant insect with long, bat-like wings through the night skies of Europe. But every time she glanced over to Annie Oakley, she saw the pretty, pretty girl sitting straight and tall, as prim and proper as riding a show mare during a judged competition. She rode the thing with ease, and this annoyed Jane. However, whereas Annie was content simply to let the beast fly, Jane wanted more control over hers.

The harness system was simplistic. Not a saddle of any kind, but a weave-work of thick straps, looping at places to put her feet and ending with two pommels for her to hold on to. Jane sat forward and extended her legs back, causing the straps to tighten around the beast. This caused the pommels to dig into the creature's skin, allowing Jane to exert more control when she tilted the pommels to the right or left. Of course, the flying creature took great exception to this.

The byakhee flew straight, but turned its head to snap its jaws at Jane. Jane snapped back, "Well, go right when I tell you to go right, ya damn mongrel! Now go left!"

Jane tilted the pommels to the left. The creature looked over its other shoulder now and reached back with its left claw, fingerlike talons reaching for Jane. She swatted the claw away and yelled, "Quitchyer bitchin' and work with me!"

After another angry shriek, the byakhee finally acquiesced and banked hard left. It then did three revolutions of a barrel roll, to which Jane squealed, "Yee-ha!"

Once she straightened her steed out, Billy hollered from behind her, "Woo-yeah! Nice flyin'!"

"There ya go!" Jane said to her ride as she patted its head. "That's more like it."

The byakhee gave a satisfied chirp, and continued to follow Jane's commands as she tested the ways to guide her steed. Up and down, faster, slower, she felt very satisfied that she could control her beast while everyone else, especially Annie, sat passively on theirs. She even got her steed to buzz closely over the head of Skaag, much to his consternation. Jane didn't like the creepy yellow fellow much, so his worrisome words were like music to her ears.

Confident that the creature knew where it was going, she commanded it to go faster. She wanted to be the first one there, to see if she could find Albert and Howard. She hoped they were both still alive and unharmed.

She growled at herself. Who was she trying to fool? Her being here went well beyond some petty feud with a pretty girl. Albert and Howard were good men fighting an evil few knew existed. Sure, she liked to flirt with Albert, because it made him uncomfortable. Great joy came from making grown men blush! But his willingness to face dangers so others didn't have to was admirable. She wasn't sure if Howard was a dandy or not, and his fussiness was irksome, but in the end, he wanted to do the right thing. Their zeal drew Jules right into their orbit. He was old enough to be her father, and had a disarming calm about him. Maybe it was because he wrote books about such adventures that he was so prepared to take them? Maybe he had been on plenty already, source material for his tales of the fantastic? Jane appreciated him and vowed that if he wasn't offended by her presence after mission's end, she would learn more about him. Billy, on the other hand, seemed to be the concept of adventure in human form. He was a fun tussle between the sheets, but that wasn't a unique experience. All she knew were men like Billy. But there was something different about him. Quick to care, to use his guns against those who sought to harm others and himself as a shield. Jane slapped herself across the face, angry that she was doing the one thing she actively tried not to do since Hickok. She was caring. Caring always led to pain.

A mansion atop a hill rolled into view as Jane's steed sliced through the air. Staying high above it, she saw men patrolling the grounds. From this height, they were small and insignificant, ignorant of her presence above them. She had an idea and guided her steed back to the group.

Gliding up next to Skaag, who reflexively pulled away when she approached, Jane asked, "These things strong?"

Skaag offered a placating smile and said, "Ms. Cannary, these wondrous creatures were born from the pits of—"

Jane cut him off with, "I'll take that as a yes. There's a mansion on a hill, past that group of trees there. I want y'all to follow me."

Jane led the way. Without so much as a word of what her plan was, she thought it would be better to show everybody. Sliding around the back of the mansion, she hovered toward the center of the roof. Once the rest of the group caught up, she showed them her plan.

Pushing forward on her pommels, Jane yelled, "Sick it, boy! Get it!"

The creature understood her intent, aiming for the bottom of the pitched roof. With a ferocity mimicked by Jane's yelling, the creature tore and bit at the roof, shredding the wood and shingles. It had formed a hole to the attic by the time the others arrived. Amidst the whoops and hollers from Jane and Billy, the dozen byakhee breached the mansion with ease. They crawled inside and along the walls and ceiling.

The insect-like creatures scurried around the attic, a few crawled along the ceiling. Jane drew her gun. One hand was enough to control her steed. "Do it again!"

The byakhee used its front claws to dig at the wooden floor. The others joined in, quickly creating a hole. Again, once the opening was large enough, they scurried through, along the walls and across the second-floor ceiling. However, this time their actions did not go unnoticed.

They found themselves in a large room. Jane assumed it was a study from the desks, chairs, tables, and filled bookshelves lining the walls. One man stood in the middle of the room, a blank look upon his face. He looked very much like one of the attackers in Le Havre, the ones who had abducted Albert and Howard. Instead of a scream, the man released a panicked moan as he shambled from the room. A few of the byakhee let loose shrieks and gave chase.

Jane found herself in the middle of the pack, mindful of her arms and legs as the creatures jostled with each other to get through the doorway as quickly as possible. A byakhee mounted by a yellowed man in front of her caught the prey. The man screamed this time, soulless but in great pain.

The creature ripped through wet meat and gulped down as much as it could before two other byakhee joined in the bone-snapping feeding. Jane tilted one of the pommels to turn her steed; it heeded her command.

The study led to a second-floor landing, a long walkway with a white banister that was more decorative than protective. On either side, a curving staircase led to a grand foyer, pristine marble floor gleaming. More of the wide-eyed, mouth-gaped men flooded into the foyer.

The byakhee all screeched as they skittered to the first floor. Jane's crawled along the wall, making it difficult for her to guide it. Not being one to use a challenge as an excuse, she fired at the men anyway. Four shots, three hits. She was upset that she missed one, and that two of the men were still able to move.

The wave of enemy attackers slammed into the yellowed men and their mounts on the first floor. Sharpened claws clacked against the marble floor. Jaws snapped open and closed as the monsters met the men. Armed with only their hands and numbers, the dull-minded men fought hard. A single byakhee could rend a man to gory strips like ripping apart a slop-filled rag doll, but it had a difficult time fending off multiple attackers. A team of men overwhelmed a byakhee and its yellowed rider, both swept under by the crashing wave of flesh. Two yellowed men commanded their mounts to dive onto the pile. The act was met with limited success. As torn body parts flew through the air, the numbers of minions dwindled, but not quickly enough. Within the span of a few anguished screams, both byakhee were felled and their riders found themselves in blood-soaked skirmish, flailing in panic.

"Don't let them swarm!" Jules bellowed.

"More are coming!" Billy yelled, shooting as another dozen men ran into the room.

Jane, as with her comrades, tried to stay along the perimeter, away from the chaotic melee in the center of the room. In between firing shots into the crowd, she glanced into every room, but then saw Zarkahn and Madame Sulola running down one of the hallways. "There! Szilveszter is nearby!"

"I see them!" Annie yelled back. "Dismount!"

Jane wanted to argue, but understood her reasoning; the byakhee would be too difficult to control should they find themselves in a situation demanding more finesse. No sooner had she dismounted, than the creature scuttled to the fighting, quickly disemboweling one of the empty-faced men and burying its face in his entrails.

As much as Jane hated to admit it, even if it was just to herself, she was impressed with how Annie handled the situation, moving forward while ignoring the carnage around her. Jane hardly believed herself to be a person who fell weak to queasiness, but the gouts of blood squirting around like crimson geysers mixed with the sounds of hungry animals tearing into their still-living meals moved her stomach in unpleasant ways. Jules and Billy both looked a bit green around the gills too as they followed Annie to a door at the end of the hall.

A man with hair like peach-fuzz exited the room. Jane and Billy drew their guns, training them on his face.

Stopping short, the man fixed his uniform and then put both hands on top of his head to show no resistance. His thick mustache did nothing to hide his sinister smile as he said, "You are too late."

Not taking kindly to his cryptic threat, Jane hauled off and slugged him across the jaw. He fell to the floor, slumped against the wall.

"Annie!" Howard screamed from inside the room. "Hurry!"

Annie led the charge into the room; Jane and the men following close behind. Howard and Albert were strapped to stockades and yelled, "Szilveszter! Don't let Szilveszter escape!"

Szilveszter and his cabal stepped through a metal archway that cast a glow the same shade of green as found swirling in the tetrahedron. The little pyramid filled with black and green liquids was now attached to the archway by wires and being held by a tall, thin man as he followed Szilveszter through the archway. Jane was confounded. When she looked at the archway, she did not see the other side of the room, but instead a whole different room. Once the tall, thin man crossed the threshold, he turned and looked outward. He cranked a dial on a handheld machine, also attached to the archway. The humming from the archway intensified, as did the brightness of the glow. Crackling ribbons of electricity danced furiously along the entire metal arch. The glowing green expanded, separating itself from the metal and becoming larger than the archway, until it was its own archway, larger than the metal one.

"Stop him!" Howard yelled.

Out of reflex, Jane aimed and shot. The bullet hit the back wall of the room. The archways—both the metal one and the glowing green one—were gone, as well as everyone in the other room.

Jane missed. She could have ended this madness, but she was too late.

Chapter 29

Heinrich Schliemann stood at the edge of the mound, the short grasses barely reaching above the toes of his boots. He stood upon the Hisarlik site and looked down at the city of Çanakkale below, the people nothing more than specks of dirt moving among the squat, square buildings. Twenty thousand of those specks lived in the city, making their daily lives in one form or another from the ports suckling at the Dardanelles.

With his left hand, he held a small plate, just large enough to support a cup of tea. As he brought the cup to his lips, he admired the majesty of nature. An explosion from behind him shook the entire mound; puffs of dust settled around him as a few pebbles bounced through the grass. Nature was fine, but the impact of well-placed dynamite was something else entirely.

He noticed that some of the people-specks from Çanakkale stopped moving, undoubtedly looking up to Hisarlik and wondering about the explosion in the distance. He sneered at them.

After placing his cup back onto the saucer, he used his thumb to gently dab away the splash of tea from his upper lip. For good measure, he ran his fingers along his mustache—both tips curling upward—and then adjusted his stovepipe hat, since the force of the explosion had knocked it askew. There were no screams of pain or anguish or anger coming from behind him, so he concluded that his men must have set the charges in the proper spots. He went back to sipping his tea.

Heinrich savored his beverage for another hour while he continued to look upon Çanakkale in front of him. Behind him, his crew of men cleared away the debris from the explosion, chattering away in their native tongue. He paid them well enough that they wouldn't stab him in the back or pilfer any prizes they found, but not so well as to ward off the complaints. They bemoaned the job, long periods of nothingness while Heinrich calculated the locations to plant the explosives, followed by periods of the intense manual labor involved with removing the rock they had just blown through. But what they mumbled about behind his back the most was what he was doing to this site. Most of the local workers felt that he desecrated this place. Each explosion gouged deeper into the mound, devastating a chunk of earth and blowing away a layer of history with it. He didn't care what they thought, because this was his site. This was his discovery.

This was Troy.

The right to dig here was granted to him by the landowner and his partner, Frank Calvert. The Turkish government had revoked his permission to dig a couple of years prior. He was content to let that decision be the reason why he moved on—there were plenty of other lost and forgotten civilizations to plunder. But after discovering the Mask of Agamemnon at a recent dig in Mycenae, he decided to ask the Turkish government for permission to return. They granted it, and he found his way back to this site earlier in the year.

Every day brought him closer to what he sought, to what he knew was deep within this ground he stood upon. It called to him the way a lost child would call out for a parent. Today would be the day he would find it. Today he would accept his prize with open arms.

"Heinrich?" came from behind him. His wife, Sophia.

Turning, he smiled at her. Thirty years younger, her sloped nose mixed with her downward smile made her look simultaneously sad and duplicitous. Two dozen ropes of gold, each longer than the prior, covered her chest from the base of her neck to her bosom. A shawl of gold wrapped around her head, holding the bun of black hair atop her head. Two tassels draped from either side, long enough to reach past her shoulders. There was a hint of concern in her voice and a look of worry upon her brow. "Yes, my dearest?"

"We have… guests?"

Guests were reserved for house calls, not for digging around the top of a hill. He tilted his head, a silent request for her to explain. She simply gazed to the motley crew standing by the mine entrance. So unusual, they would look out of place no matter where they stood, especially at the top of a grassy hill. Even the workers paused from their duties.

Not sure what to make of this, Heinrich handed his cup and saucer to Sophia and marched over to the interlopers. On his way, he shouted at the hired help to get back to work.

When Heinrich came within earshot, the smiling man in thin black robes standing in front of the pack said, "Good day, Mr. Schliemann. I trust your expedition is going well?"

"If you're with the government, I assure you that all the paperwork is in order and—"

The man's laughter cut Heinrich short. "I assure you I represent no government, Mr. Schliemann. In fact, I represent something much greater."

"Then what…?" Heinrich began, but trailed off when he saw the four others accompanying the young man.

As pleasant as introducing new friends, Szilveszter said, "I am Szilveszter Matuska and these are my associates. May we go inside your tent to talk?"

Not knowing what else to do and having many, many questions, Heinrich gave a curt nod. Szilveszter led the way and the others followed, Heinrich keeping close watch on them all, especially the large man with a jar instead of a head. Heinrich had read about clockwork creations made to resemble humanity, and wondered if this was some form of experimentation. The accompanying two men were a sight as well—one dressed like a sideshow magician while the other was lanky with a thin mustache. The woman wore head-to-toe veils, easily obscuring any form of mechanics if she were the one controlling the human-shaped machination. Yes, Heinrich resigned himself to believe that was all this thing was—a work of new technology, nothing more.

Each member of the small group carried with them a large sack, bulging in various areas. Clearly the sacks held many small items. Heinrich wondered if these items pertained to the workings of the mechanical man.

In the center of the tent, a large table overflowed with stacks of books, small mounds of dirt-encrusted treasures, scattered instruments, and assorted maps. Szilveszter moved to it; his robes creating the illusion he was gliding. His fingers skimmed merrily across many of the items, as if he were searching for something specific and could only identify it via touch. He stopped and smiled. Lifting a gilded mask of a stern face, Szilveszter said, "Aah. The Mask of Agamemnon, discovered at Mycenae."

Szilveszter's knowledge of his findings plucked a pleasant tune from the strings of Heinrich's ego. The archeologist said, "So, you're familiar with my work?"

Regarding the mask, Szilveszter answered, "I am a student of history."

"Then you will be excited to know what I'm searching for on this Hisarlik mound."

"The Mask of Helen. But you won't find it."

Sophia gasped. Taken aback by such abruptness, Heinrich snapped, "How did you know what I'm looking for? What do you mean I won't find it?"

While returning the Mask of Agamemnon to the table, Szilveszter looked to Heinrich like a hungry snake finding an unguarded nest of eggs. "I've read your journals."

"My journals? I have scrawled in them just this morning. How could you possibly have read my journals?"

"As I said, I am a student of history."

Frustrated to the point of clenched fists, Heinrich quaked as he spat, "Make sense, man!"

Szilveszter offered a theatrical sigh, made more dramatic by his impish smile. "I am from the future, a future that sees you as a bumbling fool. You advance the field of archeology, but only through ineptitude. Your findings are serendipity at best. But I am here to help you."

Through clenched teeth, Heinrich growled. "How dare you! Leave."

Gliding closer, Szilveszter said, "All I ask is a chance to prove myself."

"Leave!"

The man wearing the top hot and the humanoid machination started to move closer to Heinrich, but Szilveszter waved them off. "Right instead of left, Heinrich. That simple change in decision is the difference between failure and unparalleled power."

Heinrich inhaled, nostrils flaring. "I have already used my supply of explosives. The time and cost to garner more is—"

"Unnecessary," Szilveszter interrupted. With a grandiose hand gesture more to be expected from the likes of the garishly dressed magician, Szilveszter reached into the gaping sleeve of his robe and pulled out a tetrahedron, green and black liquids swirling inside, yet not mixing. "We will use this."

Had his ire left room for any other emotion, Heinrich would have laughed at the ridiculousness of the stranger's claims. The young man's eyes held lunacy, his words even more so, and now he stood there holding a pyramid filled with inks of two different colors and viscosity. Absurd! But if Heinrich wished this man to be gone, he must yield to his request. If not, then Szilveszter would use his comrades to exact his will. Once in the tunnels of Troy, Heinrich would have more than enough workers at his disposal to neutralize the interlopers' threat, even the large man-shaped thing supporting a jar upon his shoulders. That trick Heinrich had yet to figure out, but now was not the time. "Very well. After your little toy fails, though, I expect that you will be on your way and never to come back here again. Now, follow me."

Heinrich led and the others followed. Sophia remained close to her husband, casting furtive glances back to the strangers during the entire walk. Along the way from the tent to the dig-site entrance and all through the tunnels, Heinrich gathered his helpers; over a dozen joining them by the time they arrived at the point in question, deep within the tunnels. There should be plenty of hired hands to remove the intruders, were it required. It would cost extra, which was unfortunate, but necessary.

The workers were doing a fine job removing the stones from the recent explosion, chunks of earth ranging from the size of a fist to that of a chest. Heinrich even noticed the shattered remains of an ancient column, but decided against mentioning it to anyone. Instead, in the dank and dusty tunnel, roughly hewn by fire and greed, Heinrich gestured to Szilveszter that this was where he wished to be.

"I suggest stepping back," Szilveszter said as he approached a misshapen wall of rock. As everyone shifted about, the multitude of oil lanterns cast dreadful shadows upon the wall, Szilveszter being the origin point of all of them. Still wearing a Cheshire smile, Szilveszter held the pyramid before him like a diviner, a shield, a weapon.

While all eyes focused on Szilveszter, Heinrich drifted to the back of the group, to where his workers stood. Their faces masks of worry, they shifted their weight from leg to leg, whispering to each other in their native language. Heinrich didn't need to speak it to know that they discussed fleeing. He was about to command that they not only stay for this unusual charade, but to attack those perpetrating it after it was over. However, before a single word could depart his mouth, a thrum filled the tunnels.

Everyone not a part of Szilveszter's group looked around, trying to discern the source. The noise grew louder, an unmentionable beast humming its favorite dirge. The pyramid! The noise was coming from the pyramid.

Sophia moved closer to Heinrich, partially behind him. Angered that Szilveszter's parlor tricks had upset his wife and workers, Heinrich opened his mouth to express his distaste. Yet again, no words formed.

Wide beams of green light emanated from the pyramid in Szilveszter's hands, sweeping across the wall of rock.

The wall collapsed.

Everyone gasped and jumped backward, not from the need to avoid the wall splitting into boulders, but from the primal xenophobic urge to run away from the unknown, from perceived danger. There was nothing imminent yet, so everyone stood their place and watched the green light continue to wash over the boulders. Just as the wall, the boulders themselves collapsed into smaller chucks of stone, as if they simply lost the will to be anything larger.

No explosion. No pops or cracks of splitting stone. Just the sounds of smaller rocks settling, those on the top of the mounds rolling their way to the bottom.

Even though Szilveszter looked drained, sweat pouring over his clammy face, he still smiled. Making a feeble gesture to the pile of rocks, he said, "Your greatness is just behind those stones."

"Come! Come!" Heinrich waved to his workers as he ran to the rubble. So excited by the prospect of finding what he so desired, he actually helped his workers. He moved the rocks, handing off the ones he could lift, rolling the ones he couldn't down the mound. "Faster! Faster!"

He climbed the mound, shoving aside stones, pushing away rocks. He braced his shoulder against the topmost stone and put his whole body into a push. It moved, rolling down the other side and granting access to a chamber that had been forgotten for centuries. Heinrich's sweat-drenched hair blew back, flapping against his face from the burst of air rushing past him, as if the entire room had held its breath until this moment, and then exhaled. He looked through the hole but saw only darkness. "There's a room!"

Adrenaline fueled his muscles as he pushed more stones down the mound to make the opening larger. When he finally cleared away enough to allow access to any person here, even the larger-than-life monstrosity with its brain in a jar, Heinrich held out a hand and demanded, "A torch! Give me a torch!"

Sophia snatched the closest torch she could find and ascended the rubble mound to hand it to Heinrich. Too excited to offer a pithy statement or even a simple thank you, he stepped over the threshold.

The other side of the mound that he descended was just like the side he had climbed to get there—chunks of rock forming an uneven slope. Despite the fact that he never once looked down, too rapt by what the light of his torch illuminated, he made it to the base without so much as a stumble, Sophia in tow.

The chamber was huge. More torches were added from the others climbing through the newly made hole, but the light of the flames couldn't touch the walls or ceiling.

"Heinrich," Sophia whispered with such awe in her voice, it seemed that her husband's name was the only word left available to her, the only word synonymous with the vastness before her.

Heinrich heard his wife, but could not respond, enraptured by the enormity of the situation, distracted by the notion that he would have missed this had he continued along his original course. He flummoxed as to how a young stranger and his associates not only knew where to look, but used such bizarre and mystical means to uncover it. He pushed those thoughts from his mind as he walked along the uneven floor of the chamber, toward a newly glinting light.

Not a light, Heinrich soon discovered, but a reflection of his torch. Gold! Hoping beyond hope, Heinrich hastened his pace, almost running. But, yes! It was that which he so sought, resting atop a stone pedestal, more glorious than he imagined. The Mask of Helen, her perfect visage frozen in time, gilded immortality.

Bringing his trembling hand to his mouth, lips quivering, he gasped and shed a tear, held fast by her beauty. He heard Sophia approach, and explained to her as if she were unaware, "I found her. I found her. My life's work is complete."

"You mustn't think so small," Szilveszter said, approaching as well, his face glowing from the torches reflecting off the mask.

Heinrich didn't think it would be possible to stop looking at the mask, but Szilveszter's preposterous statement demanded his attention. How could the culmination of a lifetime's work be considered too small? Insulting! The younger man chuckled, and used his torch to guide Heinrich's attention to the area behind the mask. Heinrich jumped back when he saw a gaunt and hollow face, distended in permanent scream.

The eye sockets were dry and the skin too leathery to move, but the petrified face made Heinrich's heart race. Standing as tall as he, this offending creature wore the armor of a warrior from millennia ago, but held the form of a shriveled man. No hair under the helm, no life within the bones, even though they were sturdy enough to keep the dead man standing.

Szilveszter waved his torch, the fire's light touching upon face after face after face of more warriors long dead. Amazed, Heinrich used his own torch to guide his way forward, he walked among hundreds upon hundreds of these mummy-like soldiers, all standing rigid, all with shield and sword in hand.

Szilveszter's cadre walked among the garden of the dead as well. The tall, thin man with equally thin mustache pulled two small nodules from the bag he carried and placed one on either side of a warrior's neck. He moved to the next warrior and repeated the process of placing two nodules on its neck. Then to the next warrior and the next, continuing along the line. Dr. Sivkas and Zarkahn each had sacks of nodules as well, attaching two to the neck of every soldier. Even the veiled woman participated in this task.

"What… what are your people doing?" Heinrich asked.

Szilveszter glided to Heinrich and made a grand, sweeping gesture. "Preparing to show you the true power of the Mask of Helen."

"The power of…? What can the mask do?"

"You shall soon see."

"How? How do you know this?"

Szilveszter turned and smiled at Heinrich. In the dark, dry cavern, his smile still beamed brightly, lips glimmering and moist. "Let me tell you about my master and the glory to come.…"

Chapter 30

Albert was tired. Not just physically, although that pain was certainly undeniable. After being trussed up to a modified rack by thick ropes, his muscles burned, his joints throbbed, and parts of his skin stung from being rubbed raw. Having been bludgeoned into unconsciousness before that was hardly the same as a good night's sleep. What exhausted him was greater than all of that.

He missed his wife.

He missed his son.

He missed his home.

He even missed his time period, though not to the same extent as Howard. Visiting this time period made him appreciate that he came from a world of richness and wonder. If nothing else, his trip to the past made him contemplate how his time period would be viewed by the eyes of those who would consider his time the distant past. The advancements in electricity alone were astounding. In his time, the leaders of innovation were attempting to nurture the newborn science of aviation, and that Ford fellow in America was trying to get everyone in the seat of an automobile. Albert wanted to explore these possibilities, examine the philosophies, and pontificate further with his peers, yet had no access to them, another aspect that he missed while on this mission, another brick removed from his pillar of fortitude.

Howard often proved more than apt for such musings and conjecture. However, now was not the time; the mission still lay before them. This wore on him as well. Not only did he and Howard find themselves thirty-one years in the past because they were attempting to stop a mad god of chaos from coming to their dimension, but they seemed to be uncovering and discovering a new creature born of darkness every other day. Right now, sitting in the great room of the mansion owned by Alois Hitler, Howard scribbled in his notebook while Annie described the... demon?... god?... monster?... she had implored to assist her in becoming a rescuer.

Albert knew that every name Howard wrote down had the potential to manifest into another mission. The fact that Howard refused to even mutter this creature's name also weighed heavily upon Albert.

"Nothing else you can tell me about the Yellow King?" Howard asked, shading in parts of his recent sketch.

Soft smile upon her face, Annie answered, "I told you all I know."

Glancing up, Howard tilted his head. "Why are you smiling?"

"Because your left eyebrow furrows a little deeper than your right when you sketch."

Albert wished he could free the chuckle that wanted to be released, but pain and fatigue were harsh wardens at the moment, and he would simply have to retain the memory of Howard blushing.

Stammering, Howard went back to his sketch, adding the final touches. "I... umm... never knew that about myself. Thank you for such an enlightening revelation."

Annie giggled and the pinkness of Howard's cheeks deepened. He cleared his throat and then revealed what he had drawn in his notebook. "Is this what he looks like?"

Looking at the picture, Annie's smile faded as if the Grim Reaper himself had claimed it. Voice as chilled as death's touch, she said, "Yes. That's him exactly."

Howard closed his notebook, breaking the spell. "Very well. Now, I implore you, please tell me what transpired during your meeting."

Annie's smile returned, however Albert deemed it to be fake. A worrisome attempt at mirth. "I shared that information as well."

"I find it difficult to believe that this monster would offer the services of his followers simply because of jealousy."

"Now, Howard, I assume you to be worldly enough to know that the more power one accumulates, the pettier their motivations become. We are talking about kings and gods after all."

Howard must have seen something that Albert missed; a twitch, a shift, some subtle clue that Annie attempted to hide her left hand. As fast as a viper strike, Howard snatched Annie's wrist, and she gasped.

The two stood frozen; Howard looking at her left palm, Annie looking everywhere other than at Howard. Falling helpless to the siren call of curiosity, Albert moved to a different part of the room in an attempt to see what caused such a horrified look upon his partner's face. Alas, to no avail, but he did hear Howard say, "This marking. This is his claim on you, isn't it? Your soul?"

Still unable to look at Howard, she said, "Not my soul. Use of my fame. I'm to carry his word wherever I go, to help him gain more followers, build an army."

"Help him create more of these jaundiced cretins? Unacceptable."

"Howard, it was the only way to secure transport to find you and Albert."

Howard always maintained a visible level of consternation upon his countenance, so most people who met him assumed that he was angry. Always angry. Albert knew better, though, learning it to be untrue by forging a relationship through written correspondence. After working with Howard and forming a friendship with the young man for so many years, Albert had learned to see the subtle differences in mood. Now Howard was angry, truly angry. Albert assumed it was due to the level of helplessness regarding the situation. Albert wanted to assuage his friend's anger, wanted to stride over to him and say the right words to ease his churning mind, but none were to be found within his lexicon, for they simply did not exist.

"Then that burden should be mine," Howard said as he retrieved one of the dark energy guns from his satchel. A twist of the casing's base, a turn of the rear coupling, and Howard released the battery. From a small kit he kept in the satchel, he pulled forth a needle and pressed the tip into the pinpoint nozzle, releasing a single drop of green-black liquid. He let it drip onto his palm and then pressed his hand to Annie's.

"Howard?" Annie asked, voice shaky and uncertain.

"I'm taking it." Unwavering, Howard repeated, "I am taking it, your burden, the price you paid. I am taking the mark of Hastur!"

Upon uttering those words, an unseen wave flowed outward from Annie in all directions, only made visible by the disruptions it caused—knocking books off shelves, toppling items around the room, slamming Albert in the chest as it passed through him. In the time it took Albert to catch his breath and regain his footing, the wave of energy returned, smacking him in the back and almost dropping him to his knees as he saw the air ripple and funnel into Howard.

"No. No, you mustn't. I do not approve." Annie's words warbled, choking her. Tears rolled from her eyes.

"It is my burden now," Howard replied.

Annie pressed her left palm against his and rubbed. "Then I take it back. I take back the mark of—"

"Annie," Howard interrupted. "The price is not yours to pay."

Eyes red and cheeks slicked from tears, Annie looked up. Her fingers intertwined with his, her grip tight. She trembled. Words barely escaped her mouth. "Oh, Howard."

Jane and William stood by the entrance of the room, both wearing a look of utter disgust as they watched the scene unfold before them. Albert fully expected to see the sour look upon Jane's face, but William? Even in the direst of situations, Albert knew William to possess an unsettling level of zeal. Now, his eyes held a curious blend of pain and confusion.

Co-conspirators in the delicate espionage of secret emotions, Jane and William looked at each other and rolled their eyes in unison. They fell away from the doorway like peeling paint and returned to the main foyer, where the other rescuers waited. As did the prisoners.

Beginning to feel like a third wheel in the same room as Howard and Annie, now standing so close to each other that they could be considered embracing even though neither pair of arms were around the other person, Albert decided to go to the main foyer as well, but froze as soon as he crossed the threshold of the foyer, stunned.

The majesty of the foyer itself was awe-worthy on a normal day due, to the size of the space as well as the ornate fixtures of the dual curved staircases, scintillating crystal chandelier, and polished marble tile. What took Albert's breath were the nightmare-inducing beasts skittering about.

Led around by the yellowed men—also creatures Albert considered to be nightmarish—the steeds had the appearance of giant hornets with claws and eyes containing an otherworldly intelligence, far surpassing a mere insect's. Splashes of blood and gore streaked the walls and floor. The contrast between the ugliness of violence and the beauty of its design transformed the foyer into an alien gallery devoted to artwork of the macabre.

William and Jules sat next to each other on a set of stairs, engaged in a private conversation. The only company Jane kept was with one of the beasts, mumbling to it in between sips from a whiskey bottle. The yellowed men, led by the eager-to-placate Skaag, stood around the captured. The empty-eyed prisoners all looked like the men who had ambushed and kidnapped Albert. Except for one: Alois Hitler.

"Fascinating," Howard said from behind Albert, causing him to jump. Albert wondered how long his attention had been attuned to the lunacy in the foyer.

Albert regarded Howard and Annie. Howard's complete attention went to the winged creatures, while Annie's attention went to trying to hide her look of shame. Howard looked back to Annie just long enough to ask, "You rode one of these?"

"Yes," she replied. "They are called byakhee. I hope you don't mind, but I made notes about these creatures in your notebook."

Nodding absently, Howard flipped to those pages in his notebook. "Yes. Yes. I have heard of these creatures. I'm not surprised in the slightest that the Yellow King has possession of such things. I am surprised, though, that you were able to ride one."

Annie shrugged. "Without any issues, either. They came straight here. I simply had to hold tight. Although, Jane treated hers like a bucking bronco and fought it until submission."

"I am right back to being not surprised," Howard moaned as he read over Annie's notes.

Neither was Albert. He had no time to indulge in imagining that scenario, though. Gesturing to Howard and Annie, he said, "Come with me."

They followed Albert as he walked to a spot in between where William and Jules were sitting and where Jane could hear. Once he had their attention, Albert asked, "Now what?"

"What do ya mean?" William asked, arms crossed over his chest.

Jules answered, "I believe he's asking about our next course of action."

William shrugged. "Simple. We take the bee-things to wherever Szilveszter went to. They brought us here, right?"

Offering a simplistic smile, Skaag injected himself into the conversation. "That only happened because of a deal made with my master, and the deal was to find Albert and Howard, not Szilveszter."

Albert's stomach turned as the yellowed man said Szilveszter's name. Howard's face pinched, as if forced to swallow something bitter. "No more deals today."

"What about him?" William asked, nodding in the direction of Alois Hitler, sitting on the floor. Ropes bound his forearms together behind his back. "Surely he's gotta know where Szilveszter and crew went."

"I doubt very much that he would give us the information we need, no matter the threats."

"If he ain't gonna talk, then I say we shoot him and then burn this whole house down," Jane said.

"We went over this before," Howard said. "We must do everything in our power to keep time as it is. I loathe to think about the ramifications of so many deaths that we have caused already."

"Yeah?" Jane snorted. "How do you know that they wouldn't have happened anyway? I ain't no student of the physical sciences like you, but even I know that none of Hitler's slaves or any of these yellow-skinned freaks ain't gonna be fruitful and multiply. They ain't gonna give history its favorite son or daughter. It don't matter none if they're dead or alive."

Howard reeled back and blinked, clearly not expecting any form of logical argument coming from Jane. "That… may be true, but that doesn't give us the right to play judge, jury, and executioner for the court of history."

"No? And history told you this?"

"Not directly. But… well, it's no secret that everyone we have encountered so far has their own chapter in history."

"That means we should sit back and not punish them for their misdeeds? We just let them go? That Alois Hitler fella is a monster. I know this. You know this. We need to rid the world of him."

"We can't do that."

"Why? What's so special about him?"

Howard disengaged from Jane to look at Albert. Trying to be as subtle as possible, Albert arched his eyebrows. He had never heard of the man, yet everyone other than minions or lackeys or common folk they had encountered had some form of historical significance, be it good or bad.

Jane had caught on and said, "So, you two ain't never heard of him, huh?"

Albert answered, "Just because we have not heard of him does not mean that he isn't important in shaping the world."

"He's a no-good varmint! He ain't gonna turn into some saint after we leave. He ain't gonna have no kids or grandkids that are gonna be saints neither. What if his progeny is worse? What if a hundred years from now, smarty people like you and Howard are sittin' around askin' themselves, 'What if we could go back in time and kill Hitler?'"

"That is the very reason why we can't kill him now. If he has that much impact on the future, then we need to let him live to play his rightful part in it."

Jane threw her hands in the air and grunted with disgust. "I'm sick of arguin' with you two! Makin' my head hurt. My bottle's empty, so I gotta find a new one. Fetch me when we're ready to leave. Rich guy like this gotta have some good stuff."

Albert wanted to call to her as she left the room, wanted to say the right words to make her understand. That was unlikely, though, and it would be best just to let her drink herself to the desired level of comfort.

Before Albert could think of what to do next, William leapt up from where he sat and strode to Alois. Standing behind Alois, he drew his gun and placed it against the bound man's temple. With his other hand, William grasped Alois's collar and growled, "Where are your dirt bag buddies going?"

Alois laughed.

"William—" Albert started, wanting to tell him that his empty threats would be fruitless.

Then William squeezed the trigger.

Everyone jumped and gasped.

Shifting his aim right before he shot, the bullet struck the marble floor between Alois's knees, creating slivers of debris as it ricocheted away. Tone much harsher than before, William asked again, "Where are your dirt bag buddies going?"

Alois didn't laugh, but he still didn't answer, his face contorted from the pain of having a gun discharged so close to his ear.

"William!" Albert snapped, not knowing what else to say.

"You can't do this!" Howard added. "We just discussed this."

William shot again. This time the bullet hit the marble between Alois's thighs, flying chips tore at his pants.

With even more earnestness, William continued, "I know you're willing to sacrifice your life for this new god of yours, but how about your unborn children? Ready to sacrifice them? Can this new god grow your cock back after I shoot it off?"

"Billy!" Annie yelled. "This isn't you!"

Moving only his eyes to look at Annie, William smiled as he said, "Annie, when it comes to targets, you got me dead to rights. But when it comes to kills, you ain't got nothing on me."

He pulled the trigger again.

This time Alois winced as a third hole in the floor appeared closer to his crotch than the first two. Tiny bits of red stained his pants, superficial cuts from the flying chunks of marble. "Çanakkale," Alois grumbled. "Çanakkale, Turkey."

With a smile as bright as if he had told a show-stopping joke, William released Alois and holstered his gun, after giving it a good twirl first. "There ya go."

Annie stared at him with a look of complete heartbreak, and William sauntered past her without a single glance her way as he aimed for the kitchen. He stopped when Jane reentered the room with a bottle containing liquor so golden it seemed as if the Olympians themselves had distilled it. William made a polite gesture to the bottle; Jane shrugged and handed it to him. She looked around the room and then asked, "So, what'd I miss?"

Chapter 31

Billy watched Howard, watched as the arrogant fop incessantly fidgeted atop his mount. Hundreds of feet above ground, the byakhee flew, each carrying one rider. Howard and Albert lacked the prior experience that Billy had. They also lacked the disregard for death that Billy had. After all, Billy was certain that the future would not remember him as perishing from falling off a giant insect over the country of Turkey. Although Albert and Howard were steadfast in trying to preserve history—even if it meant keeping killers like Hitler and that Borden girl alive, instead of meting out present justice against future atrocities—and they both got a little squirrelly about Billy's fate, far more so than that of anyone else. Maybe Billy *would* fall to his death? Maybe he would die somewhere along this mission? Billy's education was nowhere near the extent of other men, but even he knew that it was the survivors who wrote history and told the tales. Just to be on the safe side, Billy gripped the rudimentary pommels a little tighter.

Albert fared at riding the byakhee far better than Howard, and Billy loved it. He enjoyed watching Howard experience difficulties. So unsure and frightened of falling off, Howard would lean in close to his steed, almost to the point of hugging it, then he would push himself away, perilously close to knocking himself off. The process repeated, and Billy laughed each time.

As he watched, he wondered what Annie saw in Howard. It still stung, painfully so, to think about the kiss. It was deep, meaningful. A connection between two kindred spirits. They both knew what the world was like, what they needed to do to survive. Although Annie seemed far more unaffected by it, choosing to rise above the filth, she still knew that it was a dirty world. Howard didn't know, didn't understand. In Howard's mind, anything not Howard was dirty, filthy. Annie could get her hands dirty; Howard couldn't. Annie could care about others mired by the ways of the world; Howard couldn't. Yet she turned to Howard for help, embraced him immediately after rescuing him. Billy never needed to be rescued. He did the rescuing. He could never be so weak. Or could he?

Billy looked over to Jane, guiding her mount as if she had been riding one of these things all her life. If Billy were honest with himself, he would have admitted that he was weak, so easily swayed by the allure of the fairer sex, even if it were Jane. Rough and uncouth Jane. All it took was a few shots of whiskey and a shake of her ass, and he fell right between her thighs in bed. On the floor. Against the wall. The mere thought of that night made Billy's trousers uncomfortable. He shook his head and reminded himself that Jane had used him, and not for the sole purpose of rubbing one out either. She used him to hurt Annie, and he was weak enough to let her.

Then there was Annie, riding with her back straight, steady posture. As if riding a prancing show pony. A queer thought squirmed through Billy's mind—what if this were Annie's story? All motivation seemed to center around Annie, the performer desperate for stardom. Maybe this adventure was just her moment on stage? Billy and Howard being the two points of the love triangle; Jane her bitter rival. Both Jules and Albert respected her and looked at her through paternal eyes, characters supporting the intrepid heroine as she ascended through the story, through life. And what if she was? She certainly deserved it, and Billy would happily do what he could to see her succeed.

No. No, he could not just blindly follow along some preordained script. He wanted more. He wanted to do more. He wanted to be more. It all came back to that kiss; a kiss between a traipsing woman and a rambling man. What could that lead to?

Billy pushed aside his stray thoughts of uncertain futures to refocus on the seriousness of the present. They had arrived at their destination.

The byakhee brought them to the top of a large hill. After everyone dismounted, Billy assumed it to be a messy campsite, but most of the others talked about it being an archeological dig by the tools and equipment strewn about. Billy walked along one of the dirt-worn paths among the tents. Most of them were tattered and fallen, stray flaps twitching in the light breeze. Everyone wandered around the camp as well, speculating about what had happened, what Szilveszter was looking for. The conjecture yielded no conclusions, just more questions, and that made Billy's head hurt. Needing to investigate further, he strolled along a path that became a deeper groove in the ground as he followed it, leading to a hole in the earth.

Billy knew nothing about archeology, but the hole looked like a sloppy mineshaft, an open wound into the planet itself. Wondering how far into it he could see, Billy approached, but almost fell over as the wind shifted.

Death. Not just death, the stale putrid stench of an animal rotting away. More than one animal, judging from the overpowering smell. Eyes watering, Billy lifted the front of his shirt over his nose. He turned to tell the others about what he had found, but a noise caught his attention. From the mouth of the cave, a dry rustling noise sounded from as if the Earth itself were wheezing. Billy moved closer, trying to see past where the sun's rays stopped. The noise reminded Billy of a doddering old man shuffling across a dirty tavern floor. Then he saw movement.

Drawing his gun, Billy approached the cave entrance. Curiosity could not push aside the fear within him; it just spoke to him louder. Every heartbeat radiated from behind his chest to his fingers and toes. He could even feel it in his ears. Yet, he still crept closer to the opening. Sweat rolled down his face. He moved the gun to his left hand so he could wipe his right hand on his pants, wicking away the moisture. Another step closer and he could make out a shape. A person? A person stuck on something, tugging to get free.

"Hello?" Billy asked, but the word came out small and cracked. Embarrassed by the flimsiness in his voice, he asked again, "Hello? Are you stuck?"

Still cautious, he tightened his gut to try to stymie the flutters happening inside and took another step. A pop. A snap. The sounds of something more substantial than just cloth tearing. Hands and teeth rushed toward Billy.

Yelling, Billy jumped away and shot. His bullet struck rock as he stumbled and fell. Using his elbows and heels, he scuttled out of the gouged pathway onto the soft bed of grass. Once he was sure that he was far enough away, he stopped and trained his weapon on the thing that attacked him. A corpse.

Laying face first in the dirt was a shriveled and dried husk of a human being, missing part of its right leg, from the knee down. The sunlight played upon the opening of the shaft just enough to show the lower leg stuck between two jagged rocks. Feeling foolish, Billy stood up and put away his revolver.

"Jumpin' at boogey-men now," Billy mumbled to himself as he walked over to the long-since dead man. Crouching in front of it, he marveled at the ancient armor the corpse wore. Then he noticed something out of place—two metallic nodules on its neck, buzzing with electricity. Billy reached for them.

The corpse reached for Billy.

Billy yelled and jumped to the side, drawing his gun to shoot this undead abomination that chased after him. Except... the creature wasn't pursuing Billy.

Slack-jawed, it lifted its head as if it could see out of its empty eye sockets. Using its hands to claw along the ground, it dragged itself along the path. Billy stood dumbfounded. What motivated this thing to break free from the chains of death and drag itself away from its tomb? Then its head exploded.

The creature's head burst into chunks of brittle bone and desiccated skin; Billy jumped back at the echoing crack of gunfire. Jane, wide eyed and shaking, was holding a smoking gun. "What the fuck was that?"

"Don't know," Billy answered. "Came outta the hole."

The others ran to the scene, all their guns drawn as well. Howard looked toward the dig site opening. "It came out of there?"

"Yep."

Howard looked to Albert and said, "At least we know what they were after now."

Albert knelt next to the body and examined it. "Look at this armor. When... could it be?"

Howard joined Albert and asked, "What are you thinking?"

"I once read that an archaeologist named Heinrich Schliemann discovered the tomb of King Agamemnon, but that wasn't what he ultimately wanted to find. Do you think that this site, this place could be...?"

"Troy?" Howard asked. He looked to the opening to the dig site, then to the headless corpse. He grimaced. "It certainly wouldn't be the strangest thing we've encountered on this mission."

Jules gave a nervous laugh. "Troy? As in Helen of Troy? The face that launched a thousand ships?"

Billy stepped up and said, "If that's true, then this must have been a soldier from one of those thousand ships. How is it possible that he was still able to move?"

Albert carefully prodded one of the nodules still attached to the base of the decapitated corpse's neck. "These. While held captive by Hitler, Howard and I saw his minions assembling these things. Hundreds of them."

"Enough for a whole army," Annie speculated.

"So…" Jane said, holstering her gun. "Where's the army now?"

Billy walked toward a freshly cut path leading from the hard-packed dirt. "It was crawlin' this way."

Everyone joined Billy and followed the path, muddied grass matted flat, random chunks of dirt missing. It led to the edge of the hill and followed the slope downward. Everyone stopped when they saw where the army had gone. To the town below.

The town burned.

Chapter 32

Eerie. Eerie was the only word Annie could muster to describe the situation. The scene. The noises. The smells. All conducive to making the tiny hairs of her arms all the way up along her neck stand at attention. A year prior, if anyone, no matter how close she held them to her heart, had told her that she would be traversing through the newly scarred remains of a Turkish town with future men for the sole purpose of stopping a demented god from destroying the world, she would have accused them of being stricken with madness. Now, she was questioning her own grasp on sanity.

Senses heightened, attuned to her surroundings, she could hear the soft crunch of the dirt road beneath her feet despite the crackling of various fires and the constant wails of anguish in the distance. She could still smell the spices used in local cuisines, meals uncooked, as she passed by the stone-walled buildings of residences, yet the odors of charred wood and burned flesh were unyielding. She could see the beauty of the harbor town; so foreign to the towns she had visited in North America, even though anything that was once wood was now ash. She did her best to ignore the lumps of shredded clothing, some still leaking blood, along the streets. She knew this to be Hell, and the guilt of allowing Howard to take this future curse from her felt like a wire tightening around her heart.

Howard walked alongside her, his futuristic gun in hand just like the revolver in hers, and she felt too ashamed to glance his way. The others were moving along the streets of the town, in a tight group, among the emptied and lifeless buildings like ten explorers—her allies as well as four yellowed men—walking though the skeletal remains of a newly dead behemoth. No one spoke, simply moving toward the water, toward the noises of pain.

Annie tried to remain focused, but her stray thoughts made her reckless, and she turned a corner too quickly. Withered and dried hands clasped around her neck before she could even register that they were there. A choked squeak escaped from her as an undead creature slammed her into a nearby building. An opened mouth filled with rotted teeth and dehydrated tongue moved close enough for her to hear the faint buzz of the nodules on the zombie soldier's neck.

Being long putrefied did not detract from its speed. Annie couldn't fight back, couldn't defend herself. All she could do was watch impotently as the fetid maw of death sought her demise. A gun shot thundered, and a bullet powdered the creature's head.

Howard rushed to Annie and used his shoulder to slam into the decapitated zombie, knocking it away. Even though every muscle in his face angled into a frown, she could see concern in his eyes. "Are you okay?"

Annie nodded, running her fingers over her neck, feeling phantom hands still grip her. Satisfied that they were indeed gone, she whispered, "Yes. Yes, I'm fine."

"Well, so much for keepin' quiet now," Billy said as he looked down the street. Four more soldiers shuffled closer at a surprisingly brisk pace. "We woke the neighbors."

"Good!" Jane yelled as she pointed her gun at them. She squeezed the trigger three times, her aim true each time. Before she could put a bullet in the head of the last soldier, Albert put his hand on her shoulder and said, "Jane. It is now a matter of conservation. We don't have enough bullets for all of them."

Yanking away from his touch, Jane holstered her gun as she walked toward the remaining undead soldier. Halfway to it, she paused and procured a thick hunting knife from her boot. In a flash of rage, she jammed her hand under its jaw, pinning its mouth closed. With efficient grace, she sliced twice and removed the neck nodules. They dropped harmlessly to the ground, as did the lifeless corpse after Jane released it. She turned to her companions and gestured to the withered husk of pruned flesh. "Better?"

"Much," Albert replied. Annie could not discern if he were being serious, or simply making the statement because there was no other possible answer.

"Hope you got more knives," Billy said as he pulled a small knife from his boot. "'Cause I only got one."

Four more undead lumbered down the street toward them. Jules found a length of wood as thick as his leg, once part of a door. He and Billy approached the soldiers, all four still maintaining enough faculties to reach for their enemies. Jules used his weapon as a battering ram rather than a spear. Putting his weight into thrusting the chunk of wood, he smashed an undead's face. The force was enough to remove its head from its neck. The creature fell into a heap. Billy cut the nodules off one of the other undead, while Jules bashed a third soldier to uselessness. A green flash of light streaked down the street and reduced the fourth creature's head to a puff of dust. Billy and Jules thanked Howard as they returned to the small group.

"We need to keep moving," Howard suggested. "Toward the piers."

Toward the screams. Toward the subsequent nightmares Annie would have, if she lived through this experience. She assumed she would since the men from the future knew of her. The only way a professor from Germany and an American misanthrope could have possibly known her was if she achieved a greater level of fame than her current tier. Could the past be altered? She hoped not. But she hardly thought it an excuse to be careless. She certainly did not wish to go toward the unending screams, yet she followed the group anyway.

They made it down two more streets without incident. Trees had lined one side of the way, most charred black and fallen. Albert and Howard found sturdy enough branches to use as bludgeons, supplementing their ray guns. Annie never asked Howard about the futuristic guns, but she assumed they held a limited number of shots, judging by the fact that both men were hesitant to use them too often.

Jules kept the large chunk of wood. Although he was strong enough to wield it, he was the oldest of the group, and sweat flowed along the perimeter of his face from hefting the weapon. Howard found a two-foot piece of metal, a bar that had been torn off a gate, and gave it to Annie. The yellowed men made do with smaller sticks and palm sized rocks they found along the way.

After two more blocks, their luck ran out. Following Albert and Howard, they turned down an alleyway that ran toward the sea, close enough to smell the salt air. Before they could reach the end of the alley, a small contingent of undead soldiers poured in. Billy and Jules now led the party as they all turned and ran from the mummified soldiers. Out of the alleyway, down the street, another street. No escape. More soldiers flowed from surrounding alleys and side streets.

Jules crushed skulls while Jane and Billy slashed their knives with purpose, engaging only when forced to stop undead hands from grabbing someone, or to break through a mummified wall of papery skin to create an egress. Annie found that if she did the rather unsettling act of shoving her metal bar far enough into an empty eye socket, it had the desired effect. She'd never forget the momentary resistance the skull gave when she yanked her weapon free only to repeat the process. They all did their parts to keep moving through the city, even the yellowed men.

While running across streets and turning corners down short alleyways, the yellowed men hurled anything that had sufficient weight to it, their missiles mostly stones or debris from buildings. One fellow did not fall back with his comrades fast enough. Bending over to pick up a jagged piece of detritus, he stepped too close to the open doorway of a nearby house. A set of bony hands reached from the darkness of the abode and grabbed clumps of the yellowed man's shirt. Nothing more than tatters to begin with, there was enough of the shirt to serve as a tether. The yellowed man thrashed about like a wounded animal caught in a trap as a second member of the undead army approached. A third soldier followed and ushered a small group behind it. Annie thought it impossible that so many hands could appear from one spot, yet they did, all grabbing a part of the yellowed man. He screamed as they pulled, loud enough to cover the noises of joints popping and meat being torn apart. Amid the horror, Annie found a macabre sense of comfort that the color of blood spurting from the yellowed man was indeed red. There was no time to mourn him, though, barely enough time to even acknowledge that he was dead. She and the others kept running.

Annie felt like they were running in circles. The squat, single story buildings of the same beige stone all looked alike. Some of the damages started to look familiar, too. Had she seen that pattern of burn marks before? Did these bloodstains on the walls look exactly like the blood-stained walls from a few blocks ago? Recall was becoming harder as they ran. They turned a corner. Jules bashed. She stabbed. Billy and Jane sliced. Howard and Albert poked. The yellowed men threw stones. All to turn the next corner and repeat.

Her legs hurt. Her arms weakened. Fire swirled in her lungs with every ragged breath. She pushed herself to keep moving, unwilling to test the theories of time travel causing splintered realities by dying on the streets of a Turkish city. Fight. Move. Run. They turned the next corner. This time, they couldn't make it any farther.

Crashing into the building wall across the street like a wave of horror, dozens of undead soldiers flowed from a nearby alleyway. Jane shouted, "Hurry! We can take 'em out before they get oriented."

Albert grabbed her arm, stopping her from unintentional suicide. "No. We can't. Their numbers have been increasing with every street we run down."

Frustrated to the point of animalistic howls, Jane drew her gun and fired. All of her bullets hit their targets, but the results were quickly swept under by the approaching mass of undead flesh. She screamed again, as if the anger in her voice was the power needed to obliterate her enemies.

"Here! Over here!" Billy yelled as he ran toward a nearby house. A tree had fallen against it, giving just enough of a ramp to the roof. Billy and a few of the yellowed men scurried up first, then helped the others. Once all nine of the still-living made it, they kicked at the top of the tree, knocking it from the roof. The undead soldiers congregated at the base of the house, all looking up with hollowed out eyes.

The roof was constructed of roughly hewn wood planks, but Annie was thankful that, even though it was uncomfortable and creaked with every step, it seemed sturdy enough to support them. She was also thankful for a chance to rest, to massage her burning muscles. She cursed when she realized their respite was going to be very brief.

"They're still comin'," Billy said, looking over the roof edge.

Everyone joined him and watched as the gathering drones proved that having numbers was more important than having a mind. The undead continued to reach up for the living, pressing against the building, pressing against themselves. Those closest to the wall fell, inadvertently serving as a step for those around it. As more fell, more climbed.

Howard followed the perimeter of the roof, still looking below as he moved along. "They are still coming, all moving to join the larger group. There must be over a hundred. Maybe two hundred."

"More, I'm afraid," Skaag said from the other side of the roof. He looked over as well and continued to walk along the edge, away from the main group. "Maybe three hundred."

"We can take 'em," Jane spat, leaning over the edge and jabbing her knife at the closest face. She was within inches of making contact.

"It seems that we may have no other choice," Jules replied. He shortened his grip on his battering ram so he wouldn't drop it, his attacks now merely pokes. The closest creature toppled off the pile, but arose from its fall and joined the writhing mass at the base.

Annie struck with her bar as well when an undead soldier made its way too close to the rooftop. In between strikes, when she had no target, she looked to see who needed help. Howard and Skaag continued to walk along the roof's edge, and eventually met at a spot on the other side of the roof.

Then they both disappeared.

Chapter 33

Skaag helped Howard to his feet. Once standing, Howard quickly yanked his hand from Skaag's and dusted himself off. Skaag smiled and asked, "Are you okay, my friend?"

"Yes," Howard replied. Skaag was a friend to no one except for his fellow minions, if they were even capable of feeling friendship.

Howard examined the small room that he and Skaag had fallen into. An inventory room in some sort of store. There were no windows and only one doorway leading out, not including the newly made hole in the ceiling. Howard assumed that the store either repaired or sold furniture, as more than a dozen chairs were crammed into the doorway. The shop owner lay slumped against the far wall, gun in his limp hand, brains splattered on the wall. The owner must have known his fate had he not chosen this option.

"Howard?" he heard Annie's voice faintly from above.

He knew that she could not leave her position, lest the invaders gain an advantage. Cupping his hands around his mouth, he shouted as loud as he could, "I am standing and uninjured."

Skaag pointed to the barricade. "We must hurry out of here. The soldiers are surely coming."

Skaag was right. Howard could hear the moans from dozens of dead men, lost commands issued from beyond the grave. Through the various gaps in the furniture blockade, he could see the soldiers start to make their way into the front of the store. "Get away from the door, you fool. It's the only thing separating us from them."

"What other choice do we have?"

Howard smirked. "Well, let's ask your master. Hastur!"

"No!" Skaag shrieked.

"Hastur!" Howard called again, more than a little curious by Skaag's reaction. Apparently he'd rather face being ripped apart by an undead legion than be in the presence of his own master.

"I beg of you, please do not call him."

"Hastur! Show yourself!"

The room darkened as if the light fled, afraid of an ominous presence. Yellow-tinted smoke seeped in from the corners of the room, Hell making its presence known. The smoke began to swirl along the walls. As it coalesced, a noise akin to an aggravated groan formed. The noise grew louder as the smoke flowed into different shades of gray and yellow. Darker plumes formed a mouth and gnashing teeth along one of the walls. An angry face formed and growled, "Who dares call upon the Yellow King?"

"I do," Howard answered.

The eyes of twirling fog looked to Skaag. "Servant! How could you allow him to disturb me?"

Skaag fell to his knees, sniveling. "I tried to stop him! I tried! He was insistent. He called upon you before I could—"

"Enough! I will deal with you later. You!" The Yellow King now addressed Howard. "What is it you want?"

"My companions and I find ourselves in a dire predicament."

The Yellow King shifted his gaze past Howard, as if the surrounding walls provided no hindrance to what he saw. He chuckled. "Yes. Yes, it seems that you have."

"Get us out of it."

Curls of smoke turned inward to form a scowl. "What gives you any right to make such demands?"

"This!" Howard shouted as he thrust out his palm. "I bare your mark."

The smoky face reeled back and disappeared within itself. When it reformed, it sneered. "How? How is that possible?"

"I claimed the responsibility from your debtee."

Even though the face was a nebula floating over a miasma, Howard could tell that its full focus was on his hand. "So, she dies and owes me nothing. You die and I have lost next to nothing."

"You made a deal for her fame, have you not? For her to spread your word and assist you in making more of your horrid followers."

"A fame you do not possess. You have neither the access to the number of souls for me to convert, nor the true proclivity to follow through with the delivery of my message should I rescue you from your predicament. I choose to let you die."

"Then let's adjust the terms accordingly."

"Bah! What have you to offer me?"

"The future! I have come from thirty-one years further along than the present."

"From your words and actions, I can assume you have traveled here with the knowledge of me, meaning I exist thirty-one years from now. I can simply wait."

"If your adversary escapes his prison, then you will exist in a future that will never happen, if you even exist at all. You have no means to defeat your adversary. Your army is a pittance compared to his."

Like gathering thunder clouds, the sickly smoke pulled together into a frown. "What are you proposing? I save you and then sit with you for tea and tales? You give me information I cannot use for over three decades?"

"Hardly. I'm offering you *access* to the future. My body. Existing in this realm is desirous to you, yet you have yet to do so. I hardly understand the dark machinations controlling you or the eldritch governance that you abide by, but you can circumvent that by inhabiting my body, that I willingly offer up. But—only after I die, and you can only inhabit it for the same length of time I have. The longer I live in this body, the better the odds of you walking the Earth in the future, and the longer you can keep it after Life's ember gets snuffed out, which should be any minute now unless you wish to act. For the sake of full disclosure, I have yet to see my twentieth birthday. Were I to die today, you would have less than two decades to be a king in a world ruled by your adversary."

The Yellow King focused solely on Howard. "I am no genie. I do not grant wishes on your whim. If I do this, there must be a price to pay."

Howard did not have a response, content to stare in silence until the Yellow King made an offer. Judging by the way the smoky lips twisted into a wicked smile, Howard assumed he would have to make a difficult decision.

"He will die by your command," the Yellow King said, shifting his gaze to the prostrate Skaag.

Confused, Skaag pulled himself off the ground and stood. Pleading, he extended his arms. "Master? Why have you forsaken me?"

"It is no longer my choice, servant. It is your fellow human's."

Skaag turned to Howard. For the first time since their meeting, Skaag wore no smile. Instead, his bottom lip quivered, and tears streamed down his cheeks. "Please. Mercy, please."

"Despite his grotesque appearance, he is a human being," the Yellow King said to Howard. "Your decision is premeditated, and I am nothing more than your implement. Should you choose to escape this mess, make no mistake, it would be murder. Shall we continue?"

Skaag's whole body trembled as he wept. A stinging formed behind Howard's eyes, but he pushed away the tears before they could form. He knew that if he eventually found a way out of the Yellow King's deal—and by God he would try—he would never be able to remove the stain of murder from his soul. There was a higher importance, though. A priority greater than he or his soul. One he must choose, no matter the cost. "Yes."

Before his mouth finished making the word, Skaag burst into flame, bright yellow as if the sun had fallen from the sky onto him. He screamed so fiercely that he could no longer form words. Howard was certain the only one he would have spoken was, "Why?"

The flames shriveled his skin and vaporized his hair, yet Skaag still remained standing. Screaming. He turned and tore through the barricade, tossing the furniture about, yet the only thing that burned was him. The only thing screaming in pain was him.

Skaag ran from the storage room into the throng of undead soldiers. They, too, knew the touch of the yellow fire. However, the fire consumed the undead, reducing them to ash within seconds while Skaag continued to boil, his skin bubbling as he ran out the front door of the store. Screaming.

Howard no longer heard the screams, just the Yellow King's laughter. Walking out of the storage room, Howard didn't bother looking back; he just needed to get away from the laughter.

By the time Howard made his way to the street, the battle was almost over. Skaag merely stood in the center of the street while the contingent of soldiers swarmed to him like moths, with the same effect—as soon as a soldier got too close, the yellow flame consumed it.

Bursts of fire flared up, a demonic fireworks display, around a flaming totem. Flame and ash swirled around Skaag. The man burned white hot, yet still found a voice for his screams. Finally, after Howard could take no more of Skaag's anguish, the screaming stopped. The pain ended. Fire still burned the crumpled remains of Skaag, but diminished in intensity. What had been attacking soldiers were now mounds upon mounds of harmless dust.

"What the fuck was that?" Jane yelled from the roof of the building; seven other faces slack from disbelief and confusion.

"It was Skaag," Howard answered.

"How?" Annie asked.

Howard looked into the store, back into the storage room, to the unmoving form of the shopkeeper who had taken his own life. "The Yellow King intervened."

The remaining pair of yellowed men murmured between themselves and said a quick prayer for their fallen leader, allowing the others to leave the rooftop first. Once they finished their words, they joined everyone else on the streets.

As soon as her feet hit the ground, Annie ran to Howard. She whispered, "What happened?"

"I'd rather not discuss it at the moment," Howard whispered back, averting his eyes from hers.

She grabbed his hand and turned it palm up, exposing the Mark of the Yellow King. "I knew you would still bear it, but I had hoped that somehow… somehow the burden would have shifted back to me."

As if hearing the punch line of the cruelest joke imaginable, Howard offered a weak chuckle. "Me bearing this mark actually saved us all."

"We should get movin'," Billy said as he glared at Annie and Howard.

"Yeah," Jane said, standing next to Billy. "Wouldn't want no one else gettin' hurt now, do we?"

Trying to push aside the vivid images of Skaag's torched body, Howard followed everyone else as they continued toward the harbor, toward the noises of torture. He remained close to Annie. Even though she had her revolver in her right hand, she still wielded the metal bar like a sword in her left hand. Much to Howard's chagrin, she still needed it.

Deep down, Howard knew that Skaag had not eliminated all of the undead soldiers, but he still prayed that there would be no more. Making a deal with a devil didn't preclude him from asking God for favors.

Groups of undead warriors moved about in small packs. They were disposed of with ease, the yellowed men taking point and dispatching the enemy with the zeal of vengeance.

One more street. One more alleyway. They kept close to the buildings and moved with caution. Finally, they reached the harbor, and Howard wished they hadn't.

Standing at the end of a pier as if it were an altar, Szilveszter gleefully recited incantations in an arcane language. Like wicked deacons, Heinrich and Sophia Schliemann stood on the pier as well, arms raised in the air. Above his head, Heinrich held a mask of gold, the visage of a beautiful woman, one Howard assumed to be Helen of Troy. He also surmised that the power of the mask was what controlled the undead warriors. But the happenings around the pier brought more dread to Howard's heart than the shuffling of reanimated corpses.

On the street near the pier was Nikola's teleportation machine, electricity crackling about the wires that snaked around the metal hoop. Green lightning flowed from the machine to a swirling whirlpool in the sea. The whirlpool was red. Blood red.

Like an assembly line of the damned, hundreds of animated corpses stood and formed a path from nearby buildings to the water's edge. They would snatch a denizen of the town from within a building and pass them along, a head of chattel to be processed. The townsperson wailed and struggled, but to no avail; the number of hands involved were too numerous. Down the line of the undead the person went until they reached the water's edge, where they were handed off to dozens of crimson-stained soldiers. They ripped the townsman apart, limb from limb, using skeletal hands to tear into their bellies and pull the entrails free. After the living became dead, they were tossed into the murky water, viscera and all. The raging whirlpool mixed all the parts together like a stirring soup.

Judging from the deafening screams rising from the buildings, Howard assumed there to be thousands of sacrifices left. Doing his best to keep hidden in the alleyway, he pressed his luck and leaned out farther.

Muscular arms crossed over his massive chest, Dr. Sivkas stood guard by the machine. Zarkahn and the veiled woman moved from building to building, working their dark magics to keep the citizens in the structures. Nikola... Nikola paced in small circles between the machine and the Schliemanns while chewing on his fingernails. Howard hoped that was a sign of gnawing regret.

"Oh my God," Annie whispered as she witnessed the grim scene. Jane uttered a string of profanities so obscene that Howard didn't know the meanings of half the words. The others gasped and offered softly spoken prayers. Even the yellowed men were taken aback by the atrocity that played out before them.

"We have to save these people," Billy said, tightening his grip on both his gun and his knife.

"We have to stop Szilveszter," Howard replied.

"Seriously?" Jane spat. "You're willin' to sacrifice people—human beings—to complete your mission?"

"Jane," Jules said, the calmness of his voice belying the horrors happening close by, "If we stop Szilveszter, we save the people."

Jane set her jaw as she stared at Szilveszter. "I can get 'em."

"From this distance? Are you sure?" Billy asked.

"Yup."

"Are you sure?" Annie asked.

"Yup."

"You've been drinking."

"I'm always drinkin'."

"I think I should try."

Jane turned to look Annie directly in the eyes. Through clenched teeth, she said, "Look, girly. This ain't the carnival where the props are all set up nice and neat. Yeah, I'll admit, you might be able to outshoot me that way. But not this way. Not in the real world. Not with wind and arc and distance and people dyin' all around us. I. Got. This."

Howard hoped that Annie would argue more, find the right words to convince Jane to stand down. There must have been some unspoken conversation between the two while they stared at each other—either woman-to-woman or gunslinger-to-gunslinger—because Annie acquiesced.

Holding his breath, Howard felt helpless as Jane used both hands to hold her gun. He wanted to inform her that she only had one shot; once she squeezed the trigger, their position would be compromised. But stating the obvious would only be distracting. Though he wished that they would have at least thought to reposition themselves.

Jane squeezed the trigger.

Even though he logically knew it was impossible, Howard swore he saw the bullet leave the barrel of the gun. As if possessing some form of supernatural sight for a fraction of a second, he saw the trajectory of the projectile, aiming right for Szilveszter's disgusting smile. Howard knew, deep in the places of his soul he examined only when alone, that Jane's shot was true and accurate. Had it not been for an undead soldier turning at the last instant.

The bullet struck the walking corpse, dropping it. The echo of the gunshot could be heard by all along the docks, even over the screaming in the buildings. Szilveszter didn't stop the ceremonial incantation, but his voice became richer, bolder, more triumphant.

Heinrich responded to the gunshot by commanding some of his soldiers to attack.

"Run!" Howard yelled, but no one needed to be told. They made it down only one alley before they were swarmed by the undead. The numbers overwhelmed them, overwhelmed Howard's mind, as if Skaag's sacrifice had never happened.

Hands. Dead and decaying. Bony hands with dried skin sloughing away, grabbed Howard and his companions. He could no longer see Annie. Or Albert. He heard random shouts, specifically Jane's foul mouth.

Howard struggled; they all did. One person against a hundred hands was nothing. The soldiers moved, shoved, pushed, guided Howard and his companions closer to the water's edge. Closer to death.

Just a piece of flotsam trapped in the current created by a river of rotting flesh, Howard watched as other undead soldiers brought forth more and more townspeople from the buildings. Just as helpless as Howard, dozens of people were now being dismembered and disemboweled, and tossed into the water for whatever awaited in the center of the whirlpool. Howard could no longer watch the horror, and turned away as best he could. He caught Nikola's eye.

Wringing his hands together, Nikola watched, eyebrows arched with worry, face etched with fear. Howard called to him. "Nikola! Help us!"

Nikola's focus danced around, weighing odds and playing out scenarios. Howard yelled to him again, "This is not the way to be remembered for greatness! This is not how to usher humanity into the next evolutionary step! Please believe me when I say that this is not the way."

"But the vision of my future. It was unthinkable!"

"The future is clay, not stone. Now that you know it, you can sculpt it into whatever shape you wish it to be!"

Fear had turned Howard duplicitous, his words betraying the sacrosanct message of maintaining tomorrow's secrecy. But it had worked.

Being taller than Heinrich made it easy for Nikola to snatch the Mask of Helen. By the time Heinrich turned to assess what had happened, Nikola clutched the mask with both hands and commanded, "To the Mask!" With as much effort as his lanky body could muster, he tossed the gilded face into the sea, as close to the whirlpool as possible.

"*Nooo!*" both Heinrich and Sophia Schliemann screamed, as if Nikola had ripped an organ from their bodies.

Howard decided to contemplate his proclivities toward religion as the undead soldiers released him from their grip and began marching into the sea. Droves of corpses shambled to the edge of the docks and fell into the sea. They bobbed like tea bags as they swirled along the flow of scarlet water, disappearing down the funnel of the whirlpool. Howard didn't know if the stream of undead soldiers helped the process or hindered it. At the moment, he didn't care, simply too happy to be free.

The confusion caused by losing control of the undead army was enough to break the concentration of Zarkahn and of Madame Sulola. Whatever illusionary terrors they were showing the trapped townspeople ended, as did their hold over them. Cries and screams continued to ring forth as the residents poured out from the buildings. None stayed to fight or witness, all ran from the scene.

Taking advantage of thousands of people fleeing from the hundreds of undead soldiers marching to the sea, Howard turned to assess the situation. Szilveszter was alone at the end of the pier, both Heinrich and Sophia fled with the crowd. Nikola was gone. The control over the undead had been broken, yet Szilveszter continued to chant. The swirling within Howard's guts rivaled the raging whirlpool. This wasn't over yet.

Chapter 34

Insanity. That was the only word Billy could come up with to describe this situation. He didn't even have time to curse the bad luck of one of those graveyard soldiers taking Jane's bullet meant for Szilveszter. As soon as their position was compromised, the world turned upside down.

The catacomb warriors were everywhere. Billy fought. He kicked and punched, elbowed and kneed. He drove his knife through their skulls and even ripped off the neck nodules with his bare hands. Not enough. The numbers were endless.

Then, the reinitiated dead stopped, releasing the confounding pressure.

Instead of the walking corpses trapping him, they now jostled him as they ambled past on their way to the sea. He didn't care. Looking for his companions, he pushed his way past the zombies as they trundled along with monomaniacal purpose. Catching a glimpse of raven hued curls, he yelled, "Annie!"

"Billy?" he thought he heard her cry out.

Billy continued to shoulder his way through the flow of corpses. As he got closer to Annie, he saw her turning and turning, spinning. Billy pushed past the creatures, knocking over any that got in his way. As she spun one more time, she turned herself right into Billy, slamming against his chest. Gasping, she stepped back, her eyes wide with confusion and shimmering from tears. Billy reached for her, to embrace her, to let her know how happy he was to see her alive. As he wrapped his arms around her, she kissed him.

A deep, desperate kiss.

Just as immediate as it started, it ended. She pulled away and looked even more surprised by her actions than by once-dead soldiers shuffling all around her. "Billy, I'm sorry—"

"Don't be. We—"

"—I shouldn't have done that—"

"—are just happy to see each other—"

"—now is simply not the time. We must find the others." With the end of her statement, she turned and pushed her way through the flow of undead to look for everyone else.

Billy shook his head as if it would dislodge the confusing messages rattling around inside. No such luck. He lied to himself and said that he understood; she simply wasn't equipped to handle this form of lunacy. Albert and Howard had dealt with situations like this before. Jules wrote about such flights of fancy. Jane was probably thinking that she was just in an alcohol-induced dream. And himself? He was willing to do anything for Annie, even letting her confuse him if it helped her process the situation.

There was mass confusion as the fleeing townspeople crashed into the flow of the undead, but Annie and Billy managed to find the others, less one yellowed man. The unlucky abomination of humanity had fallen to the ground. Too many footfalls led to a punishing death. Even Billy couldn't help but feel a touch of pity for the poor fellow.

He was happy to see the others, but still concerned about the direness of the situation. The undead were destroying themselves and the townspeople were escaping. Szilveszter and his band of freaks were still alive. And the whirlpool in the sea was getting bigger and faster.

Howard said, "Albert and I will stop Szilveszter. Everyone else, dispose of the circus freaks."

The group spilt into two. Howard and Annie exchanged glances of relief and longing before attending to the tasks at hand. Billy chided himself for allowing that to irk him.

Billy led the way to the buildings where the townspeople were being held hostage. He felt like he was swimming in two different rivers, with the current of the living, against the current of the dead, almost drowning because of both.

"Jane!" Annie called out above the screams of the escaping people. "Do you have a clear shot at anyone?"

"No!" Jane yelled back.

Billy knew it was the four of them and a yellowed men against three freaks. Their adversaries had some form of supernatural advantage, but Billy had shooting skills as well as two women who surpassed him in ability. But they could barely see their enemies, appearing for a glimpse in the crowd and disappearing just as quickly. Fighting through the crowd was tiring, and he feared being too fatigued to lift his gun when it came time to need it. He found the one place where the number of bodies would be diminishing. "Inside this building!"

Fighting against the horde of people spilling from the wide entrance, Billy pushed his way through. Inside the building, he still had to push past the thinning crowd, but was able to break free into a vast, open space. It was a warehouse to store the many goods being shipped from across the waterways. The roof was twenty feet above his head, and shelves reached up from the floor to touch it. A few shelves were broken and toppled. Burlap sacks of various grains were stacked on the shelves, most torn open, their contents spilled along the floor like granulated, beige blood. Crates and casks of different kinds of liquids lined the one wall, also in various conditions; some pristine enough to read the manufacturers' names etched into the shining glass bottles, others had been reduced to saturated splinters floating in aromatic pools. Bolts of materials, from commonplace to exotic; some spooled, some shredded.

"Billy!" Annie called from behind him. She burst from the crowd and ran to him, but disappointment stabbed him in the chest when she stopped out of his reach. No embrace. No kiss.

"The veiled woman! She was right behind...." Annie's words faded as she looked behind Billy. Something distracted her. Billy was ready to shoot whatever it was until Annie smiled. "Perfect!"

She ran toward tools and furniture. Billy was confused. They had guns and the veiled woman was unarmed, so they should be planning an ambush. Waves of screams crested by the doorway.

The people still inside the warehouse stopped trying to shove their way out. Cowering and covering their faces, they parted, moving out of the way of something terrifying. As the last row of people moved aside, Madame Sulola entered, holding the silken scarves away from the wrinkled crone side of her face. Billy went to train his gun on her but was too late. She looked his way.

Caught by her gaze, Billy froze, his limbs petrified. The world rippled; the warehouse walls melted away like hot wax. All that remained was blood. A blood-red sky. A sea of knee-deep blood. Blood-covered creatures baring their fangs, clawed their way toward Billy.

He opened his mouth to scream, but before he could lend voice to the terror, an angel appeared. Annie, running past him. How was she here? Did the veiled woman capture her within this nightmare as well? The blood world swirled around him. A woman screamed. Annie? No. A different woman was screaming. Then the horrific world dissipated like steam on a cold day, returning the warehouse to Billy. His head throbbed with questions, but Annie was the answer to them all. She had rescued him.

Standing in front of the veiled woman, Annie held an oval mirror, one that would look perfect on a stylish vanity. Billy didn't like being rescued by a woman, but he didn't try to fight the feelings of relief. Until Annie drew her gun and pointed it at the veiled woman's head.

"Annie?" Billy asked. "What are you doing?"

Tears streamed down her face. "I may not be able to put an end to… to… to all of this, but I can at least put an end to her!"

"You already did that," Billy said. Half of Madame Sulola's face was frozen in horror while in a standing coma. "Anything else would be murder."

Annie shook her head. "No. No. No. It wouldn't be. It would be in self-defense. If we kill anyone now, it would be considered self-defense."

"No, it ain't, miss prissy-pants," Jane said, walking into the warehouse. The number of people trying to get out had gone from hundreds to dozens. Jane approached the others and waved her hand in front of the veiled woman's face. "And you know it. She's a turnip right now, and it might be a mercy to kill her, but it'd still be murder."

"You wanted to kill Hitler earlier. Why is this any different?"

"He was a man with power. Real power. He could get more and more and more people to kill for him. Not some cheap hypnosis tricks like this bitch. Look at her now. Helpless as a baby."

Billy placed his hand on Annie's. It was cold, and he helped her lower her gun. "Motivation is everythin'. You gotta be one hundred percent sure. You don't wanna bear the burden of doubt for ending another person's life."

"The way I see it, ending your lives now will be a mercy killing," came from the doorway. The warehouse was almost empty of townspeople, but the last few left cowered as Zarkahn strode in.

Billy drew first, but immediately dropped his gun. With the wave of a hand, Zarkahn turned the gun into a fist sized spider. He waved his hand again, and Annie's gun turned into a chattering centipede the length of her arm. Panicked, she flung it to the floor. "Impossible!"

"Oh, my dear girl," Zarkahn said as his fingers caressed the curls of his handlebar mustache. "Because of the god that I am helping Szilveszter summon forth, all things are possible."

Billy and Annie stepped back as Zarkahn continued to advance. Jane held her ground.

When Zarkahn came within ten feet of Jane, he stopped and removed his garish top hat. Annie released a horrid amalgam of a gasp and a shriek. Billy's stomach lurched. "What in the hell...?"

Zarkahn's forehead did not stop where the hat had been resting; it continued upward, transitioning from smooth skin to wrinkles and folds, slicked with a maculate sheen. Dozens of tentacles sprouted instead of hair, each moving independently. In the center gaped one large eye, tears of pus escaping over its bottom lid. "He is my master. He is with me at all times, giving me the power to do this!"

With angry flourish, Zarkahn waved his hand in front of Jane. Nothing happened. All parts of his forehead angled down into a frown as he waved his hand again. Still nothing. "What is happening? Why is my magic not working?"

Jane pointed her gun right at the center of the third eye and said, "I don't believe in magic. I believe in bullets."

She squeezed the trigger.

The screech of an inhuman nightmare filled the warehouse, high pitched to the point where Billy needed to cover his ears. Advancing on the fallen body, Jane shot the top of Zarkahn's head again. And again. The whining stopped.

Jane turned to Annie, pointed at the unmoving body of Zarkahn, and said, "Now, that was self-defense."

Billy and Annie stared.

Jane frowned and said, "Quit gawpin' like a couple of frogs tryin' to catch flies and pick up your guns."

Billy felt like a simpleton, needing Jane to tell him to pick up his gun, because he would never have thought to do so. A tiny piece of his mind expected to see the spider. Instead, his revolver lay on the floor.

Before the trio had a chance to formulate a plan, commotion by the door caught their attention. All of the civilians were gone, fled looking for safety. Dr. Sivkas lumbered in through the entrance, engaged in fisticuffs with Jules and the remaining yellowed men. The chiseled muscles of Dr.

Sivkas twitched and jerked as he swatted at the yellowed man wrapped around his waist. Having some heft himself, Jules landed punches to Dr. Sivkas' ribs. If not for the incredible musculature of Dr. Sivkas, they would have been effective. With a meaty right hand, Dr. Sivkas grabbed a fistful of Jules' shirt and tossed him aside.

Jules' legs tried to keep up with the backward momentum but failed. He stumbled and fell, sliding to a stop by Billy's feet. Billy looked down and asked, "Need a hand?"

"In more ways than one, I'm afraid," Jules said, using Billy's outstretched hand to get himself back to his feet.

"Well, at least the little freak is keepin' the big freak busy," Jane said as she aimed her gun at the brain of Dr. Sivkas. She squeezed the trigger. Again, her aim was true. And again, it didn't yield the desired results.

The bullet ricocheted off the jar, barely a scuff mark for the effort. Growling, Jane shot three more times. Each bullet struck the jar Dr. Sivkas called a head, and each time the bullet impotently bounced off. "God damn it!"

"He certainly has," the mechanical voice of Dr. Sivkas reverberated through the warehouse. "Or he will once I get to you."

As simple as plucking a flower from its stem, Dr. Sivkas removed the yellowed man's head from his neck. Nothing more than a sack of meat now, the decapitated body fell to the floor in a gush of blood.

"We need to think of somethin'," Billy said, wincing from the sound of breaking bone, the slap of a dead body hitting the floor followed.

"I'm doin' the only thing I know how," Jane said as she reloaded her gun.

Jules tore a strip from the bottom of his shirt, and then tore that into eight smaller thumb size strips. Handing two to everyone, he said, "Here. Put these in your ears. Jane, when the time is right, shoot. Billy, keep his hands away from me."

Billy balled up the cloth and jammed one in each ear. He followed as Jules advanced on Dr. Sivkas and punched him a few times in the gut. No effect, but it did afford Billy enough time to round behind Dr. Sivkas. Billy jumped and placed his hands on the top of Dr. Sivkas' head as if preparing to leapfrog. Before going all the way over, Billy brought his legs over the shoulders, hooking his heels under Dr. Sivkas' armpits. Dr. Sivkas tried to extend his arms, smashing Billy's crotch against the back of the jar and bringing forth tears, but he could not bring them forward.

Jules went after the speaker set in Dr. Sivkas' chest. Deftly, he popped off the casing and fiddled with the wires.

Wrapping both arms around the jar, to maintain balance and make a feeble attempt to relieve the crushing pressure in his groin, Billy prayed that whatever Jules was doing would work.

"Now, Billy! Let go now!" Jules yelled.

Not needing to be told twice, Billy used the jar as leverage to untangle his legs and jump free from Dr. Sivkas.

A mechanical whine filled the air, growing rapidly in pitch and volume. Even with the ersatz earplugs, Billy covered his ears, as did his comrades. Dr. Sivkas brought his hands to the jar, trying to settle it. To no avail.

The jar vibrated. Even though there were no facial features around the floating eyeballs, Billy swore he saw panic in them. Then the jar shattered.

The fluids splashed over Dr. Sivkas' shoulders while his brain and eye stalks seemed to hover in the air as if they refused to believe they were no longer protected. Before gravity could take over, a bullet from Jane's gun struck the brain, gouging away part of it. Despite the body being made of pure muscle, without a brain it wobbled, then collapsed in a useless heap.

Billy removed the balls of cloth from his ears, and the sound of his blood flowing through his veins beat to the same rhythm as his heart. He looked to the others, primarily Annie, and they were fine. Billy allowed himself a smile to accompany the relief flowing within him; cut short by the crack of thunder from outside.

Chapter 35

Albert aimed at Szilveszter and squeezed the trigger just as the ground rumbled. His shot went wide, as did Howard's.

Hands still raised reverently above his head, Szilveszter had the smile of a man who was intimate with madness. He chanted but one word over and over again with such vigor that his entire body tensed each time he said it. "Ia!"

Any hint that the sky was once clear became a memory as clouds the color of death billowed, roiling like bubbling soup. Lightning flashed, but instead of colors that nature intended, the electrical streaks flashed bright shades of green. The sky was a black beast with emerald blood coursing through its veins.

The lightning struck the water, closer and closer to the whirlpool. Once one arc struck the center of the spinning water, all subsequent bolts struck the same spot. The green flashes mixed with the blood to give the water a fetid brown hue.

Albert aimed his gun at Szilveszter, but lost his balance as the ground shook again. A groan filled the air as a tentacle large enough to crush a horse emerged from the center of the spinning water. More activity took place around the agitated water's edge. Smaller waves formed contrary to the natural splashing. The mounds of water took shape, until forms surfaced. The undead warriors.

Albert and Howard both gawped in dread as they watched heads break the surface of the water. First a few, then dozens, then hundreds. They still had gape-mouthed expressions, but now Albert swore they all had anger and determination within their empty eye sockets. As they continued to rise from the water, their malevolent appearance did not stop with faces frozen mid-scream.

Their flesh and muscles were no longer dried. Even though they were still wrinkled and folded, they bore a new sheen, a coating of fresh mucus. Some wore patches of human skin, torn from the sacrificed townsfolk and displayed like prized pelts. Others had different trophies. Working lungs inflated and deflated behind mummified ribs. Hearts pumped and twitched within half-rotted breastbones. Loops of intestines spooled around petrified spines and trailed like streamers. Each of the undead soldiers marched from the water wearing some part of a recently mutilated townsperson like a piece of trash caught in a fishing net—a jaw stuck on a shoulder, a severed hand dangling from a hip bone, toes jammed in between exposed ribs.

Madness. The once-dead defiled the remains of the once-living, and madness was the lone path available for Albert. It wasn't until his throat hurt and his lungs burned that he realized he was screaming. He vaguely heard Howard yelling for him to stop.

Walking toward the army of ghouls, Albert fired his gun. Crying and screaming, he pulled the trigger again and again. Energy beams the same unnatural green as the lightning, the same green as the electricity coursing from Szilveszter's tetrahedron to the whirlpool. Albert's beams tore through the heads and faces of the undead soldiers marching forth. The soldiers fell, never to move again. Albert's efforts weren't enough.

He advanced. The closer he got to them, the faster he could drop them. Knee deep in the murky water, Albert shot and shot and shot. A second tentacle appeared from the whirlpool as a gurgling laugh emanated from within the swirling waters, deep enough to rattle Albert's chest. Yet he continued to shoot the warriors encircling him, reaching for him. A third tentacle appeared. Albert shot at the tentacles; the energy blasts having no effect. Still raging, Albert maneuvered farther into the water, closer to the whirlpool.

Before he got close enough to feel the tug of the swirling waters, he was able to see into the center, see what the tentacles were attached to. Had he been any less monomaniacal, he would have heeded Howard's screams of, "Don't look!"

Albert looked. He stared into the eye of the god of madness.

Fear.

Harrowing, bone-shattering fear.

Albert couldn't breathe, couldn't blink. A million icy pinpricks stabbed up his spine to his scalp. The world fell silent and still for a split-second eternity. Until a hand pulled him away.

Jules grabbed Albert by the arm and pulled. William grabbed Albert's other arm, and together they dragged him out of the water through a path created by the blazing guns of Annie and Jane. Howard used his weapon of dark energy to keep the undead soldiers from clutching Albert's rescuers.

Once back on shore, Albert dropped to his hands and knees. He became acutely aware of everything. He felt every piece of sand and dirt digging into his palms. He heard every voice of his comrades, yelling. Every ounce of blood rushing through every inch of his body felt like river rapids crashing against cliff walls. The mad god in the whirlpool moaned, the harrowing sound announcing the arrival of Hell on Earth. But above all, he heard Szilveszter's cackling. It had to stop, no matter the cost.

"The tetrahedron," Albert mumbled.

"What?" Jane yelled over the sounds of her gun.

"The pyramid!" Albert yelled back. "Shoot the pyramid!"

Jane and Annie did as Albert commanded. With no result. The bullets merely bounced off of it. Szilveszter laughed even harder.

Quivering muscles fought with aching joints as Albert stood. Despite his arm not wanting to move, he lifted his gun and aimed it at Szilveszter. Then he changed his target. He squeezed—and held—the trigger.

An unbroken beam of green emanated from his gun to the tetrahedron. The green and black fluids within the pyramid swirled faster. Szilveszter screamed, "No!"

"Howard!" Albert called, implying that he should do the same thing. Without hesitation, Howard brought his weapon around and fired. The inky fluids within the pyramid swirled faster; the container sides began to throb.

Szilveszter screamed again, now caught in the shifting storm of green electricity. Another ground-shaking moan bellowed from within the whirlpool.

"Albert!" Howard shouted over the cacophony of the thunderous storm and undead moans. "The tetrahedron may be our only way back to our time!"

"We must stop him, Howard! No matter the cost!"

"Your wife! Your son! Are you absolutely sure of this?"

Albert thought of his family. Despite the hell swirling around him—the black clouds shooting lightning bolts, the deity trying to birth itself from the sea, his companions shooting nightmarish creatures—he thought about nothing else other than the warm and loving arms of his family. Tears rolling over his cheeks, he answered, "Yes! It is for of them that we must do this!"

The steady beams caused the colors of the pyramid to swirl so fast they blurred into a putrid dark green. The electricity now formed a nonstop circuit, circling from the sky to the whirlpool to the teleportation doorway to the whirlpool. The longer that Howard and Albert concentrated their beams on the pyramid, the faster the lighting moved, the more the walls of the pyramid throbbed. The more Szilveszter screamed. The louder the world protested.

Albert wondered if he would be able to walk away from this with any form of sanity. Just as he doubted he would, the tetrahedron shattered. Without the protective walls of the structure, the dark energies within dissipated, nothing more than a foul colored cloud fading away with the wind. With one final crack of thunder, Szilveszter disappeared within the boundaries of the archway, as if the lightning flowing over it reached out and snatched him away. The whirlpool stopped; no creature to be found within the waves. The undead things fell back to their lifeless states, the sea pulling their bodies into it, moving to conceal the memory of their existence. The clouds parted to reveal the sky, the devil's curtains parting to reveal the window to God.

Weeping, Albert fell to his knees, unable to stand any longer. The weight of necessity in stopping the madman lifted from his chest and allowed him to gasp in a large gulp of clean air. But the devastating crush of losing his family hurled the air right out of him again. This he could not bear. Blackness consumed his vision as he fell unconscious.

Chapter 36

One week. It had been only one week, and Albert could already see the gray. Leaning in closer to the mirror for a better look, he realized "gray" was not accurate. White. Peeking up from the base of his scalp, covering the entirety of his head, was a centimeter's length of white hair.

Albert chuckled. He knew that surviving his encounter with Szilveszter and his mad god would leave a scar, but he never expected it to be white hair. That and sleepless nights.

Still looking in the mirror, he needed to touch the purple bags under his eyes to prove that they were real and not some bad makeup job. He checked his teeth and gums, happy that they seemed normal. He stuck out his tongue, for reasons unknown to even himself. Maybe he did leave a little of his sanity behind at Çanakkale. Maybe it was the lack of sleep. He chuckled again, thinking about Jane's homespun remedies for garnering slumber, especially since she had only two suggestions—alcohol and sex. He hardly thought that constant inebriation was the answer, and he still considered himself married with child, despite being thirty-one years removed from the last time he saw his family.

Standing back from the mirror, Albert smiled. He would get more sleep tonight than last night, because he slept longer last night than the night before. Despite the atrocities he had witnessed, he knew, deep in his heart, that he would find his way back home. He wasn't sure how, but if he could come here, to this time, then he could return to his home. But what would he go come back to?

A mild pain formed behind his right eye at the thought of trying to untangle the knots of the space-time continuum. When a minute passed here, did the same minute pass there, at his home? Or was that inconsequential, because he could plunk himself back into any minute of any day of any year? Or was that an impossibility because he was standing in an alternate timeline, one independent of his own? Whatever the answer was, he knew two things about it: he and Howard would invest hours of conjecture over the topic, and they would find a way back home.

That would have to wait for another time, though. Albert hardly felt up for the task. Howard, on the other hand, had been poring over his notebook this past week, adding more sketches, trying to make sense of the madness found within its pages. Feeling sorry for his friend, Albert went to go check on him.

Howard was in the living room, sitting by himself on a couch, reading and rereading the things written in his notebook. The others were there as well, all looking pensive, still shaken up from the events of a week ago. Unfortunately for Albert, all eyes turned to him for leadership. William gave voice to what everyone was thinking, "So now what, boss?"

Albert smiled. "I'm hardly anyone's boss, William."

Standing by the largest window overlooking the French countryside, William shrugged. "You and Howard are the only two who really know what's going on, and I'd follow you a lot sooner than I'd follow Howard."

Howard looked up from where he was seated and cast a snarling glare at William. It lasted no longer than a few seconds before he lowered his head back to the pages of his notebook.

Albert looked around the room. Jane stood on the other side of the window from William, the morning sun giving them both a healthy glow. The angle of the light through her whiskey bottle created a tiny rainbow on the wooden floor every time she brought it to her lips. Annie sat in an armchair upholstered with red velvet and laced with spirals of gold filigree. She sipped tea. Jules sat in a loveseat with the same pattern as the armchair. He, too, had a small cup of tea.

Albert didn't like that he was standing, giving him the appearance of the leader he did not wish to be. He might have little choice now, considering how the others viewed him at this moment. "It's not so much one person following another. It's more about information gathering and disseminating what we do with it."

"All right," William said. "So, what information do we have?"

Without looking up, Howard answered, "We're in the middle of a war."

William snorted. "What? Like a war between Heaven and Hell? Good and evil?"

"No." Howard looked up. "It's a war among evil and evil and evil and evil. And we're caught in the middle, viewed as allies to some, enemies to others, and pawns to all."

William gulped down a dry swallow. "So... I guess that brings me back to my first question. Now what do we do?"

Albert answered before Howard could sour the mood any further, "Howard and I will continue to fight against the dark forces while looking for a way to return home, to our time period. We apologize for intruding on your lives, and appreciate all that you have done. We encourage you all to go back to your regular lives."

"Balderdash!" Jules barked. He placed the saucer and teacup on a nearby end table. "I for one cannot go back to a 'regular life' knowing that this kind of malevolence exists. If you two leave this house or leave this time period, it does not mean that these dark forces will cease to be. I will be aiding you in any way possible, including the use of this château. No one knows about this property of mine: not family, not friends. You will stay here as long as you need. If anyone else would wish to stay, there are plenty of accommodations."

Albert and Howard looked to each other, a wordless conversation playing out without so much as a twitch. Albert felt the adamancy behind Jules' words, and assumed Howard recognized it too. With a soft smile, Albert said, "Your offer is gracious, and you seem as unbendable as iron, so I see little other option than to accept."

"I'm in, too," William said with wry smirk, "I ain't got much to return to, other than desert towns and scorned chicitas."

"I'm stayin' as well," Jane said. She offered only a long swig from her bottle as explanation.

Everyone looked to Annie. Albert didn't like that he felt the pressure of the room weigh on her to make a decision, but if there was one person who could handle pressure, it was Annie. Like Jules, she placed her drink on an end table. However, she stood and ran her hands over her dress a few times. "I am still uncertain where my fate lies and which path I must follow. I sent a telegraph regarding my whereabouts to my betrothed a couple of days ago, but I have yet to receive a reply. I believe I will go into town."

As if she were a kiss blown from a goddess, she floated out of the room.

A big smile spread across Jules' face after she left. "This is exciting! Exciting indeed! It's not often one who writes fantastical fiction gets a chance to live it. I will take inventory of our supplies. I will rouse those who I know to dabble in such eccentricities. I will make sure we are prepared for whatever we face next!"

With a speed belying his girth, Jules leapt from his chair and dashed out of the room.

William chuckled, then turned to Jane. A devious smile slid across his face as he asked her, "A little boot knockin'?"

Jane took a big swig of whiskey while keeping her eyes on the window, as if seeking advice from the outside world. She put her bottle on an end table and walked out of the room, pausing just long enough to gesture with her head for William to follow. He did.

Albert didn't know what to make of any of that, and he was quite certain that he didn't want to. So he put it out of his mind and joined Howard on the couch. He looked at Howard's notebook and said, "It appears that we have some allies in this fight."

Howard wrote a single word on a previously blank page and closed the notebook. "It does. Although I do not think they know what they might be in for."

"They fought alongside of us and survived. I think they might have a good enough idea."

"True."

"Any idea of what to do next, my friend?"

"Nikola Tesla was involved, and he helped us at Çanakkale. If there is anyone who could help us with this, or help us get back home, might it be him? We could even weigh the pros and cons of revisiting Thomas Edison."

"I like those ideas. But after Çanakkale, I think we may still need a few more days of rest."

"This is very true. We have a lot ahead of us."

Albert couldn't agree more. He leaned back, allowing the plushness of the couch to comfort him. Even though he had woken up less than hour ago, he eyes burned with the desire to sleep every time he blinked. He took that as a good thing, his body yearning for slumber. He closed his eyes and gave into warm unconsciousness, pondering the last word that Howard had written in his notebook:

Cthulhu.

Epilogue

Szilveszter awoke with a start; water lapping his face, both biting cold and reassuring. His robes clung to his body, water-logged and heavy. He felt moist, rough dirt against his face, the hardness of the ground he lay upon. Most importantly, he felt. If he could feel, then he was alive. If he was alive, then his god had not forsaken him.

He moved his arms and legs, aching soreness radiated from every joint. He smiled at that, feeling that he had all of his limbs. Opening his eyes, he stood.

Szilveszter found himself on the shore of a large stream, one winding through countryside and forest. Nothing like the port town of Çanakkale. Instead of dryness and dirt and stone, he was among wild grasses and trees. "What is it you wish of me, Master?" he whispered to himself.

Looking for any clue, any form of a sign, Szilveszter slowly turned to get a better understanding of his environment. He saw someone standing near him from his peripheral vision. Panicked, he spun quickly to face his potential attacker. He almost laughed when he turned to face a boy, about age ten. The boy simply stood there, at the threshold of the forest, his hands fiddling with one another. However, the earnestness found within the boy's stare put Szilveszter at unease. Eyes set close together under a heavy brow; they held notions beyond his years. Intelligence. Wisdom. Insanity. With a small mouth as straight as a knife cut, the boy asked, "Who are you?"

Szilveszter recognized the language as Russian, and assumed that was the country where he had found himself. He replied, "My name is Szilveszter Matuska."

"What is your mission?"

"To usher in a new world, to prepare it for the arrival of the great god that I call my master."

The boy stood quietly, staring at Szilveszter, pondering the words as his fingers folded together and unfolded. Repeatedly. A sense of discomfort bloomed within Szilveszter's chest, and he pondered what to say next.

"Would you teach me of this god?" the boy finally asked.

Szilveszter smiled. "I would. I would like that very much. Tell me, boy, is your village nearby."

"Yes. It is but a small one called Pokrovsoye."

"Wonderful. Lead me to this village. Lead me to your parents, so that I may bathe myself and find dry clothing."

"No. I do not think my parents would like you very much."

Szilveszter frowned. "Then I'm afraid I will be unable to teach you about the great god I call master."

"But I do know people who would like you, as long as you teach them about your great god as well."

"Truthfully?"

"Yes. They are of soft mind and unsturdy will. Those are who your great god seeks, right?"

Szilveszter admitted to himself that he was quite taken aback by the boy's intuitiveness. "You want to aid me? Why?"

"I believe your eyes are a lot like mine. They hold… secrets. I wish to know what they are."

Szilveszter smiled again. "So, boy, what is your name?"

Stoic beyond his years, the boy said, "My name is Grigori Yefimovich Rasputin."

Szilveszter laughed out loud. His great god had shown him a sign, a wonderful sign indeed.

Milton Keynes UK
Ingram Content Group UK Ltd.
UKHW010643020624
443357UK00002B/26